FULL DISCLOSURE

— A NOVEL —

BEVERLEY McLACHLIN

PUBLISHED BY SIMON & SCHUSTER

New York London Toronto Sydney New Delhi

Simon & Schuster Canada
A Division of Simon & Schuster, Inc.
166 King Street East, Suite 300
Toronto, Ontario M5A 1J3

This Simon & Schuster Canada edition May 2018

For information about special discounts for bulk purchases, please contact Simon & Schuster Special Sales at 1-800-268-3216 or CustomerService@simonandschuster.ca.

Manufactured in the United States of America

3 5 7 9 10 8 6 4

Library and Archives Canada Cataloguing in Publication Data
McLachlin, Beverley M., author Full disclosure / by Beverley McLachlin.
Issued in print and electronic formats. ISBN 978-1-5011-7278-6 (softcover)—
ISBN 978-1-5011-7280-9 (ebook)
I. Title.
PS8625.L33F85 2018 C813'.6 C2017-906236-0 C2017-906237-9

ISBN 978-1-5011-7278-6
ISBN 978-1-5011-7280-9 (ebook)

For my mother, who taught me to love stories.

ACT ONE

CHAPTER 1

WHAT DO YOU DO WHEN your client goes to jail?

You do what you can, then forget.

I look down the long corridor of the detention center and wonder how it will be this time.

The guard, a burly man in uniform, spies me at the end of the hallway. A shadow crosses his hardened features. He doesn't like lawyers, particularly women lawyers with saucy haircuts and eyes that refuse to look down or away. The steel door behind him opens, a grating sound of metal on metal, and my client appears. Vincent Trussardi. Scion of the business world, patron of the arts. And as of yesterday, widower charged with the murder of his wife.

Trussardi walks toward me, steps measured, shackled wrists crossed in dignified mien. Did he kill his elegant wife? *Probably*,

I think to myself—I can hope, at least at the beginning, that I'm wrong, but a decade in criminal law has made me jaded. Not that it matters. My job is to get him out and get him off.

The guard's right hand moves to his holster as the flat of his left nudges the prisoner forward. My client stops, half turns to resist, then resumes his calculated stride. For some perverse reason, they've put Vincent Trussardi—upstanding citizen, no criminal record—in cuffs. Whether he killed his wife, he's hardly likely to take the guards down and make an unscheduled run for the door. Prisons run on the dignity game—we take it; you keep it if you can. Most people can't.

Maybe this man is an exception. Even in prison reds, he commands. The guard backs off a little, averts his eyes as he bends to unlock the cuffs. A uniformed woman appears from nowhere—a slight creature with brush cut hair—and scrabbles a key at the door of an interview room. Trussardi moves into the room; the guard waves me in. The door clanks behind us. We are alone, unless you count the shadow of the guard's face behind the window high on the wall.

There's not much in the room—a table, two plastic chairs. They dehumanize these places. I motion to my client to sit down; he complies with a graceful shift of the torso. He's caught on quick; cuffs change the way you move. I scrape back the chair opposite and slide into it.

"Thank you for coming, Miss Truitt," Vincent Trussardi says, his voice low and gravelly. His eyes—green, gold-rimmed, heavy like an ancient icon—assess me. I'm not used to my clients studying me. "Just get me out of here," they tend to say. I decide to stare back.

Despite the onset of middle age, toned muscle shows beneath Trussardi's prison reds. His face is even featured, conventionally handsome. A mane of white-streaked black hair flows from forehead to chin; a black-russet mustache and beard frame full lips, the square of his jaw. His bearing is proud, his gaze lamenting. *Why not*, I think. If the papers are right, he has much to grieve for.

I break eye contact and flip open the briefcase at my side.

"Joseph Quentin called me," I say, signing in to my MacBook Air. "He says you want me to act for you." I open a document and type "Vincent Trussardi."

"Yes, they tell me I must fight this charge and that to fight it, I must have a lawyer. I understand you are competent, Miss Truitt." His voice sinks to a whisper. "You will do as well as any. Who knows, perhaps better."

I glance up from my screen. Is he guilty? Does he just want to get this over with?

"I look forward to getting to know you," he says, as if we're agreeing to a merger.

I launch into my spiel. "Mr. Trussardi. The law presumes you innocent, but a murder charge is serious. I'm here to help you." First lesson in client management: *calm them down. "Relax, you're in good hands."*

He nods.

"I understand you've been questioned by the police."

"I told them the truth. I came home and found my wife dead."

If Joseph Quentin, renowned counsel to Vancouver's elite, had had the sense to call me at the outset, Vincent Trussardi would have sat tight on his right to silence. No point in telling him that now. What's happened has happened. I just hope he hasn't sunk his case by revealing something he thought didn't matter.

As if sensing my disquiet, he leans forward. "You shouldn't worry, Miss Truitt. I am not a fool—I know that innocent people go down. Not infrequently, despite your vaunted justice system. I appreciate your help, hope for the best—but you should know, I am prepared for the worst. If it comes to that."

"And you should know, Mr. Trussardi, I distinctly dislike losing. If I take your case, I will win, or exhaust myself trying."

He sits back. "Good, Miss Jilly Truitt. I approve. In fact, I think I am beginning to like you."

I ignore the sortie. *Don't patronize me.* "The first thing we need to do is to secure your release—get you out of here. Then we can talk about the case and whether you want us to take it. If we work that out, we'll discuss what the Crown has against you and how we should handle your defense. We'll look after everything. All in due course."

My little speech, honed to perfection, washes over him like water. He gives me an empty smile.

I remind myself of the second lesson in client management: *insulate yourself against failure.* "I would be less than frank, Mr. Trussardi, if I did not tell you that on charges as grave as this one, the judges do not favor release on bail. However, we will do our best."

"So what precisely do you need, Miss Truitt? To secure my release. Or try."

"We need personal information—residence, income, someone who will act as surety, passport, that sort of thing. And we may need cash to make the bail."

"Hildegard," he intones. "Hildegard Bremner, TEC Tower." He recites a phone number, and I write it down. "My personal secretary in the ancient sense of the word—keeper of the family vaults."

"I see." But I'm not seeing at all. "The judge may want a tidy sum for bail." I think again of what I've read in the papers about the death of his wife. "Given the circumstances."

He regards me levelly. "A matter of no consequence."

"And I'll need a retainer. Ten thousand to start. More later." The third rule of criminal defense work: *get the money up front.*

"Only ten?" He allows himself a soft laugh. "I'm sure you're worth much more than that, Miss Truitt. Hildegard can arrange the payment."

"Very well." I slip my laptop back into its case. "Unless you have further questions, I'll get started. My associate, Jeff Solosky, will contact Hildegard and look after the details. With luck, we'll have you out of here today."

"That would be much appreciated." His voice catches. "My wife's funeral is tomorrow afternoon. I wish to attend."

"The press will be there. Paparazzi, photos all over the papers, wall-to-wall coverage on the six o'clock news. Are you sure you want to go, Mr. Trussardi?"

"The funeral is for her—for Laura. For those who loved her." Once more, he fixes his eyes on mine. "For *me*."

I consider the optics. Grieving husband at wife's funeral. Not bad.

"Fine," I say. "Just wear black and keep your head down."

CHAPTER 2

I EMERGE FROM THE POLICE station to shafts of sun streaking through the morning mist. I push a button and the top of my Mercedes glides back. I like how it moves, smooth and certain of its destination—a comfort in the world of chance I inhabit.

My mind fills with Trussardi. I'm too busy to spend hours each day reading the newspapers. Still, I scan my iPad daily for the recent crimes—business that might be coming my way. The murder of Laura St. John Trussardi has all but obliterated the week's usual assortment of knifings, rapes, and pornography charges. Gruesome details of her death (as much as they're allowed to tell) vie for attention with glamour shots from the social pages. It's not every day that a prominent socialite is murdered.

Nasty stuff, but I feel only elation. It's the crime of the month—maybe the year—and I'm on it. Sure, chances of an acquittal don't seem good. The victim was shot in the matrimonial bed with her husband's gun, after all. But it's early days. Much is unknown and much lies ahead; in the end, all we need is a reasonable doubt. The offices of my little firm—grandly titled Truitt and Company—lie to the west of the jail, but the one-way street takes me east, into the narrow lanes north of Hastings: street pubs below, broken glass above, where the detritus of the previous night's hooking, drinking, and snorting lies scattered on the sidewalk. I make a right toward the genteel Georgian brick of Gastown.

I park and take the elevator up to my office. Three years ago, in a leap of doubt, I signed the lease on a walk-up in a former warehouse. Faded brick on the walls, skylights in the ceiling. Not fashionable like the towers uptown, but close to what's important in my life—the courthouses, the criminals, and a clutch of trendy restaurants. *Build it and they will come,* and so they had—Jeff Solosky and Alicia Leung, my erstwhile associates. And, of course, Debbie, to let in the people we want and keep out the others.

Debbie's pasty face peers up from behind the plastic panel that shields her from the random interference that floats through the door. She carries her age bravely—lined eyes, bright lips, chin-length bob too blond to be true. I try to breeze straight to my office, but Debbie's blue eyes hook me in and bring me to a standstill.

"Did you get the case?" she asks, the lilt of her accent belying her tough-girl manner. Debbie followed a man to Vancouver from Liverpool two decades ago. He disappeared, but she stayed, claimed she liked the rain and the clean air.

"Think so."

"What about the retainer?" she asks, getting to the point.

"Ten grand, enough for the moment."

"Jilly, Jilly," she clucks.

I know what she's thinking: I should have asked for more, but what can you expect of a child who never had a proper mother to teach her about money?

"Jeff here?"

"Yeah, just got back from the sentencing on Dragoni."

"Great. Ask him to come in."

Except for the paper that clutters every surface and the document boxes in the corner, my office is just the way I like it—arched window facing onto the street; glass table; black chair; and a couch in the corner, upholstery perennially pristine. Only one painting on the high brick wall, but a good one—a big Gordon Smith that lets me hear the waves in the Strait of Georgia in the rare moments I allow my mind to wander from more pressing matters of guilt and innocence and how to get my clients out from under the law.

I shove a stack of documents to the side of my table to make way for my laptop, plug in the printer cord. A few keystrokes, and the Trussardi file—what there is of it—rolls off. I sweep the pages from the machine. Jeff enters through the open door, and I hand them off to him.

"Your job is to get him out on bail," I say. "Preferably today."

Jeff and I have been working together four years and don't need many words. He nods and sinks to the chair. He is slender and favors skinny charcoal suits worn with dark shirts and matching dark ties—today's choice is navy on navy. His long neck cranes and his glasses—round and black and thick—fall forward to the tip of his nose as he tries to make sense of my notes.

"So I get to meet Hildegard, 'keeper of the family vaults.'" He gives me a mock grin. "Not a bad turn of phrase." Jeff has his PhD in English (majored in Tennyson) and an IQ north of 150.

"Not my phrase," I reply. "The client's."

"That rarity—a client who uses metaphors. This guy may yet prove interesting."

"Mmm," I muse. "He's very cool, controlled. But unreadable."

"In denial."

"Or maybe innocent. We're defense lawyers, Jeff. At least entertain the possibility."

"I'll try."

"Spring him if you can, as quickly as you can—he wants to go to his wife's funeral Friday afternoon." I glance at my calendar. "If you can get him in here Friday morning, we'll draft a retainer, give him an idea of how things may or may not go, find out what he wants to tell us."

"The victim's funeral? Macabre touch."

I shrug. "Well, there you have it. Maybe he actually loved her—I hear there is such a thing."

"Bail won't be easy," he grumbles. "This murder's brutal, from what the papers say."

"I know; I tried to curb his expectations. Still, he has no criminal record, a good reputation, and can put up any amount of security. Do your best."

"Once more into the breach," Jeff says, sighing. "How'd he pick us, anyway?"

"Joseph Quentin."

"Who?"

"Senior partner at Shaw, Quentin, and Furlow—patrician clientele, all the old families and some not so old. Traditional finders and fixers. They get their clients whatever they need—in this case, a criminal lawyer." I grimace. "Although sadly he didn't look after his client quite as well as he should have. Instead of calling us right away, he sent a junior litigation lawyer down to hold Trussardi's hand during the police questioning."

There's no need to say what we know—that most murder cases are won or lost right up front, in the initial interrogation.

"No confession, I hope," says Jeff.

"Quentin assures me Trussardi kept denying he did it. But it's the details that worry me. We'll see how much damage he did when we get the transcripts."

"Still don't understand. How come Quentin called *us*?"

"Apparently Trussardi asked for us. They'll find some other firm if we don't keep them happy. You know the judges, Jeff. Don't let me down."

"Thanks," he says. "Where are you this afternoon?"

"Eight hundred Smithe—pretrial on Cheskey. Maybe I'll talk to Cy about a plea."

Cy Kenge. Number one Crown prosecutor. Tough as nails and no holds barred in his passion to keep the city streets safe. But I like to think he has a soft spot for me.

"Cheskey," Jeff mutters, "another disaster in the making."

"What's your problem with Cheskey?" I know, but I want to hear Jeff say it.

He leans forward. "'It may be that the gulfs will wash us down.' To use the vernacular, Jilly, we're going to take the fall. We should plead Cheskey out to manslaughter."

"Yeah, sure." I glance at the clock and start packing papers. Got to get to the courthouse. Another day without lunch.

Jeff places his hands on the chrome edges of the chair and pushes himself up. "It's just a case, Jilly—just a job. Don't kill yourself trying to prove the kid's innocence."

"Gotcha, Jeff." I head past him and out the door. "Just keep me in the loop on Trussardi."

—

IT KILLS ME TO SEE the innocent go down. And that's what Damon Cheskey is: an innocent. Twenty-one months and three days over the age of consent. Damon Cheskey stands charged with first-degree murder of Jinks Lippert, street pusher and chief enforcer for the drug kingpin known as Kellen. Everybody knows that Damon fired five shots from a single-shot .22 pistol into Lippert, three of them potentially lethal. *Guilty*, the law calls Cheskey. But I call him innocent. Innocent of life. Innocent of mind.

"I'm going down," Damon whispered when I met with him yesterday. He's back from rehab, looking better. Still, three shots into a prone figure are three shots into a prone figure. No way to change the facts. "Thanks for trying, Ms. Truitt," he said as I left.

The Cheskey pretrial—no Damon, just lawyers arguing about evidence—goes as expected: a roster of witnesses for the Crown, nada from me. Our plan is to see what the Crown can prove and then decide what witnesses to call. Cy sent his junior—Emily McFee, she of Titian hair and blushing skin. So much for my hope of a plea bargain.

The pretrial winds to its weary end. I exit and take the stairs to the library at double stride. The Arthur Erickson building that houses the Supreme Court of British Columbia is light and airy, and there's a portrait of the chief justice of Canada on the wall (when she was young and looked good) to remind me that sometimes, occasionally, women actually do rule.

Halfway through a draft of my opening statement, I take stock. My finger hits the delete button. I'm getting nowhere; Trussardi has laid claim to the entire frontal lobe of my brain. The trajectory of his trial stretches out before me. Disclosure, when the Crown tells us what they have. Investigations, timelines, alibis, weaknesses in the Crown's case, alternative suspects—whatever we can dredge up. The preliminary inquiry, and, finally, the trial. Could take years, could take months. Either way, it's sure to consume a big chunk of my future.

My cell phone, silenced but omnipresent, vibrates with an incoming text. It's Cy.

Meet me at the Wedgewood for a drink at six. Need to talk about Trussardi.

I look at my watch—five forty-five—text back, **See you there.**

I'm happy to talk about my new case. If he has something to say about Cheskey, all the better.

I shut my laptop, push my papers together, and head for the street.

CHAPTER 3

LAWYERS LOVE THE WEDGEWOOD'S DARK corners, its secret alcoves. A place to meet, greet, and, should the need arise, whisper propositions in private. Story has it that a beautiful lady from central Europe got the building as a parting gift from an entrepreneur she had briefly enchanted. It wasn't much at the start, but the lady, with a keen sense of what makes the world go round, transformed it—old rugs, antique couches, heavy velvet swags—bordello without the you-know-what.

Mitchell, the maître d', greets me at the door and flashes me a Colgate smile. "Ms. Truitt, such a pleasure."

"Is Mr. Kenge here?"

"Not yet, but let me have Olivia show you to a table."

I am aware of eyes following me as I cross the lobby. In my early days, I tried the whole pantsuit, no-makeup look, but I couldn't pull it off. So, at thirty-four I dress like who I am—dark suits, white shirts, crimson lipstick and nails (if it's not a court day, maybe a bright jacket over a strappy dress) always with black heels. When I move, it's chin up, shoulders back.

Mitchell hands me over to a statuesque young woman clad in black hose and the briefest of miniskirts who ushers me past the social shrieks of the lounge.

"House Chardonnay," I say as I slide into a nook shrouded in drapes.

I hear Cy before I see him: the click of his artificial leg, the sound of his brace, the audible expulsion of breath with each step. Life is an effort for this man. Years after polio was eradicated here, Cy contracted it in Uganda, where his father went on sabbatical. Cy makes light of his limp, says it's made him strong, but the burden of his body shapes his life and colors his moods. Most think of him as acerbic, some view him as shifty, a few call him downright mean. *Slippery Cy*, they whisper in the corridors of justice, and walk the other way.

Not me. It wasn't easy, learning to be a criminal lawyer. I bumbled, lost more often than I should have. I was on my way down, another dropout from the cloistered criminal bar. No one cared. Except Cy. After pummeling me in court, he would offer coffee and a postmortem. Between banal bits of legal gossip, he slipped in morsels of advice: *Think through your case, know your defense, look the jurors in the eye, don't talk down to the judge. And, by the way, never let the bullshit get you down.*

Why are you telling me this, Cy? I would ask after each session.

An arch of brow, a twist of lip. *I consider it my duty to toughen you up, Jilly.*

And he did. These days our conversations are sometimes

friendly, sometimes not. Though it's our lot to do constant battle, he is forever, in some place in the back of my being, my mentor.

"Jilly," his deep voice booms, "good to see you." He pivots his body forward on his arm brace, lets it fall to the bench beside me, and motions to Olivia, who hovers in the shadows. "Laphroaig, straight up, no ice, double." He's a big man. His round head sits low on his thick neck, his forehead so broad he seems hydrocephalic.

"How's Mike?" he asks.

"Great. Awash in apps and applications. Traveling too much for my taste."

"When are you two going to make it official?"

"Soon." I shrug. "Probably."

"Jilly, dear Jilly. Take some advice from an old and bitter warrior. There's more to life than courtroom skirmishing." He pauses. "And Martha and Brock and the boys?"

"Thriving. Don't see them enough, though." I spare a fond thought for my foster family. I'm an orphan, abandoned by who knows whom, who knows where, appropriated, sort of, by a kindly United Church minister and his wife who took me into care. I was twelve when they died within months of each other. I try to avoid thinking about what followed—a series of foster homes where I discovered an impressive capacity for rejecting horror shows and getting thrown back into the system. My final home was with Martha and Brock Mayne. I am forever grateful for their kindness (not to mention financial underpinning), and for their four sons, from whom I garnered such street smarts as I possess.

I change the subject. "How's Lois?" Cy's wife, who more than once has offered me a homemade meal on a late trial evening, has been unwell of late.

Cy's shining skull moves side to side. "Want the good news or the bad?"

"You know me. Both?"

"Well, the good news is she's stopped drinking. The bad news is her liver is shot."

"So, what do you do now?"

"We go for a transplant."

"But if she's—"

"You're right, Jilly—big *but*. She's sworn off, though. Doing detox. So she's on the waiting list."

"How long?"

"Who knows? In the meantime, let's just say she's not deliriously happy with the world."

Our drinks arrive. I feel the first sip of Chardonnay slide down my throat, spare a thought for the misery of life. Cy and Lois seemed a perfect match at first: feisty country girl paired with only son of the late and revered academic, a force of a man. They had a son; twelve months later, he died. Cy buried his sorrow in a fueled-up passion to convict the sons of bitches who run afoul of the law while Lois sat alone in her grief. A nip to make the evening pass, then another. *Get a divorce, end the charade*, I'd told him, *you're killing her.* But something—maybe guilt, maybe love?—has held him to her.

"Jilly," Cy says. "You know I like you. I need to give you a word to the wise."

What I need is a deal that will save my skin on Monday, not advice, I think.

"You've been on a roll. The Smith verdict, then the Nugent drug-conspiracy trial you torpedoed for the prosecution. Your win in the Court of Appeal the other day."

He shifts the weight of his torso on the bench. "Ten years, and you've built a reputation. You're hot, Jilly. But it could all be over like that." He flicks his finger against his thumb. "A couple of losers and you're gone."

I shoot him a look. "There's always legal aid."

"You can't go back to that. It would kill you."

"Your point, Cy?"

"You're starting to take chances, Jilly. I've seen it happen before. Cheskey—it's a loser and you know it. Yet you're taking it to trial."

"If I'm not mistaken, *you're* taking it to trial, Cy. Last time I looked, you were the prosecutor."

"Cut the bullshit. I offered you second degree."

"Not good enough," I say. "Second degree gets my client parole in ten years. Nice boy, no record, scared shitless when he fired the shots. He's a kid, Cy. It's a waste if he goes to jail. With luck, I get manslaughter or an acquittal." I let the words hang.

"Acquittal, Jilly? You're crazy. He blasted five shots into the victim. Point-blank. You know I can't go to manslaughter on this one."

"Then I guess we go to trial."

"I guess so. But it pains me to see you lose."

"Spare me." I know Cy loves to win as much as I do. Needs to win. Lives to win. He shifts gears.

"I hear you're defending Trussardi."

"We'll see. I'm meeting him tomorrow."

"Another loser." Cy takes a deep draught of the single malt. "He's guilty as sin, Jilly. No one could pull an acquittal for your guy out of that crime scene. And it'll be big. National, maybe even international."

I shake my head. Does Cy care about me? Or is he worried I might win?

"It's my job to defend the accused, Cy. In case you've forgotten, he's presumed innocent. Anyway, from what I read in the papers, you have a problem. The identity issue. In street talk, *whodunit.*"

"He's going down, Jilly. His bed, his gun. And the photos—let's just say when you see them, you'll understand. Just thought I'd try to warn you."

"Cy, if fear of losing were enough to make me quit, I'd never have started in this business. Every case, somebody loses. I know how to pick myself up."

He cracks a small smile. "I thought that's what you'd say." His eyes lock on mine, unblinking. "I see it all now. Back at your condo on the Creek. Open a can of tuna, crank up the jazz. Google *Trussardi.* Enough on the web to last you until midnight. At least."

"And you? Home to cold roast beef and a bleak evening with your ailing wife. Don't worry about me, Cy. I'll survive."

He's about to order a second drink, but I motion for Olivia, who eyes us discreetly from behind the velvet drapes. "The check," I say, "and a cab for my friend." I flip a twenty on the table, rise. "Thanks for the advice, Cy. See you Monday."

CHAPTER 4

CY KNOWS ME WELL. AFTER a salad from Urban Fair, I settle in behind the blond desk that sits at an angle in my living room window and spend the next few hours ignoring the ocean sunset and getting to know my client.

I start with the wife, Laura Trussardi. There she is, looking up at me from the social pages of the *Sun*, taking the steps of the Hotel Vancouver on the arm of her husband, radiantly arrayed for the Beaux Arts Ball, gloved hand raised in silent greeting to some unknown acolyte, bared shoulder framed in silk. Blond hair sweeps up from her long neck in an elegant coif held in place by a diamond comb, and the emeralds at her throat shimmer in the klieg lights. The social bloggers do not reveal her age—bad form—but I can guess: forty, tops.

I learn that she kept busy, sat on the boards of arts groups and ran drives to raise money for causes as diverse as cancer and Bard on the Beach, an annual Shakespeare festival. *The perfect wife.* I scan further. *No mention of children, though.*

I hit a link—LEAF, short for Women's Legal Education and Action Fund. There she is, a woman who never cracked a law book, handing a check with big numbers on it to the president of the local chapter at a fundraising breakfast. LAURA TRUSSARDI CONTRIBUTES $25,000 TO THE FUND FOR MISSING EASTSIDE WOMEN, the headline reads. I lean back in my chair. So, Laura Trussardi was a woman of conscience. A while ago, I was part of LEAF, might have even met Laura, but I've been off causes lately. These days, I'm more likely to be defending the guys accused of crimes against women than lobbying for their victims.

I find fewer photos of my client. Google says his parents came to Canada via London in 1945, fleeing the chaos of postwar Italy. They had a daughter named Raquella, and a decade later—an afterthought, maybe—a son whom they named Vincent after his father, Vincenzo. Vincent lived a charmed life—Oxford, cars, World Cup sailing. No shortage of women, judging by the photos. After a decade or so—his mother dead, his father ailing—he returned to Vancouver from abroad to take over the family business. Surprising the doubters, the playboy buckled down and steered the family firm in new directions. Not content with purveying Italian shoes and furniture, he diversified, acquiring banks and a chain of pharmacies. One of the banks failed in the dark days of the early eighties, but he picked himself up and went on to remake his fortune. Along the way, he started collecting Aboriginal art, amassing the best collection of bentwood boxes and baskets in the world, barring the Museum of Anthropology. Then, ten years ago—late in life, as these things go—he married a woman fifteen years his junior from a prominent Vancouver family. I follow a link to *Western Living*, scan Laura and Vincent standing together in their West Vancouver home, a gallery of paintings in the background.

I consider hitting the chat sites, seeing what the masses say about Trussardi now that they've probably found him guilty beyond a reasonable doubt, but I decide not to bother. I already know enough from the front pages of the papers. LAURA TRUSSARDI, DEAD IN HER BED OF GUNSHOT WOUND, the *Sun* had proclaimed, leaving the details to the imagination. I shut my computer down. I am all too aware of what they've concluded.

Something doesn't jibe. My mind keeps going back to the man I met in the interview room—dignified, distant, stoic, moved to passion only at the end when he spoke of the need to attend his wife's funeral. The eyes haunt me, sad and grieving—one minute telling me he's overwhelmed by what he's done, the next that despite the damning evidence, he's innocent. I try to wish the thought away—it only makes the job harder to know that if my efforts fail, an innocent man will go down.

The jangle of my cell phone interrupts my thoughts. I pick it up. "Yeah, Jeff?"

"Got him out."

"Difficult?"

"Piece of proverbial cake. Didn't even have to put up money. Out on his own recognizance. 'Surrender your passport, stay around town. No boating south of the forty-ninth parallel, and, oh, by the way, show up for trial.' The usual warnings, 'Your undertaking is sacred da-da-da,' and the judge signed the paper. Done. Finito. Home free."

"Home, but not free. Anyway, good work, Jeff. Where is he now?"

"Headed back to his house. Driver picked him up."

"God."

"Yeah. I know. I wouldn't go near the place. Not if I was innocent."

"Ours is not to judge, Jeff."

"Whatever you say, boss."

The line goes dead. I stare at the mute phone in the hollow of my hand, wondering if Trussardi will spend the night in the matrimonial bed, assuming it's been cleaned up. Eleven thirty, the red light says. Time to sleep, or try to. Tomorrow is another day.

CHAPTER 5

NINE A.M., FRIDAY. I'M AT my desk poring over papers when my line blinks. "Vincent Trussardi has arrived," says Debbie.

"Show him into the boardroom," I reply, referring grandly to the twelve-by-fourteen-foot cubicle we use for meetings. "And get Jeff—Alicia, too, if she's in." I want to make an impression.

When I enter the boardroom, I see Trussardi standing at the arched window, gazing out on the street below. He turns. "Miss Truitt."

He is wearing a silk ascot and a jacket of finely checked wool over dress trousers. He looks exactly like what Google says he is: entrepreneur cum cultivated collector of fine art.

I cross to him, offer my hand. "Mr. Trussardi. Good to see you."

He releases my hand with a nod. The melancholy mood of our prison interview is replaced today with a veneer of courtly manners. His eye travels from me to the Inuit bear carving on the table and the Toni Onley prints on the wall. "I see you are interested in art."

"My foster parents introduced me to fine art. They insisted on trekking the family through galleries on weekends. I got into it. The colors, shapes, stories."

"Art is my passion," Trussardi muses. "I've had other loves, from time to time. But I always return to art. Beauty in all its fascinating forms."

I don't know what to say. Not much art—nor beauty—in prison, unless you count the graffiti on the walls.

Jeff enters, followed by Alicia. *Here to take notes,* she pats her laptop. Alicia is first-wave Chinese, she likes to remind us—descended from the men who came to build the Canadian Pacific Railway a century and a quarter ago and who paid a head tax to the government to bring their wives over. She wears her long black hair pulled back from her smooth face. She looks delicate, but I know better. She was second in her law class last year. I feel lucky to have her. We slide into our chairs. But before I can launch into my spiel, Trussardi speaks.

"I expect you want to know if I killed my wife."

"Not unless you want to tell us," I say. Why do they always think it's about the truth? "Our job is not to decide whether you're innocent or guilty—it's to give you the best defense we can."

"For the record, I didn't. I didn't kill her." He must see the wheels going round in my head. "Nor did I hire anyone to do it. I loved my wife."

"That's good to know, Mr. Trussardi. But unfortunately, it's not enough to get you off." I think of the mountain of evidence Cy will amass against him. His wife, his bed, his gun. Circumstantial, sure, but evidence nevertheless. If he's telling the truth—and I want to believe he is—he has a lot of explaining to do.

"Do you have any idea who killed your wife?"

A moment of hesitation, then he shakes his head. "None."

Alicia stops typing. Jeff's eyes meet mine, *I told you so.*

"Mr. Trussardi, we need your help. You must have thoughts about who could have killed her, who could have wanted her dead."

"She was a good person."

"Too good, Mr. Trussardi?" I ask. I think of my Google search. "Too many causes, too many missions?"

"I admired what she did, tried to support her causes."

"But it wasn't always easy?"

"No." Then the words come out in a pent-up rush. "Sometimes it drove me mad. She was always trying to help this person or fix that wrong. 'It's not your problem,' I used to tell her, 'not our problem. Why can't we just live our lives, you and me, why do you have to save the world?' " He pauses for a breath. "But I didn't kill her. Sorry," he whispers. "Never speak ill of the dead."

"Don't be sorry. We need to know her, know you, know how it was." I lean across the table. "Who did she try to help?"

"Everyone. Crazy kids, missing women. *Me.*" He offers a tortured smile. "She took a playboy and gave him a conscience, or tried to. She took my sister, Raquella—in a wheelchair and beset by inner demons—and gave her a reason to live. The boy who used to hang around—" He breaks off.

Jeff, Alicia, and I watch Trussardi's bowed head. "I'm not a saint—sometimes it drove me mad. But I loved her. I didn't kill her."

I clear my throat. "Sometimes bad people kill good people. Do you have any enemies, Mr. Trussardi? Anyone who would want to hurt you by murdering Laura?"

"I have business rivals, of course, but no enemies, no one who would do . . . this."

"Do you have an alibi?"

He leans back, relieved to retreat to neutral territory. "Yes. I was sailing. Came home. Found her. Her body."

"Were you with anyone? Do you have any way to prove you were away when she died? Someone who saw you? A cell phone trace that puts you on the water when she was killed?"

"I turned my phone off—I wanted peace and quiet. I sailed alone, but there were people at the yacht club. Someone must have seen me."

"And what about the gun? Where do you keep it?"

"In my safe, but when I came home, the safe was empty."

I make a note. "Mr. Trussardi, let me be frank. This will be a difficult case. Perhaps impossible. If we are to have any chance of success, you will need to be open with us, work with us. No secrets, no games, no holding back. Any of those things and you find yourself another lawyer."

Alicia's keys, clacking furiously as I speak, fall silent as Trussardi takes his time to answer. "I understand. No secrets, no games, no holding back."

"Then we'll do our best for you."

He nods, then asks, "How do you see this unfolding?"

"Too soon to know," I say. "We wait for the Crown prosecutors to tell us what evidence they've got. Disclosure, it's called. That will take a few weeks, maybe more. Then there's a preliminary inquiry, where the judge decides if there's enough evidence to send the case for trial."

“And how long does all that take?” Trussardi drums his fingers on the tabletop.

“We can make it take up to a year just for the preliminary, if you want.”

His gold-rimmed eyes lock on mine. “That long?”

“Depends on the prosecution, of course. They could prefer a direct indictment. Or they could dillydally so long we can get a *Charter* stay because you haven’t been brought to trial within a reasonable time.”

“Perpetual purgatory.”

“There are worse things. Like jail.” Cy’s premature verdict comes back to me, *Guilty as sin*. He’s got Trussardi in his sights. “I have a feeling the prosecution won’t let this case drag.”

“I don’t want to rush to trial if it means a verdict of guilty. But I don’t think I can wait two years for this to be over.”

“In that case, let’s get down to business, Mr. Trussardi. We’re going to need access to your house, your friends and family. We need to build a picture of your late wife’s life, get an idea of who she was and who could have done this. We need to know everything about her.” I drop my voice. “Everything about you.”

“I understand.”

“I’d like to start by looking at the crime scene.” I flick through my electronic calendar. “I’m tied up in another murder trial all next week. As soon as it’s over, I’ll contact you.”

His mouth twists. “Under the circumstances, it is highly unlikely I shall be straying far.”

“I’ll want to talk to your sister, Raquella. Is there anyone else?”

“The housekeeper, Carmelina Cappelli. My sister lives in a suite on the ground floor of my residence, so you won’t have to go far." He sags in his chair, all at once tired. "Can we leave the rest until later?"

"Fine." I shift. "One more thing. We'll need a deposit to keep working on the case. Fifty thousand—in trust, of course—for now." *Debbie would be proud of me,* I think.

"Certainly, Miss Truitt." He takes out his fine Italian-leather checkbook, writes out the check, and hands it to me as he gets to his feet. *Meeting over.*

"I look forward to seeing you the week after next, Miss Truitt. May I offer you dinner when you come?"

Don't get close to the client—rule number four of criminal practice.

"We'll see," I say.

CHAPTER 6

VINCENT TRUSSARDI IS SCARCELY OUT the door before my cell phone buzzes.

"Hi, Mike."

"Jilly, can you meet me at Carrall and Hastings at two? Got some stuff on this afternoon, and I'd like you to come with. Maybe we can do dinner after?"

Stuff, I think, *how enticing*. Still, I haven't seen Mike for weeks, what with my cases and his trips to San Fran chasing legal apps for IBM.

"Sure," I reply. "I'm finishing up here soon."

Michael St. John and I have been together since first year law, best friends and occasional lovers. He went the high-tech IP route and now earns a fortune on apps. I went into criminal law.

At the appointed hour, I'm standing at the street corner,

surveying the sea of traffic that stalls, comes at me, stalls again. I spot the ancient silver BMW that once belonged to Mike's mother. I wave and Mike does what he can, which is nothing, to angle his vehicle in my direction.

I cut through the lane of traffic, ignoring the angry horns, breaking all the rules.

"Hi," I say, when I get into the passenger seat of Mike's car.

Mike's eyes slide from my face and down my legs to my strappy black shoes. "Hi, Jilly. Long time no see." He's a man of few words, and those he does offer take a while to come out.

"What's with the suit?" I ask. Mike is given to cladding his lanky form in jeans and sweaters—maybe a jacket thrown over for a really dressy occasion. Today he wears a suit and tie like he was born to it. Which, I remind myself, he was—they teach young men these things in the preppy schools he attended in his youth. "Where are we going?"

"Patience, Jilly, never your strong suit."

I smile at him. He has irregular features and a beaky nose, but he looks good to me. "Come on."

He gives me a strained grin. "To a funeral."

"Really? Whose?"

"Third cousin. You know."

I don't know—I possess no cousins of first, second, or any degree; no mother or father for that matter. But something latent within my brain stirs. "This funeral, it wouldn't be—?"

"Laura Trussardi. Terrible thing. Murdered. Not pretty, I understand. They say her husband—"

A sudden opening appears in the press of cars and Mike's BMW surges forward. I brace myself against the dashboard. Mike. Laura. Cousins. It was all there on Google. Had I bothered to register what I read, I would have picked up on the name, figured out that Laura St. John Trussardi inhabited the fringes of Mike's extended family.

"Interesting," I say, digesting the news as we sail south on Richards.

"What's the matter, Jilly?" Mike glances over as he slows for a light. "You've gone white."

"I'm acting for him. For her husband. Vincent Trussardi."

"Tell me you're joking."

"No. Dead serious."

He gives me another side look. "You can't take this case, Jilly. It's too close to me. I mean—"

"It's not like we're married or anything, Mike."

"Be that as it may," Mike says tightly. "From what I hear, it's open and shut—he did it. Why would you want the case anyway?"

"Because he's entitled to a defense." I'm aware my voice has risen. "I defend people. That's my business. Whether they did it or not isn't relevant to me."

Mike's a lawyer, but the right to a fair trial doesn't rank number one in the rariefied world of designing apps for commercial solicitors. "Besides," I mutter, "he says he didn't do it."

Mike, slow to speak and slower to rouse, asks, "You believe that, Jilly? From what I hear, whoever did it might as well have written jealous rage on the wall. Who else would have done that to her?"

"I don't know. A lover, a stranger?"

"Yeah, a lover or stranger with access to the connubial bed," he says flatly.

I shrug. No point in replying even if I had an answer. Mike

changes lanes abruptly and noses the car into an underground parking lot. As we emerge from the car, it comes back to me. "He's going to be here."

Mike halts and we stare at each other in the gloom. *Forget it, Jilly,* he's going to say. *You shouldn't be at her funeral—and definitely not with me.* But he reaches out and gives my shoulder a quick squeeze. "Let's go."

WE SURFACE FROM THE WELL of the parking garage onto the bright street and cross to Holy Rosary Cathedral—a dignified structure of stone and stucco pierced by tall stained glass windows beneath a lofted roof. People crowd the steps that lead to the blackened doors, although the funeral won't begin for another half hour. Journalists press against the cordon as ushers do their best to fend off the busybodies. A bald, officious man spies Mike through the crowd and waves us toward him. I take the hand Mike offers and follow him through the throng. Ignoring the flashes from the cameras, we move up the steps, down the long center aisle, and into the dimness of the cathedral.

My forensic brain kicks into gear as I peer into the nave. No urn or box—with a murder trial in the offing, Cy has had enough sense to nix cremation. Much may turn on the story the body tells. For Cy's sake, I hope he's told them to take it straight back to the morgue after the service; I could make something of a precipitate rush to burial.

As befits third cousins, we are seated three rows back on the right. I scan the benches around us—pew after pew of family, ahead and behind. I've been with Mike for a decade, on and off, and yet I've met only a handful of them. The front pew is empty. I wonder if the priests have reserved it for my client.

Mike's doing the right thing, acknowledging the glances, whispering polite greetings, introducing me to cousin this and aunt that. *Nice to meet you, Miss Truitt,* they say. *And good to see you, Mike—you look well.* I am aware of their speculative glances—*So this is Michael's friend.* Fortunately for Mike, I happen to be wearing my usual black suit upgraded a notch by the Hermès scarf he bought for me on a trip to La Jolla last year. Inspections completed, they smile thinly and turn to the matter at hand. *Terrible business. She was so lovely, such a good person. Unbelievable waste. What a crime.* I nod, taking care to remain noncommittal.

The organ sputters alive in an uncertain drone, and the casket, a rich mahogany affair, is wheeled in. Priests in lace mantles swing censers.

"High mass," Mike whispers.

"I thought you were Anglican," I whisper back.

"Same thing, except Catholics don't do eulogies until after mass. Kneel, Jilly."

Peeking between my fingers, I see the front pew is now occupied. Some side door must have opened to admit my client. The back of Vincent Trussardi's head glows in the soft light of the stained glass windows, his streaked mane falling elegantly over a starched white collar. Beside him sits a woman in black, a fringe of jet hair visible beneath the veil of a hat—Raquella, Vincent's sister, I assume. Her neck swivels as she looks back toward the aisle, but I make out only a shadow of profile beneath the heavy veil. *I'll come to know her soon enough,* I think.

The priests take their positions behind the high altar. Words float by, *Laura, baptized in the church, married in the church, blessed by the church. Lord have mercy.* We confess our sins; we pray. The bishop gives a homily on the brevity of life. We pray again. I know some of the prayer—my first foster parents taught me the Lord's Prayer—but the ups and downs of the mass unsettle me. I do my best to follow the cues, but I miss a few. "Not much good at this," I mumble as I belatedly rise from a crouch that's killing my knees.

Mike's head is bent, eyes closed; he is lost in the incantatory rights. And then the obvious hits me—he is saying his farewell to his cousin. They must have played as children, laughed, perhaps fought. The images pass before my eyes—family dinners, adults sated and tipsy, children liberated to scamper to this attic or that basement of whatever St. John mansion had been chosen for the Thanksgiving or Christmas celebration. And now his cousin is gone. I touch Mike's hand. His fingers absently entwine with mine as his lips move silently in final communion.

The bishop intones the benediction, swings the censer over the coffin, and sprinkles the holy water. *We commit the soul of Laura St. John into thy care, oh Lord.* No mention of the name she has used for the past decade—in death, it seems, Laura Trussardi has once again become Laura St. John.

I am relieved that someone—presumably my client—has had the sense to dispense with post-mass eulogies; from my point of view, the less said about the deceased's exceptional qualities and premature death the better. The pallbearers wheel the coffin down the aisle, and Vincent Trussardi swings in behind, his sister beside him in a wheelchair. I make a mental note.

My client follows the coffin, eyes lowered, just as I instructed him. *Good,* I think. As he passes, he looks up and sees me standing next to Mike, offers the hint of a sad smile. But it's the sister's stare that transfixes me even from beneath her veil. Mike picks up her gaze, follows it to me. Then the cortege passes and the family shuffles, pew by pew, into the aisle.

Outside, the sun hits us in a blinding wash. As my eyes adjust, I make out the black cars in front—one for the body, one for Vincent Trussardi and his sister, a suite of limos for the St. John clan. Cluster by cluster, they make their goodbyes—hushed tones, decorous hugs, a few tears.

A group of well-dressed women has moved down the steps and stands by the hearse as the undertakers close the doors with a solemn thud. I recognize a few lawyers from LEAF, here to mourn their fallen sister. I stood with them on similar occasions in my day. They will not be pleased when they learn I am defending Vincent Trussardi. Criminal lawyer or militant feminist—whoever said you could have it all lied.

Behind the LEAF ladies stands yet another group, this one shabbier, a few of the women gaudy in short skirts and net stockings. One or two carry signs, STOP THE CARNAGE, FIND OUR MISSING WOMEN. I remember Vincent's bitter tone—*Laura and her causes*.

Vincent Trussardi, having ushered his sister to the far seat of their limo, moves round the back of the car to the opposite door, while the driver folds the wheelchair and stows it in the trunk. He bows decorously as he closes the door after my client.

The procession of cars inches forward. The crowd, now hushed, steps back.

Then I see him—a tall, slender man stepping out from the crowd toward the hearse, his right arm out, as though willing it to stop. But the car pulls away and the man's arm falls. His artist's tam sits askew. He's wearing a corduroy jacket. When he lifts his face, I see that it is wet with tears. He stares after the departing vehicle for a long moment before stumbling back to the sidewalk, turning, and pushing through the crowd.

"Who was that?" I ask Mike.

"Who knows? Some guy who loved her, I guess."

I want to run after the man, get his name, talk to him, but Mike has my elbow and is steering me away.

CHAPTER 7

TWO HOURS LATER, MIKE AND I are sitting in a private corner of Bishop's on Fourth, a small restaurant known for the fastidious excellence of its refined *cuisine de nature.* Mike usually takes me for granted, as I do him. I like it that way, but today, I sense something different in him, and it's not just saying goodbye to his cousin Laura.

"Mike, what's going on?"

"What do you mean?" He reaches to smooth his already sleek cap of black hair.

"I mean, you actually went shopping. For a painting—not chopped liver or socks at the Bay. You never shop. And you made a reservation. At a *restaurant*. Usually, it's just, what do you want, pizza or Thai?" I reach to cover his hand with mine. "And the suit. I know it was a funeral and all. But you still have it on. Even the jacket."

"Ditched the tie in the car."

I take in his open collar. "Don't miss it a bit."

"I'm trying to do better."

"Must have been some blog you read," I say.

"You could say that." A darting flash of grin, before he changes the subject. "Do you like the painting, Jilly?"

"Mike, when it comes to paintings, it's whether *you* like it. But yes, it's a lovely painting. It will look fantastic over your fireplace."

After the funeral, Mike had taken me to see a painting he had his eye on at the Bau-Xi. I was impressed. A Joe Plaskett—lovely angles, soft colors, doors and mirrors—a painting where your eye walks in and wanders along and you forget what it was you came for.

"It's not something you would buy, Jilly," Mike had said, and he was right. My taste is brighter, bolder.

"It's right for you," I said. "If you like it, buy it." *It's not like you have to think about it*, I'd thought to myself, rolling my inward eye, *with what you inherited and what you make.*

In the end, he bought it and made arrangements to have it installed on Monday.

"This is a good buy, Mike," I told him as we headed back to the car. "It's perfect. A lovely start to filling all your empty space."

Now, over pre-dinner nibbles, he says, "I actually really like it, Jilly."

I lift my glass of Prosecco. "To the Plaskett, and to the pleasure it will bring you."

"Bring us," he says as he clinks his glass against mine.

We drift into small talk, and Mike fills me in on the doings of friends from law school. Tom and Sally are divorcing. Meanwhile,

Ainsley and Fred, who have been casually dating for a decade, have decided on a big July wedding.

"We'll be invited, Jilly."

And so it goes. Those who pledged young separate. Those who were more cautious decide it's time to take the plunge. There's a lesson in there somewhere, if I care to look for it.

Mike and I are both orphans, in different ways. It's what drew us together; it's what keeps us together. I'm a *real* orphan. Mike is a *virtual* orphan, the only son of wealthy parents who consigned him to the care of nannies and private schools while they wintered in Nice or caught the opera season in New York. We're both damaged goods, but we've both come through, if not intact, at least without diagnosed afflictions. Along the way, we've pulled each other out of bad places.

I think about my dark time sometimes. Nights on the street where packets changed hands and needles were shared. Why did I do it? Life wasn't so bad. I liked law school and the Maynes cared about me, gave me everything I could ever want. Sure, I wanted to experiment; it felt good, eased the pain. But why? *Some angst gnawing at you*, said the counselor Mike took me to. *Some inchoate longing for the mother you never knew*. All I know is that, with Mike's help, I pulled myself together and came out of the black place that almost claimed me. *I will be a lawyer*, I vowed, thinking of the deeds I had witnessed on the street, the lost souls I had met. *A criminal lawyer*.

I permit myself a moment of tenderness. "I'm going to Naramata for a week with Martha and Brock at the end of July," I hear myself saying to Mike. "Why don't you come? They'd love to have you."

"Yeah?"

"Martha thinks you're good for me."

"Then how can I refuse?" He cocks his head—*what Martha wants is what Martha gets*—but his look turns intense.

"Tell me about Laura," I say, changing the subject, my curiosity getting the better of me.

"Not sure I want to talk about her."

"Maybe you need to," I press gently.

"She was a nice girl. The usual schools, good grades, socially active, nothing exceptional for our sort." He pauses, fork poised. "Except, looking back, she had a way of making unusual choices. She studied art history in New York—nothing different there—but instead of the Italian Renaissance, she focused on Indigenous art, came back and did a masters in Salish carvings at UBC."

He takes a bite, chews, swallows. "She did all the charities, balls, the lot. But then, in the last couple of years, she got really intense about feminism and missing women on the Downtown Eastside." He puts his fork down. "Way too deeply, some of the family felt. It's one thing to cut a check here and there for some charity; it's another to work at the shelters, hand out money on the street. She always seemed pretty much mainstream on the surface, but when you looked closely you could see she was restless."

Bent on changing the world, I think, remembering Vincent's lament. Maybe she got too close to someone bad, someone who wanted more than a twenty on the street corner.

"You were close to her?" I pick through the arugula.

"When we were kids. She was a little older than me—beautiful, kind. I sort of revered her."

"And Vincent?"

"Didn't ever get to know Vincent Trussardi," Mike says thoughtfully. "Family wasn't pleased when she announced she was marrying him. They could see what brought them together—her interest in Indigenous art, his passion for his collection. Quite exceptional, I understand. It was just that"—he looks down—"well, he was not quite right for the St. John clan. His family came from Italy after the war. Milan, I think, somewhere in the north."

"First-generation wealth," say I, who cannot claim a generation, much less wealth. "Never quite good enough."

"No, that's not it." Mike meets my gaze. "The Trussardis were hardly your typical immigrant family that lost everything in the war. They were very upscale, some distant offshoot of the old manufacturing clan—leather goods, that sort of thing. Rumor has it Vincent Senior got too cozy with Mussolini's Black Shirts, and the family had to flee when the Fascists lost the war and the Allies took over. Just gossip, but it didn't endear him to Laura's father—old Cedric won a Victoria Cross for valor in the Italian campaign."

"Impressive." I mull over Mike's inside knowledge. "You're much more informative than Google."

"Pleased to be of service," he murmurs, as our waiter returns to drop off our entrées. When he's gone, Mike reaches for my hand. "Don't take this case, Jilly," he whispers. "Too close. Too nasty."

"Mike—"

"Okay, okay, your business." He lets go and digs into his *confit de canard*. "This isn't bad. We should eat out more often, Jilly."

I nod and we move on—no need to spoil a perfectly good evening with a spat. We've learned over the years when to push, when to let go. I take his cue, rattle on about the campy café that just opened across the street from my office and how I can't seem to keep Debbie happy.

But my mind won't let go of the case. The sun is setting, low light filling the restaurant. I'm looking across at Mike's face, but thoughts of Trussardi and Laura race through my mind.

Mike senses my disquiet. His hand moves across the linen to cover mine and he gives me a lopsided smile. "Let's go, Jilly," he says.

CHAPTER 8

After dinner, we drive to the leafy crescents of Shaughnessy where Mike lives alone in his big mansion.

When Mike's parents died a decade plus ago, he called the Salvation Army and told them to take out all the furniture except the grand piano and a love seat. We were in law school then, and as I watched him shunt the class notes I delivered each night across the barren floor of his room, I would plead, *Mike, do something.* In time, he recovered enough to order a bed, a TV, a desk, and a bank of computers, which he installed in two of the rooms upstairs. That's how it's been ever since and how it always will be. Correction—come Monday the gorgeous Plaskett will hang over the massive marble fireplace.

I settle in on the couch and Mike disappears in the direction of the distant kitchen. He returns with two glasses of something bubbly, hands me one, and takes the other to the Steinway. He starts slowly, his long fingers stroking the keys tentatively, a few chords merging into my favorite, Debussy's "Girl with the Flaxen Hair."

I sit back, eyes closed. My thoughts inevitably float to Trussardi and Laura St. John, my lover's beloved cousin. A rich woman, yes, but also a restless woman not content with the safety of her affluent life, a woman drawn to dark streets and unaccustomed byways. My mind catalogues the possibilities—an affair, an addiction, a sentimental susceptibility to those who prey on the naïve. A woman who might somehow put herself in harm's way. I remember the grief-stricken stranger outside the church. Is he connected? My case suddenly seems slightly less hopeless than before.

I catch Mike's gaze moving from the piano to me—soft, the hint of a crooked smile. Then he turns back to the piano and moves on to something else—Chopin, I think, a nocturne. I know the routine better than the music. In a while he will leave the piano and come over to sit beside me, put his arm around me, kiss me, and take me upstairs to his bed.

Lying quietly in Mike's arms afterward, I feel his kiss on my shoulder.

"That was nice," I whisper.

"It's always nice, Jilly. With you."

"Yes, but this time was different."

"What do you mean?"

"We've been together so long, Mike, thirteen years. It's like we've fallen into a rut—you know, cordial and businesslike. Tonight felt meaningful."

"As in the 'L' word?"

"Yeah," I say, pulling his arm tighter around me. "Might even go that far."

Somewhere, in my hair, I hear him murmur. "You and your words, Jilly—*cordial and businesslike*—make us sound like an old married couple. Maybe it's time we talked about the future."

I turn toward him, prop my head up under my hand. "I like it just the way it is, Mike. You're my best friend and lover."

"Yes. But it could be even better."

"Like?"

"Like you could move in with me, see how it goes. If you like it, we could get married."

So this is what it's all been about—the casual introductions to the St. John clan (what better occasion than a funeral?), the Plaskett, the dinner, the tenderness of lovemaking. Sure I said I might go as far as the "L" word, went along with *like an old married couple*. But that was sentimental play. To alter my life, share it with Mike on a full-time basis—I can't go there, not yet. I think of my work, the perpetual careen from crisis to crisis, of my condo, full of bright light and pictures. I think of never having to ask permission or say I'm sorry.

I feel my throat filling. *Get a grip, Jilly,* I tell myself. *Handle this situation.* I push myself higher against the pillows.

"Mike, I would make a terrible wife. I won't inflict that on you."

"It's not like I'd expect you to make dinner for me every night," he whispers. "I understand your work and how important it is to you. We'd have a housekeeper, maybe a maid or two. You could come and go as you like."

"You just want more sex," I say, trying to lighten things.

"I admit that would be nice, but it's not just sex. I want you—your *company*, Jilly."

"You know I'm there for you, like I've always been. But—"

"Then marry me, Jilly. We don't have much time. If we want to make a life together, want to make a family, it's now." He stops. "Or maybe never."

I bury my head under the sheets.

"Jilly?"

"Don't push me, Mike. I'm not ready. Not ready for forever, not ready for marriage." I hesitate, offer a sop. "Maybe when the Trussardi file's closed."

Mike's voice cracks when he answers. "There'll always be a case, Jilly, always be something more important."

We lie still for a long, anguished moment, room for two bodies between us. Then he reaches toward me, places his hands on my naked shoulders. His eyes are closed. I cannot read his mind. He pulls me in a fierce embrace, lets me fall back. I search for his gaze, for his lips, but he's turned away from me.

"Jilly," he whispers.

I know what's coming. He's going to tell me how much he needs me, and for once I, Jilly Truitt, wizard of words, will have nothing to say, no way to say *I can't deliver.* "Mike, hush."

He falls asleep, or pretends to. No matter. I lean over his back, kiss his cheek. He does not move.

I slip out of bed and search the floor for my shoes and scattered pieces of clothing, stoop to retrieve the Hermès scarf for old times' sake. I glance back at his recumbent form, the shape of his back still impassive beneath the sheet, before I close the door behind me.

I find the bathroom down the hall, shower and dress. I fish my iPhone from my bag and call a cab. For some reason I'm crying. I slam my bag on the sink and find a tissue to dry my face, a compact to restore my façade. I am Jilly Truitt, defense attorney, thirty-four years old and seasoned in love and the ways of the world. *Suck it up*, I tell myself, and make my way downstairs to the waiting car.

The cabbie cranks the car into gear and cranes his neck to inspect me—a knowing leer as he takes in my face, tear-streaked in the light of the street lamp. "You okay?" he asks. *A call girl*, he's thinking, *bad gig at some rich toff's place.* We pull out of the porte cochere.

I paste my face against the window. Gray dawn, bleak shadow, light but no light. The leafy crescents of Shaughnessy blur into the black fronts of Granville's empty shops. Around the corner from my condo, the cabbie passes a news shop, brightly lit in the dark street.

"Let me out." I hand him a bill and wave off the change. For some reason I feel the need for the Saturday paper. I reach for the *Sun* on the rack, but what I see sends me hard back against the newsstand. There we are, top corner of the front page, Mike and I, climbing the steps of the cathedral, hand in hand. MICHAEL ST. JOHN AND JILLY TRUITT ENTER HOLY ROSARY CATHEDRAL FOR FUNERAL OF LATE LAURA ST. JOHN. Then below, in smaller print, MR. ST. JOHN IS A COUSIN OF THE VICTIM; MS. TRUITT IS SAID TO BE ACTING AS DEFENSE COUNSEL TO VINCENT TRUSSARDI, CHARGED WITH FIRST-DEGREE MURDER IN THE SLAYING.

I pay the cashier and numbly stumble home.

CHAPTER 9

"IMPRESSIVE GAMS," CY SAYS AS he slaps a copy of the *Vancouver Sun* on the counsel table in courtroom fifty-six. It's Friday, the last day of the Cheskey trial. Typical Cy. Saves the paper for seven days so he can throw me off my game just as I'm set to address the jury. Emily, who has been waiting patiently for Cy, looks up inquiringly, pretending she hasn't seen the photo.

"A little early in the day for sexist comments, my friend," I respond.

"How about something PC and legal, then? Like"—Cy rolls his massive head back so he can stare at the ceiling—"let's see, St. John–Trussardi, conflict of interest?"

"Mike and I are no longer an item, Cy. No interest, no conflict." A truth I'm slowly beginning to comprehend. For the first time in a decade plus, Mike won't text me, won't return my calls.

"Poor Mike, excess baggage under the circumstances. No choice but to throw him over. Always liked him, though."

"It wasn't quite like that," I start to say.

I could tell Cy, if I had the time and inclination—which I don't—how it really was, how it is. Or could I? How do you describe *absence,* how do you explain *empty*? Maybe *hollow* does it, maybe *numb. Diminished*. I still walk, still talk—but I am less than I was before. A part of me has been severed, a part for which I ache in the night. Gone forever is that quiet place I could visit without invitation and find a crooked smile and a cocked brow—*What's it now, Jilly?*—a place where gangly arms reached out and gathered me in.

In the early hours of the morning after I left Mike's house, it came to me that perhaps it was not too late. I could go back, tell him it was all a mistake. I went to my closet, hauled my suitcase from the upper shelf, threw in my jeans and a suit, and zipped it up. As I heaved the suitcase out the door and into the corridor, it hit me. *What about Trussardi?* he would ask as I stood at his door, and I would turn around and leave. I hauled my bag back in.

All for the best, I thought as I waited fitfully for sleep. What future is there for a girl with a word for every situation and a guy who hardly talks? A girl who faints for a Motherwell and a man who just bought, tentatively, his first gentle Plaskett? A girl who likes the edge and a guy who can say "like an old married couple" and think it's a come-on? I told myself we were doomed from the start, told myself it was time to move on. *Next week you'll be in court, a life in your hands. Get over it, Jilly.*

But the ache went on.

A door slams and brings me back to the present. Cy heaves his body into his chair. Across the room, the guards are leading

Damon Cheskey to the prisoner's box. His face is down, *You can drag my body wherever you want, but you can't make me look at you.* I think of my foster homes; I know the feeling. Then, unexpectedly, Damon looks up, searches the benches, halts at his aging parents. They stare back, uncomprehending in their bewildered pain. How would it be, I wonder, to have parents bound from birth to care, love, suffer? I will never know. Damon's blond coif, carefully clipped for the trial, falls over one eye. He's trying to look cool and collected in his sharp blue blazer, but the fear and shame show through.

It's been a tough trial, a tough week. The prosecution has been measured, the judge has been fair. The jury has listened attentively. The problem is the evidence. Five bullets pumped into the body while the whole street watched.

We sit waiting for the judge. Maybe Cy's bored, maybe he's planned it. Whatever the reason, he makes his second move. It's hard for him to get out of his chair, so he motions to Emily to bring something to me—a plain brown eight-and-a-half-by-eleven manila business envelope. I open the flap, tug at the pages. What I glimpse is enough and I shove them back inside. Photos, crime scene, Laura Trussardi. *Color* photos—the ashy white of dead flesh, the scarlet red of spattered blood.

I shoot Cy a venomous look and bury the envelope under my Cheskey papers as Justice Orrest marches in. *This is neither the time nor the place.* Cy smiles, then shifts his attention to the legal pad in front of him.

I'm up. Ninety percent of the job is getting the sympathy of the jury—convincing them they want to find for your client. Ten percent is showing them how. We've got an uphill battle on both counts.

I leave the defense table and cross to stand in front of the jury box. I take a deep breath and look at each of them in turn before launching myself.

"Ladies and gentlemen of the jury." I pause. I want what comes next to sink in. "The fate of a young man—a promising young man with his whole life before him—lies in your hands. But on the evidence you have heard, you will find your decision easy. There is only one verdict the law permits—you must, and you will, find Damon Cheskey not guilty of the charge he faces."

The insurance executive sits back in apparent disbelief; the salesman and the mechanic exchange a skeptical glance. But our forewoman—Betty O'Shea, a housewife from east Van—is listening intently. *All it takes is one.* I plow on.

"Damon stands charged with first-degree murder, the most serious offense known to our criminal law. The Crown must prove every element of that charge beyond a reasonable doubt. The simple fact is, the Crown has failed to do this. This case is rotten with conjecture, riddled with doubt."

Behind me, Cy gives a cynical snort, and twelve heads turn in his direction. I've lost them. *Cy, you bastard.* I lean in toward the jury.

"It's clear that Jinks Lippert, the dreaded drug enforcer who had killed and maimed so many before, died as a result of bullets fired from a gun by Damon, and that the lethal bullet was fired while Lippert lay prone on the sidewalk. The defense does not suggest otherwise."

Then how can you say he's innocent? the jurors' stares ask. I need to hook them in.

"What is in doubt—grave doubt—is the state of Damon's mind when he fired those bullets." I offer the hint of a sad smile, as though I'm talking to my friends. "Before you can convict this young man of murder, you must conclude beyond a reasonable doubt that he deliberately fired the lethal bullets with the intent to kill Lippert. On this point, the evidence—the only evidence—is that Damon did not intend to kill Lippert."

I'm on a roll. The adrenaline kicks in. The jury shifts in their chairs; they're with me. "Damon was terrified that Lippert would kill him because Damon had inadvertently sold drugs on the territory that Lippert's boss, Kellen, claimed. Damon, if he wished to preserve his life, had only one choice—to get a gun to defend himself. And so that is what he did."

I slowly walk along the length of the jury box. "Damon Cheskey—a nice boy from a God-fearing family—told you what happened that fateful night. Scared out of his mind, he had hit up on amphetamines. He doesn't do drugs now—he's been to rehab and put that behind him—but then he was sick. Put yourself in Damon's mind—imagine his terror. Lippert swaggered over to him and told him he was dead meat. Damon saw him reaching for his gun. Damon panicked and fired. It was fire first or die." I reach the end of the box, stop. "There can be no doubt—Damon Cheskey fired on Lippert in self-defense. If Damon shot to defend himself, you must acquit him."

I see the jury softening, bending my way—some of them, anyway. The insurance man looks straight ahead, unmoved. But Betty O'Shea's brow is creased in a sad way, and the barista sends Damon a teary look. Damon gives her a tragic half smile. *Good,* I think, *no harm in a little chemistry*.

"Mr. Kenge will tell you that each shot required two deliberate acts—cocking the gun and pulling the trigger. He will ask why, if Damon feared that Lippert would kill him, did he not stop shooting after the first two shots to the chest? He will tell you that

Damon fired the fatal shots into the head of a man who, at that time, posed no threat, and that Damon cannot claim to have killed Lippert in self-defense. It is a powerful argument," I glance at Cy; he's not amused. "But it overlooks the evidence that those last three shots were a continuation of the first two. You listened to Damon tell you, tears in his eyes, that the shots came in blind succession—it was all a blur. Other witnesses put only a second or two between the shots to the chest and the shots to the head. Dr. Effington, one of this city's most respected psychiatrists, testified that you or I might have made a measured decision that Lippert no longer posed a threat, but Damon was incapable of making that judgment in his amphetamine-crazed state of panic. And to eliminate any residual doubt you might have, one of Vancouver's finest and most experienced police officers, Sergeant Petrov, told you that even with a single-shot gun, rapid fire syndrome can make all five shots virtually automatic for a farm boy like Damon, who grew up shooting gophers for Sunday target practice."

I see the jury leaning forward, hanging on each word. Even the insurance executive. Time to wind up.

"The law does not require a person defending himself against serious harm or death to measure precisely what is required to remove the impending threat. Damon could have accepted Lippert's death sentence, but he refused. He fought back to save his life. Ladies and gentlemen of the jury, that is the evidence. And on that evidence, you must, I submit, conclude that the Crown has failed to discharge its burden of proving Damon Cheskey guilty of murder."

Betty O'Shea nods; the barista wipes a tear from her eye. They have to be unanimous to convict. We may just have a chance.

I sit down. Justice Orrest gives me a sympathetic look. *Not bad, Ms. Truitt, under the circumstances.* She turns to the jury. "We'll take a short recess before we hear from the Crown."

"Nice try, Jilly," Cy says as the jury files out. "Sadly, for your client, not quite enough." If Cy's worried, it's not showing.

AFTER THE RECESS, CY MAKES his pitch.

He recaps the prosecution's case, then attacks our defense of local improvement. "Jinks Lippert," he says, pivoting toward the jury, "may have been a street dealer and enforcer. No doubt he was not the sort of man you would invite to tea in your parlor." Small smile. "But even not-so-nice people have a right to live. Canadian society has not yet—and hopefully never will—reach the point where one citizen has the right to kill another just because they don't think he is a good person."

The just society argument; a few jurors nod. "Ms. Truitt paints a picture of a naïve, well-intentioned, confused youth. But look at the facts. Damon Cheskey is a young man of superior intelligence, with a term of university behind him. Good family, no mental illness, no extenuating factors that might lead him into what Ms. Truitt so eloquently describes as his inevitable downward spiral. The truth is that Damon Cheskey, a boy with every advantage, *chose* to forget all he had been taught about right and wrong. He *chose* to do drugs, knowing what he did about the dangers of them. He *chose* to continue taking drugs and to leave university for a life on the street. This privileged young man with a world of opportunities before him *chose* to start selling drugs. That's the truth. Self-defense," he guffaws to the jury, "what a joke. Damon Cheskey, in defiance of all the street rules, *chose* to sell drugs on Kellen's territory. And, when the inevitable response came from

Kellen's enforcer, Jinks Lippert, Damon Cheskey *chose* to go out and steal a gun."

Cy shifts and sends me a steely gaze. *Watch how a pro does it.*

I glare back. *Do your best, Cy.*

"At each step, Damon Cheskey could have turned and walked away. But he didn't. Instead, he made his final, fatal choice—to seek out Mr. Lippert and fire five shots into his chest and head. The first two shots, you have heard, did not kill Mr. Lippert. If the accused had stopped there, Mr. Lippert would be alive today. But Damon Cheskey left nothing to chance. He had decided—he had *chosen*—to kill Mr. Lippert. So he went on to fire three more shots to Mr. Lippert's head as he lay helpless and bleeding on the pavement. Each time, he had to cock the pistol, pull the trigger. Each time, he made a deliberate choice. That's not self-defense, that's murder. Those, ladies and gentlemen of the jury, are the facts. And there is only one verdict consistent with those facts—guilty as charged of first-degree murder."

As Cy returns to the counsel table, he stops to look at Damon in the prisoner's box. The jurors' eyes follow Cy's and read the contempt in his look. Heart sinking, I watch as their faces harden and close.

CHAPTER 10

JEFF AND I WAIT ON a low bench in the Great Hall under slanting sheets of green glass. The jury has been out for three hours. Justice Orrest charged them this afternoon on the law and the evidence, barely a hint of incredulity as she described the theory of the defense.

"We're done," Jeff grieves. "It's the mechanic. He understands the world in pieces; you press, something happens—you don't press, nothing happens. He's not buying our rapid fire syndrome."

"Jeff, it takes twelve to convict, one to acquit. Delay is good news. Someone is having a problem with guilt." Still, it will be a miracle if whoever that someone is—I'm thinking the barista—continues to hold out.

A stray lawyer detours to tell me that the bets in the barristers' lounge are not in our favor, but I'm more interested in Sheriff Clara Klinks coming down the corridor.

"Thanks a million," I say to the lawyer, my eyes on Clara. Her stride tells me she's on her way somewhere; her expression tells me she'd like to stop but shouldn't. I decide to make the decision for her.

"How's it going, Clara?" I ask, intercepting her path.

She looks around to see if anyone is watching. "Lots of discussion. So loud it's coming through the walls." She sighs. "They want dinner, so nothing will happen before eight at the earliest. Might as well get something yourself."

"Thanks, Clara." She hurries off, and I hear a click behind me. Cy is approaching, alone. I give him a small wave.

"Long wait," I offer.

"Evidently you've managed to confuse them, Jilly. But I expect they'll overcome it." He leans toward me and lowers his voice. "That last-minute trick you pulled calling Petrov and his cock-and-bull theory of rapid fire syndrome—" He breaks off.

I take a good look at him. His skin is transparent as Meissen and black pools sag under his eyes. He hasn't slept for days. I need to talk to him about setting a schedule for Trussardi, but this isn't the time or place.

"How's Lois?"

"Wearing." He changes the subject. "Going to grab a bite with Emily. Could be a long night."

I wonder if he means the jury or what awaits him at home when Orrest finally lets us go. Out of the corner of my eye, I see Sheriff Clara descending on us.

"They've changed their mind," she says breathlessly. "They're ready to bring in the verdict now."

"Somebody couldn't stand the thought of another KFC dinner and caved," I say lightly, but this is not good news for us.

We shuffle back into the courtroom, watch while the prisoner and jury are escorted back in. Damon sits motionless, pale as chalk. I try to catch his eye—*you're not alone*—but he stares straight ahead as if in a trance.

Justice Orrest climbs the bench with a heavy step. She, too, looks weary. "Madam foreperson, has the jury reached a verdict?"

Betty O'Shea stands. She throws her shoulders back in her shiny gray suit, looks straight at Orrest. For this moment, she is totally in command, and she's making the most of it. I wonder idly how her life on Nanaimo Street will seem after this experience. Will she toss her adult children out? Tell her dockworker husband to take out the garbage on Wednesday morning? Maybe she'll leave him and find a new life.

"We have," Betty O'Shea intones. "We find the accused not guilty."

The courtroom erupts. The handful of court watchers who have stayed with us to the end let out a whoop. From the bleachers I hear a low groan that becomes a sob—Damon's mother. Damon rises shakily, sinks back to his seat, unable to believe what he's heard.

"Order!" cries the clerk.

I glance at Cy. It's his right to have the jury polled; for a moment I think he's going to exercise it, but he inclines his head. Not this time. Orrest thanks the jury and takes her leave. Behind us, the crowd disperses. It's over.

Cy is pushing himself up on his crutch, taking the aisle in a single stride. I offer my hand and a nod, but he looms over me. "Travesty of justice," he hisses. "I taught you too well, Jilly Truitt." He swings round and heads for the door. "Don't worry," he calls over his shoulder. "We'll pick him up on new charges before long. Just pray he doesn't kill again next time."

The force of his venom paralyzes me. *Get over it, Cy*, I think. But deep inside it hits me: he won't. My kindly mentor is no more; an implacable adversary has taken his place.

I feel a tug on the sleeve of my gown, turn.

"Ms. Truitt." Damon's hand trembles as he pulls it away. "Thank you."

"We got lucky," I say. "Today, by some miracle, you got the rest of your life back. Promise me you won't throw it away."

He struggles for sound, nothing comes out.

"I know you can do it, Damon. You have everything to live for." I glance at the bar that divides the lawyers from the audience, where his parents wait, faces wet with relief.

"I won't let you down, Ms. Truitt." His voice is uncertain but his eyes are bright.

I nod and watch him return to his parents and head toward the door.

Abruptly, all is quiet. I feel the letdown coming on as the adrenaline dissipates. I turn to Jeff and notice lines on either side of his mouth I never saw before and wonder how things are at home. "How's Jessica?" Jessica is a fragile flower, too delicate to be the wife of a trial lawyer.

"Last time I looked, her jeans were still on the hook."

"Jeff, I'm giving you an order. Float plane, the Island, Deep Cove Chalet. Tomorrow. On me."

He gives me a wan smile. "If you say so, boss." I watch him make his way to the elevator, twin briefcases rolling behind.

Alone behind the wheel of my Mercedes, I nose up the parking ramp and south. I go two blocks before it hits me—I'm headed in the wrong direction. It's my routine when a trial is over to head south to Shaughnessy and Mike. He pours me a glass of wine, sits me on his love seat, listens as I recount what happened, moment by moment, hour by hour, day by day, not revealing whether I won or lost until the very end. *Ah*, he will say if I've won, *that calls for a toast*. Or if I've lost, *I think you need a hug*. Debriefing, decompressing, the restoration of normalcy.

Except Mike isn't there anymore, not for me, anyway. I'm heading back to Yaletown when my cell phone buzzes.

Maybe it's Mike, I think as I fish into my bag for my phone. *Stop dreaming, Jilly, it's over with you and Mike.* The screen tells me it's Edith Hole.

Edith is my social worker. An orphan needs many people in her life. One of them is a meta-manager charged with the basic task of seeing that the orphan has a roof over her head most, if not all, of the time. When they found me on the street—in my imagination it's always just *the street*—Edith took me in. When the minister and his wife died, Edith found me a new home. When I got thrown out of the next home for altering my second foster father's food in unmentionable ways, Edith found me another home, and another and another, until finally she discovered the marvelous Maynes, who in their own inimitable, neglectful, but affectionate way, saw me through high school and university.

I think about letting it go to voicemail, but then some latent urge to connect with the closest thing I have to a birth mom surfaces. I pull over.

"Edith, how are you?"

"Fine. Just thought we should have lunch—it's been forever." Her familiar tone, even and infinitely patient, wraps around me.

"Sure. I'd like that."

"Trafalgar's Bistro," she says. "Next Saturday, twelve thirty? Call me if you can't make it. Otherwise, I'll be there."

I think of my calendar, nothing but blanks where it says Saturday. "Great, Edith. See you then."

Suddenly I'm tired. I nose the car back into the traffic and head home.

CHAPTER 11

I LIVE IN THE MOST beautifully situated city in the world, the travelogues like to brag—only Rio gives it a run for its money. Yet too often I could be in any gray place, nothing but fog and cloud and the sleet of rain as I navigate the soaked asphalt. No beaches, no ocean, no mountains. Just one bleak street after the other.

But today, as I drive through Stanley Park toward the bridge, the clouds lift and the sun shafts through. The North Shore Mountains emerge in all their snow-capped splendor. Whatever I find at the Trussardi residence, savory or unsavory, at least the view promises to be spectacular. At a red light, I input the address on my GPS and study the map that will guide me through the labyrinth of trails linking the mansions of the North Shore. Trussardi repeated his offer of dinner when we arranged today's meeting, and I reluctantly accepted. *Forget professional niceties*, I told myself. I want to win this case. If that means breaking bread with my client to get him to open up, then so be it.

It takes less time than I expect, so with fifteen minutes to spare, I pull into a cul-de-sac uphill from my destination and fish the envelope Cy gave me from my bag. I open the flap, take the photos out, and note the time and date stamped on each—Saturday, May 4, 2014, 5:38 p.m.—before inspecting them one by one.

I am used to looking at photographs of crime scenes. They are never pretty, never fail to punch me in the viscera. What was once alive is now dead; what was once human has been utterly, irrevocably dehumanized. Even when the victim is a monster, like Kellen's enforcer, the still flesh packs its punch. But these photos are worse. The forensic pathologists have likely already assigned words to what the photos show: *female, Caucasian, well nourished. Tied at the hands and feet. Bruises to the face, hips, and upper thighs. Cause of death: bullet entering base of the skull, exiting left temple.*

Those are the words. But it takes pictures to tell the story of a death. IF YOU CAN SAY IT IN WORDS, WHY PAINT? a banner on the art gallery once proclaimed. These photos paint, and the picture is evil.

Who could have done this? I push the key into the dash and rev the motor. *And why?*

The Trussardi house descends the rocky cliff in a graceful cascade of glass and cedar. It is unobtrusive, tailored to blend seamlessly into the landscape of red-streaked boulders and evergreens. I park my car in the drive and follow flagstone steps down to a massive door carved with Salish motifs. I push the brass bell and wait.

A beautiful woman appears in the doorway.

"Miss Truitt?" she asks. "I am Carmelina, the housekeeper. Please come with me."

Housekeeper indeed. More like Sophia Loren. She moves like a cat, hips swaying, as she leads me through the upper gallery. Paintings glow like lighted jewels on the white walls, and cabinets of pale wood and glass line the wall at the end of the room—no doubt they house the famed Trussardi collection of Indigenous boxes and baskets. Nearby, bathed in a cone of discreet light, green men in a clamshell row toward some mythic nirvana.

I follow Carmelina's long legs—despite the intermittent gloom, she is wearing shorts—down shallow steps to the living area. Through walls of glass, I glimpse English Bay, gray-streaked orange in the lowering sun.

Vincent Trussardi is standing on the terrace, back to me. *Taking in the view*, I think, and then his fist comes down on the railing. He utters a low animal moan that makes me catch my breath.

Carmelina hesitates, then slides the half-open glass door aside. "Miss Truitt has arrived," she says, pushing a sculpted wave of dark hair from her face.

Vincent turns, and his shoulders relax as he settles his mask of equanimity back in place. "Excuse me, Miss Truitt, I am remiss." He waves to the chair next to his. "Please, do be seated."

"Thank you," I say, sinking into the chair.

"May I offer you a refreshment?" Carmelina hands me a stemmed glass before I can answer.

"Nice place. Nice things."

"You mean the art, my collections."

"Everything." My eyes follow Carmelina's retreating figure, then swivel back to Trussardi.

"Given the choice, I opt for the aesthetically pleasing." He takes a small sip of wine. "Even in housekeepers. Why live with the mediocre if beauty is available?"

I think of the crime scene photos—not much beauty there. "Before we go further, Mr. Trussardi, I need to be certain that you want me to act for you. There are many excellent defense lawyers available in this city. You aren't bound to me."

He eyes me curiously. "Are you saying you don't want to take my case?"

"No," I reply. "But you cannot be unaware of the fact that I have been linked to a cousin of your late wife."

"If you are referring to the photograph of you holding hands with your fiancé on the steps of the cathedral, yes, I am aware. And I am not in the least concerned."

"You should know that he was never my fiancé. And we are no longer together."

He sets down his glass. "Miss Truitt, it would grieve me to think that I may have come between you and your—friend."

"No," I say. "It's more complicated than that." Why should he care? Most of my clients don't give a damn about my personal life.

"If there's something I can do to help . . ." He lets the words hang. "Forget I raised it."

The words I usually find to fill moments such as these do not come. We stare out over the sea. The sun is on the horizon; it lowers, begins to sink. When it is no more than a sliver of red on the edge of the ocean, he breaks the silence.

"Miss Truitt, Carmelina has prepared a small repast. After, whether we like it or not, we must attend to our business."

WE DINE ON *VITELLO TONNATO* and a green salad that Carmelina—now clad in a dark wrap dress—brings to the glass table. Her cleavage, as she leans to serve Trussardi, glows golden in the candlelight.

I purse my lips, focus on the food. Something in the sauce—anchovies perhaps?—elevates the chilled veal from banal to exquisite. "This is excellent," I say.

"Classic Italian dish," Trussardi replies. "But I must admit, Carmelina does it well."

It's out of my mouth before I can stop it. "What else does Carmelina do well?"

"Enough, Miss Truitt."

I accept the reprimand. "Sure. My apologies."

No point in prematurely offending him, I think. But I know one thing for certain—if Cy finds a way to get Carmelina on the stand, it will not be good for Vincent Trussardi's chances.

After dinner, we move to the fireplace, where Carmelina has set espressos on a low table near the suede banquette. "How did you and Laura meet?" I ask, finally getting to the reason I'm here.

"I don't know if I want to think about it. Don't know if I can."

"You must." I know all the jargon: *get beyond denial, get beyond grief.* But jargon doesn't get the job done.

"Very well." Eyes half closed, he begins. "I was looking for someone to help me catalogue my Haida collection. A friend in the department of anthropology recommended one of his graduate students—Laura. I contacted her; she seemed interested. I lived in a penthouse downtown at the time, and she came to see the collection. She fell in love"—a bitter downturn of lip—"in love with the collection. I hired her."

He stares into the fire. "She visited almost every day. At first I hardly saw her. I gave her the keys, and she came and went as she pleased while I went about my own affairs. It was a hectic time. I was focusing on rebuilding the business, traveling a lot. Then one day I came back from I can't remember where and I turned the key in the lock and there she was." He looks up. "Sitting among my baskets and boxes on the floor of my living room. She was wearing jeans with a T-shirt and sneakers. When I entered, she started and flushed, and her hand went to her face to push a strand of hair back." His voice breaks. "And—and I fell in love."

"Just like that?" I probe. "I mean, I've done my research. You'd had other women in your life. Quite a few."

"Dalliances, affairs, infatuations. But not love."

"Until Laura?"

He turns away. "Yes, until Laura."

Something in the way he answers makes me wary. "Please go on," I say.

Trussardi clears his throat. "I courted her madly. Took her to dinners and shows, flew her to L.A., Palm Springs, and New York. Bought her paintings and jewels. It wasn't an easy conquest, but ultimately, she succumbed. Her family was against our union. But in the end she agreed, and we were married in a small Catholic ceremony."

"How did she feel toward you?"

"Did she love me, you mean? No, she fell for my baskets, but she never fell for me the way I did for her. She always held something back, a core of reserve I tried to pierce." He sighs. "Without success."

"You were married for some time. Was it a happy marriage? Did you fight? Were there other people in your lives?"

He takes a long time to answer. "I've already told you, sometimes her do-gooding drove me mad. I suppose I was jealous, upset I wasn't enough to fill her life. But I told myself to accept it—no—to admire it. She was born to privilege, beautiful, rich, *entitled*, but she refused to accept that entitlement. She insisted on doing what she could to alleviate the suffering of those less fortunate. But then . . ."

"Then what?"

"She had an affair with the architect who designed this house, Trevor Shore." He looks at me bleakly. "I told the police about it in my statement. I failed to mention it to you earlier, at your office."

"You should have. You agreed not to hide anything."

"I'm sorry."

My mind clicks back to the day of the funeral. "The architect. Was he the man outside the church?"

"So you noticed. That was unfortunate. Their affair—meaningless while it lasted—ended long ago." His mouth sets in a hard line. "Bad taste, running after the hearse."

I need to ask about Shore, find out what the police—what Cy—knows, but Trussardi loops back to the house, to the beginning.

"I bought this piece of land a long time ago—something I picked up in a side deal on a transaction. Normally I didn't share business matters with Laura, but we found ourselves driving by on a Sunday afternoon, and on a whim I took a detour and showed it to her. She stood in the pines and looked out over the ocean. 'Darling,' she said, 'the view is amazing. We should build here, live here.' I could refuse her nothing; she was my beautiful pet. So we built the house, and along the way, Laura decided we should make it a proper place to showcase our collection. But apart from approving the plans, I had little to do with this house." He waves his hand around the room. "Everything you see is her doing. A remarkable achievement, don't you think?"

"Undoubtedly." I cast my eye over the room. "It's stunning. But getting back to the affair—was she in love with the architect?"

A harsh laugh. "She didn't fall in love with *him*. She got caught up in the aesthetics of the enterprise, and he was part of it, just as she had with my baskets and boxes. It all blurred together—her infatuation with the design and building of the house, and the man who was creating it."

"How did *you* feel about their affair?"

"Obviously I didn't like it. Things hadn't been perfect between Laura and me, but I still wanted her and hoped that we could make the marriage work." He buries his head in his hands for a moment. "I got it into my head that if we had a child, things would be better between us."

"You said the affair was over. Is it possible that she was still involved with Shore until recently?"

"No—that's what was so bizarre about his demonstration at the funeral. They had broken it off last fall. They'd been quarreling for some time. He wanted her to divorce me and marry him, but she was beginning to wonder what she had seen in him." He gives me a wan smile. "The house was built; the attraction faded. One night she came home, face streaked with tears. There was a bruise under her eye." He stops, looks up. "Do you think he could have killed Laura?"

A violent lover desperate to keep the relationship alive. *Perhaps we can make something of that*, I think. *Maybe even parlay it into a reasonable doubt.* I lock it in my mental filing cabinet and push on.

"He may have had a motive," I say. "What happened next?"

"I held her and comforted her. Told her we should give our marriage another try, that we should have a child." He shrugs. "To use the banal vernacular, we reconciled."

"Was it still that way when she died?"

"Yes. In fact, I had reason to believe that she was pregnant."

I sit back. More good news. What man anxious to have a child would kill his pregnant wife?

"Had she seen a doctor?"

"I don't think so, but she told me she thought she was pregnant."

"So, no one else knew? It's just your word?"

"Yes, I suppose so."

Not great, but presumably the coroner took blood—maybe it will reveal pregnancy.

"Did Laura's charity work involve her with dangerous people?" I ask, changing course.

He ruminates, eyeing the orange and black etchings of the Riopelle on the far wall. "She used to bring homeless kids to the house, give them a bath and a meal, and hope it would make a difference. Once . . ."

"Yes?"

"Once she brought a boy back. Sick, spaced out on drugs. She must have picked him up off the street somewhere, brought him home to clean him up and get him into new clothes. She was going to take him to a psychiatrist, but he ran away." He pauses. "I thought, *Good riddance*—he scared me. But he kept coming back, like he was fixated on her. The gardener told me he would find the boy lurking outside the house."

Another suspect if Trevor Shore doesn't pan out. "Do you know his name? How we can find him?"

"No, I don't know his name, and the chances of finding him are slim to none. There are hundreds like him on the streets and under the bridges."

It's growing late, but there is one more area I need to explore.

"You said you were sailing the day your wife was killed? All day?"

"Yes," he says. "I came back around five in the afternoon, put the boat in the slip at the Royal Vancouver Yacht Club."

Of course, I think, *the oldest yacht club in town.*

"I came home and found the body. You know the rest."

"Are you sure no one saw you at the club?" I ask.

"I had breakfast at the club. There'll be a record of that."

Not good enough, I think. Cy will argue that he could have gone for breakfast and decided not to take the boat out, or taken it out and returned early enough to kill his wife. "What about later?"

"I'm sure someone must have seen me on my return. There were people around. But I can't remember anyone in particular."

"You didn't stop at the club? Talk to anyone?"

"Sorry, Miss Truitt. I did not. I was late, anxious to get back to Laura—we always ate at seven thirty. I was looking forward to a shower, a drink with her, a quiet supper at home. I wanted to be with her." He gathers himself. "I am not a warm man, Miss Truitt, nor a particularly demonstrative one. But that afternoon I felt hope—tenderness, even."

I hold his eye, waiting for him to look aside, but he doesn't. Maybe he's telling the truth. Maybe he's just a good liar. *Lie*, I think, *but not to me.*

"It's getting late. I wanted to meet your sister, but—"

"I'm afraid that is not possible. She is out of the country."

"What do you mean?"

"My sister is—how shall I put it—unwell. She is receiving medical care abroad."

"I see. She was in her apartment here at the time of the murder?"

"Yes. She didn't hear or see anything."

"An intrusion. An epic struggle. Gunshots. And she didn't hear a thing?"

He stiffens. "Her apartment is entirely separate. And she was listening to music."

"Listening to music?" My voice rises. I force it down. "Have the police talked to her?"

"Of course. She told them just what I am telling you. Didn't hear a thing."

I swallow my frustration. "When will your sister be back?"

"I don't know. A couple of weeks. It all depends."

"What's her illness?"

"It's—complicated."

"Terminal?"

"No. She'll be here for the trial, if that's your concern."

"Let me know the minute she gets back. I need to talk to her."

"Certainly, Miss Truitt."

I stand. "Just one more thing. Before I go, could I see the room—where she died?"

"The room's been cleaned. Is it really necessary to see it?"

"It is. In cross-examination, every detail counts."

"If you insist, but you won't find much."

He leads me past a sandstone wall, down a softly lit corridor. He swings a door open, flicks a light switch, steps aside. I enter alone.

He's right; there's not much to see. Whoever cleaned up after the crime scene unit left did a good job. The pale carpet is pristine, the silk duvet spotless, the pillows fluffed and neatly stacked. I cross to the headboard, a lush affair of tufted suede, move a cushion. A small hole marks the place where the bullet lodged. I put my little finger in, move it around. I pull it out and stare at a fleck of dried blood on my nail. Clean, but not perfect.

Who did this? And why? The besotted architect? The drug-addled boy? Trussardi, driven to madness by his wife's casual causes and affair?

Back at the front door, I extend my hand. "See you next week, Mr. Trussardi. And thank you for the *vitello*."

"A pleasure, Miss Truitt, *prego*." He says it with conviction.

I climb into my car and head back to Yaletown.

CHAPTER 12

"CRAZY," I TELL JEFF AS we commune over coffee in our diminutive boardroom the next morning. "He sits there and tells me how his wife—his dear, beloved, perfect wife—was having an affair with the architect. So I ask, 'How did you feel about that?'

"'Obviously I didn't like it,' he says. I mean, really, Jeff. *Didn't like it?*"

"Clearly, you've never been married, Jilly. Sometimes you just have to suck it up. It's called 'saving the marriage.'"

"You mean you and Jessica?"

"Don't go there," says Jeff. "Just don't."

I give him a look.

"Sorry, boss—that was out of line."

"It's okay." His use of *boss* from time to time is more a figure of speech than a nod to hierarchy, which is fine by me. His face is closed. *Guess the weekend away didn't work.*

Jeff brings us back to Trussardi. "Just because he's not weeping doesn't mean he didn't care. I'd be more worried if he was carrying on."

I remember Trussardi's head in his hands as he told me of the affair. "You've got a point," I say.

"Thanks. Occasionally I do."

I down the rest of my latte. "We need to check out the architect—who is he, what's his history, you know."

"Just what every murder case needs—an alternate suspect."

"Exactly. He loved her, he lost her—became crazed, violent. Would calm, civilized art collector Vincent Trussardi kill his wife? Unlikely. Would a crazed, in-love, jilted romantic with violent tendencies kill the mistress who threw him over? Perhaps."

Jeff nods along with my ramble.

"I'll get Richard on it," I say. Richard Beauvais, our go-to private eye. Best in the business.

I tell Jeff about the kid Trussardi's wife brought home, too.

"Needle in a haystack, Jilly, but no harm asking Richard to look into it, just in case."

"Yes, and another thing. Cy. I need to talk to him about the timing of the trial. Not exactly looking forward to that conversation."

"He said too much after Cheskey. But he's still Prosecutor Numero Uno. We have to forgive and forget." Jeff stands. "Gotta get to 222 Main for a sentencing. Good luck."

Alone, I reach for the phone and tap the contact for Richard Beauvais. The ring flips to voicemail. "Richard, I've got this case, name's Trussardi." I tell him about Trevor Shore and the boy. "See what you can find out."

I move on to Cy. There's some fussing at the other end while the receptionist pretends to be looking for him. "It's important," I repeat.

Finally, he comes on.

"If you're calling about Cheskey, I'm not appealing."

So he's still angry. I let it go. "Cy, we need to talk about Trussardi."

"What's to talk about?"

"Timing. How do you see this playing out?"

"I assume you want to drag things out as long as you can."

"Usually that's what my client wants. You know that old-fashioned thing lawyers are supposed to do—take instructions from their client?"

He grunts. "What kind of time frame are we talking about?"

"My client's open. But he's innocent. The sooner this cloud's lifted and he can get on with his life, the better from his perspective."

"Some cloud, some innocence." Cy snorts. "Tell him to enjoy his bail as long as he can."

"How about the preliminary in June, Cy, trial in the fall? Complete the disclosure ASAP."

"You're crazy."

"As I say, Trussardi's looking forward to his acquittal. Sooner the better."

"You've lost it, Jilly. But what do I care? The chiefs are under the gun for court delays, access to justice, yadda, yadda, yadda. We might be able to get a slot for the preliminary this summer. Except I'm busy. Planning a vacation. First in three years."

"Feeling a little down after Cheskey?" I shoot back, and regret it. *Why am I pushing? Do I really believe Trussardi's innocent, believe we can win?* "Sorry, Cy. We can go fast or slow, either way. If you're inclined to go fast, it's just a preliminary—Emily can handle it. Or better yet, cancel it. You may not have a winner, but there's enough to tell me the judge will send this to trial. Full disclosure is what I'm after."

"As you wish, Jilly. I don't mind cancelling the prelim. And no harm in trying to get trial dates. Might even get me a bonus. My masters in the Ministry of Justice are keen on speeding up the trial process, too. Flavor of the week."

"Thanks, Cy. Appreciate it. Let me know what happens."

My phone is halfway to the receiver when I hear his voice. "You got lucky on Cheskey, Jilly. But this time, you're going down."

"Whatever you say, Cy. Just call me when you get the dates."

CHAPTER 13

TRAFALGAR'S BISTRO ON SIXTEENTH IS a nice little place on a trendy corner, suburban transitioning to urban. Leafy trees grow between the sidewalk and the street, flowers overflow baskets onto the pavement. Vancouver loves its gardens. Trafalgar's used to be a place to have pastry and coffee with friends in the morning, but now it serves soups and salads all day. Wine comes if you want, but coffee is still favored. Vancouver also loves its coffee—right up there after the flowers.

Edith Hole waits for me at a small table in the corner, not far from the window. At fifty-five, she has learned to grab the light when she can find it. Today she is lucky. The clouds that threatened to douse me as I made my ten-kilometer run around Stanley Park this morning have scuttled eastward, and the spring sun shines brightly.

Her right hand cradles her coffee mug; her left holds the newspaper open. She stands for a hug. With no lipstick and rimless glasses, Edith looks exactly as I know her to be—earnest, caring, and exceedingly proper. We settle in while the waitress, a teenager in black tights and a white apron, fills my coffee cup.

"I was just reading about you, Jilly," Edith says. "It seems you've had a big win. Congratulations." She speaks with a cheerful tone. They must teach them that in social work school—*Now don't worry, dear, everything will be all right.* Still, she has done me countless favors over the years, including saving my life once or twice.

"I got lucky. But I'm glad we won. Damon is a good kid, just confused. His life would have been hell in prison."

"That's what the paper says—the luck part, I mean. Nobody expected an acquittal." She takes a sip of coffee. "You should take credit where credit is due, Jilly. Who would have guessed you'd become a successful trial lawyer?"

I smile. Social workers see a lot of failures. They should be allowed to bask in the odd success. We order salads. She tells me she's thinking of retiring soon.

"I saw that movie a while back with Julia Roberts—*Eat, Pray, Love,*" she says. "Anyway, Julia comes to a dead end in her life and decides to travel. She ends up in Indonesia—I can't recall what she's doing there, but there's a man in the picture. I thought, why not me? I mean, I know I'm not likely to find my personal Javier Bardem, but still I want to travel, meet people . . ."

I study Edith with fresh eyes. It never occurred to me that she might have a personal life; that she might be interested in a man, or a woman for that matter; that she might occasionally long for something other than her pristine townhouse and her job of rescuing abandoned children.

Our salads arrive. I push the mango around in the arugula. "Edith, don't answer this if you'd rather not, but have you ever had anyone—like a partner, I mean—in your life?"

Her fair skin flushes. "Well, there was someone, actually—a long time ago. Not a marriage, just a liaison. But it didn't work out."

I try to imagine my social worker—the soul of middle-class morality—in bed with a man.

"You left him?"

"More the other way around." Her voice drops to a whisper. "He never loved me, just used me. When he didn't need me anymore, he left me and married someone else."

"All these years and I never dreamed," I say, wondering what Edith had that a man might need and then suddenly not need. "I mean, I'm sorry." Then brightening, "But you're right—you're healthy, attractive; you should see the world. It would do you good. And who knows? Not all men are cads, Edith."

"No," she replies. "Mike's not. You're lucky to have Mike."

"Yeah." I decide not to tell her that Mike's dropped me. Or that I walked out on Mike. Take your pick. A carapace is slowly forming over my soft, sweet zone of sorrow; I take care not to bruise it with ill-timed confessions.

We talk about the weather—an unseasonably warm spring—about how I guilt myself over my expensive new car, about how I still have the tattoo on my right shoulder that says REBEL in fancy curlicues. Every visit, Edith finds a way to tell me it's time to have the tattoo removed.

"You always were your own person, Jilly," she muses. "That's what got you through."

"*You* got me through, Edith."

"I did what I thought I should. But you always understood, even when you were little, that it's better to live your own life imperfectly than to imitate someone else's life perfectly."

"Wow," I say, smiling. "That's profound."

She blushes. "That's what Javier says in the movie."

I reach for her hand, and it just comes out, the thing I've been thinking about too much lately. "You know who my parents are, don't you, Edith? You were there from the start."

"You know I can't tell you that, Jilly. It's confidential. Why are you asking now? You've never been interested before."

"Forget it. I don't want to know."

The waitress brings the check, and I pay, but before I can begin my goodbye, Edith leans forward. "I read that you're acting for Vincent Trussardi." The intensity in her gaze takes me aback.

"That's right."

"Please drop his case, Jilly," she says, voice faltering.

"Why?"

"I can't tell you why." She clutches my hand. "But I know things."

"About Trussardi?"

"About him and his sister." She stops herself. "Just drop the case, Jilly."

This isn't the first time I've been warned off a case, but it's the first time I've heard such cautions from Edith. "Why?" I ask again.

"He should never have married her," she whispers; her hand is gripping mine so hard it hurts. "Don't do it, Jilly. Drop the case."

"Edith, what's going—"

But Edith is up and charging for the door, the strap of her bag flapping in her wake.

Outside, I search for her, no luck. I get in my car, slam the door hard behind me, and give the engine more gas than it needs. Questions swirl in my mind. *What did she mean when she said Trussardi should never have married Laura? What's his sister got to do with any of it?* And overarching them all, *What's happened to calm, unassuming, unflappable Edith?*

I make a mental note: *Visit Raquella Trussardi. The minute she's back in town.*

CHAPTER 14

TWO WEEKS LATER, I PULL up in the forecourt of the Trussardi estate. Raquella Trussardi has been detailed and insistent. While her domain is situated below and a little to the west of her brother's home, and yes, while the two dwellings are physically connected, they are separate spaces, and I'm to enter according to her instructions.

I follow the map I've been given to a stone court that looks out on English Bay. Strategically placed urns bright with blossoms frame a suite of modern sculptures—a bit of Brancusi, a couple of Arps, and, silhouetted against a wall of stone, quite probably a modest Moore. Then, fixating on where the door to this palace might be, I trip on a nude of massive proportions—a Botero, I speculate, recalling some tidbit on the arts pages of the *New York Times.* I turn and assess the massive thighs of stone—*damn,* this is something else.

A low laugh startles me, and I step back. Raquella Trussardi rolls out from the shelter of a potted palm, black eyes flashing, forefinger fixed on the go button as her motorized wheelchair bears down on me. *Joan Baez,* I think, remembering photos from my childhood of the slender, black-haired folk singer who enchanted a generation.

"So you like this sculpture, too, Miss Truitt," she says. Clearly, she is amused, although I'm not sure whether she's laughing at the fact that I tripped or at my reaction to the Botero.

"Actually, I do. She has—presence."

"A slight understatement?" Raquella comments.

I decide to take her head-on. "Any description, however eloquent, would be an understatement in the case of this work. Words are simply inadequate to the task, Miss Trussardi."

Her eyes scrutinize me. "You surprise me, Miss Truitt—in more ways than one. Perhaps my brother had more sense than I gave him credit for when he hired you."

"What do you mean?"

"Never mind."

"Miss Trussardi, your brother hired me because he needs a lawyer, and I happen to be in the business of providing the services he needs."

"Perhaps, Miss Truitt, although I would advise you never to underestimate Vincent." She pivots her chair in the direction of the house. "Shall we go in?"

I follow her through a broad door that stands open against the warmth of the afternoon—threshold flush with the terrace to accommodate her chair. The low hall gives way to the living room. I halt, blinded. The room is a sea of white sunlight dotted with islands of primary color. It's not as large as her brother's salon upstairs nor as pristine—photos vie for space on small tables and books are piled everywhere—but what it lacks in grandeur it makes up for in warmth. On the alabaster fireplace wall, an arrangement of red, blue, and yellow stripes that can only be a Newman gently vibrates.

As though following my thoughts, Raquella gestures expansively around the room. "As you can see, Miss Truitt, I am a woman of passion. Many passions. I am interested in so much; I *care* so much. There is never enough time for everything I want to read or see. I can't actually *do* much," she says, tapping the arm of her wheelchair, "but I manage nevertheless to live a passionate life."

So much for the unwell sister abroad for medical treatment. Like the Newman on the wall, the woman before me pulses with coiled energy, despite being confined to a wheelchair.

I settle on a sofa near where she parks.

"I expect you want to talk about Laura," she says. "And my brother."

"That would be a start, Miss Trussardi. I would also like to talk about what you may or may not have observed the day of the murder."

She waves her long, beringed fingers. "You will find I cannot be of much assistance, but go ahead and put your questions to me." As she speaks, she motions to the shadows. A small figure in a dark dress and white apron appears. "Angela, would you be so good as to bring us some tea?"

While we wait, I glance at the photos that stand on every surface—silver frames, black frames, fancy frames, plain frames. On the white baby grand in the corner, one portrait dominates the others—I recognize the smile of Laura Trussardi. Clearly the deceased was important to this woman—that may explain her animosity toward her brother. On the low table to my right sit sports photos showing Raquella in her youth blowing through powdery snow, Raquella arm in arm with an unknown woman on a craggy slope, Raquella on horseback, Raquella cradling a handgun in a shooting competition.

She follows my eye. "Perhaps you don't know. I was a pentathlon athlete in my day—on my way to the Olympics." She taps the arm of her chair as her eyes wander through the window toward the ocean. "Until the accident."

What accident, I wonder. She reads my mind.

"He came out of nowhere, a crazy, out-of-control skier. I flipped, my head hit a rock. The fall fractured my neck." She closes her eyes, her face a bitter mask. "It was all over."

"I didn't know. I'm sorry. The accident must have been a great shock."

"Indeed. For a long time I thought my world had ended. Then, while I was still struggling to find the courage to restart my life, my mother got cancer, died within months. Two years later, Papa went. I was alone, on my own. But somehow, I made it through, picked myself up, and decided to make a life of sorts. And so I have."

"I understand," I murmur.

Angela returns, offering porcelain cups, and the lavender scent of Earl Grey wafts up.

"Where was Vincent during all this?" I take a sip of tea.

"Floating around Europe, cruising with billionaires, dating starlets, living what they call the good life." Her tone turns from arch to bitter. "He made a brief courtesy call when I was injured, then promptly fled back across the pond."

"But when your parents died—"

"Yes, finally, when Papa fell ill, Vincent condescended to come home to check out the family finances. He had no choice—the business on this side of the Atlantic was abysmal. So he buckled down, pulled things out. To my surprise, he did rather well, until he overplayed his hand with the trust company."

"But he recovered, remade his fortune," I say.

"I see he's given you his usual line. But yes, you're right, he did." Her mouth sets in a prim line.

I decide to be presumptuous. "Why do you dislike him so?"

"We were strangers from the start." She reaches for her cup. "He came so much later. I was ten when he was born, but I was older than that inside—smart, competent, athletic. Everything I thought my parents wanted me to be. And then he came along. You would have thought he was the baby Jesus, to judge by the jubilation at his arrival. A *son.* I realized I was nothing, for no reason but that I had been born with two X chromosomes." She gives me a long look. "You're a woman, Miss Truitt—a sometime feminist, they say. How do you suppose I felt?"

I sympathize, remembering my own bewildered adolescent rages. *Is it more painful to have had a mother who turns away or never to have had a mother at all?*

"You must have felt it was very unfair. You must have been angry."

"Deeply angry. They left him the family business because he was *the son*. A trust for me—not ungenerous—but still, just a trust, enough for a daughter. I was forced to sit back helplessly and watch him wander back from Europe, dabble in this and that, play with the family fortune." She leans forward in her chair. "If you must know, Miss Truitt, I dislike him because he is *weak*."

The word, delivered in contemptuous tones, surprises me. "I would not have placed him as weak."

"He possesses a lovely façade—but underneath, he's an empty man. Life is a pleasure ride for Vincent. Not in the vulgar, carnal sense. My brother pursues only rariefied pleasures—his art, his table, a lovely woman on his arm. Even when he does the right thing, it's because it fits his image of how he should be. But he doesn't know what love is, what passion is."

I remember Trussardi's moan as he looked out over the ocean. Something doesn't fit. I take another sip of tea, put the cup down. "He never loved Laura?"

She swivels her chair dismissively. "As if."

"You disliked your brother, yet you came here to live with him—be near him. I don't understand, Miss Trussardi."

"I did not come for him. I came for *Laura*." She says the name slowly, like a caress—*Low-ra.*

"You were *friends*? You and Laura?"

"You might say that," she says, drawing herself up. "Laura was kind to me. She was growing unhappy with Vincent, more and more desolate in the wasteland of their marriage. She was lonely. So she took to visiting me in the afternoons. Not here. I lived in a condo in the West End at the time. We'd have tea, just as we are now, Miss Truitt, talk about pictures, her work, the house she was planning. 'You'll have a place in it,' she told me. 'Separate but near. Then we can visit whenever we want.'" Raquella spreads her hands. "What could I say? I let her carry on with her dream."

Vincent, apart from occasional annoyance with Laura's causes and upset over her brief affair, described a marriage of sweetness and light. Now dark stains are surfacing. "She wasn't happy?" I ask, concealing what I know. "There were troubles in the marriage?"

"I cannot say what passed between my brother and his wife. All I know is that she came to visit me more and more often."

"She never talked to you about her marriage?"

Raquella stiffens. "Why do you ask?"

I decide to confess. "I'm told she had an affair."

"Laura never loved Trevor Shore," she says, so low I can hardly hear.

"So you knew about the architect."

She makes no reply.

I move on. "What about the boy who used to hang around?"

"Laura was always picking up strays—it didn't mean anything."

"What was his name?"

She shrugs. "How should I know?"

"Do you know where he lived? Anything about him?"

An annoyed shake of the head.

"You knew Laura well. Did she have any problems? Alcohol, drugs?"

"Ridiculous. Laura's only problem was that she cared too much."

"Her causes, you mean?"

"That, too."

"What else did she care too much about?"

"Propriety," she says enigmatically.

I want to pursue, but her pursed lips tell me there's no point. I decide to take a shot in the dark—there is a question that's been nagging me since yesterday's lunch. "Do you know Edith Hole?"

I catch the sharp intake of breath before the mask comes

down. "I recognize the name." She stares at me. "I did not expect to like you, Miss Truitt, but I did not expect to find you disagreeable."

I have touched on a nerve. I ignore the insult. "How was Edith involved with your brother?"

"Some matter a long time ago. Must you pursue every private detail of every irrelevant aspect of his life, Miss Truitt?" she hisses. "Let's just say she rendered him certain services."

"What kind of services?"

She turns her head toward the window and the sea beyond. "I have nothing more to say on the subject, Miss Truitt. That pathetic woman has nothing to do with the matter at hand."

I remember Edith's figure fleeing the restaurant. *She rendered him certain services.* Something happened between Vincent and Edith, something so awful no one wants to talk about it. That doesn't sound like the Edith I know; the Edith I trust is simple, virtuous, beyond reproach.

"The time of Laura's death is estimated between three thirty and four p.m. on May fourth. Were you here at that time, Miss Trussardi?"

"I must have been."

"Did you hear anything? See anything?"

"I would have told the police if I had."

"No cries, no gunshot?"

"No, my house is separate from Vincent's in every way. Laura insisted on absolute soundproofing. And, as on most afternoons, I was listening to music." She points to a low cabinet. "I put on something serious, spend an hour or two just listening. Maybe an opera. That day it was Bruckner's Seventh."

"How can you remember what music you played and precisely how long it lasted?"

"It's very long, the Seventh. It had just ended when the police arrived. So I remember."

"Can Angela verify that?"

"No. Angela never comes on Sunday. It's her day off."

"Was Carmelina around? Did she ever come down here?"

"Never. I refuse to have anything to do with that woman. She arrived last fall—little girl from Calabria, out to see the world. Seems to have stalled here."

"Were Carmelina and your brother . . . involved?" Maybe Laura wasn't the only one stepping out.

"How you pry, Miss Truitt." A tight grimace. "I suppose it's what you lawyers get paid to do. How would I know what Vincent was up to?" Her voice drops. "Let's just say such conduct would not be against his principles—or his custom."

"Let me ask you frankly, just between you and me: Do you think your brother murdered Laura?"

"Of course," she says. "Who else would have done it?" She shakes her head grimly.

How can she be so sure? I wonder. "Perhaps it was her ex-lover, the architect," I offer.

"That milquetoast?" Her laugh is derisive. "No, it was Vincent. In his mind, Laura had betrayed him. He couldn't live with that."

"But why now? I mean, the affair was over. According to Vincent, they were reconciled, hoping for a child."

Her hands grip the arms of her chair for a moment, then unclench. "Maybe she told him something new, something that infuriated him. For all his hollow core, he's capable of considerable rage, my brother."

Her words quash any hope she might be useful at the trial. Raquella is determined to sink him.

"This interview is at an end, Miss Truitt."

"Let me at least take the cups to the kitchen," I say. She waves me down, but I already have our cups on the tray with the teapot. "No trouble."

I pass through a corridor in the direction from which Angela appeared, find the kitchen—a spotless, modern affair—and park the tray on the granite counter. I risk a quick look around. There's not much to see beyond the usual kitchen things—appliances, a brass bar cart—except, in the corner, a niche with an elevator. I cross to it. One direction. Up. So the apartment is not as separate from the house as Raquella pretends. Maybe Laura designed it so she could come down to visit Raquella whenever she pleased. Or so that Raquella could go up. Or someone else.

Raquella has wheeled in after me. "You may take your leave, Miss Truitt."

She swivels, and I follow her back to the living room.

"One more thing," I say, remembering what Vincent said about Laura. *She took my sister, Raquella—in a wheelchair and beset by demons—and gave her a reason to live.* "The picture I'm getting is this, Miss Trussardi. You were bitter and depressed, confined to a wheelchair, cut out of the family business, and ignored by your brother. Then Laura comes along and everything changes. She picks you up and gives you a reason to live. Makes a place for you in her life, in her house. You say the two of you were incredibly close. And yet you can't tell me what was happening between her and Vincent, what was going on in her mind or in her life? Something doesn't add up."

The wheelchair takes a sudden lurch toward me: I jump out of the way. "Get out. Now," Raquella rasps. *Anger? Pride? Or maybe fear? But why?*

"Thank you, Miss Trussardi," I say, and find the door.

At the corner of the walkway, I turn. Raquella sits in the sun, face of stone. I give her a smile. *You can't scare me. Off this case or anything else.*

Her chair whirls and she disappears behind the Botero.

ACT TWO

CHAPTER 15

"BOXES FOR YOU," DEBBIE SAYS, motioning to a tall stack of cardboard containers beside her console. Her tone sends the real message—*Get them out of my space ASAP.* I check the label on the top carton as I move toward my office. OFFICE OF THE ATTORNEY GENERAL, and then in smaller print, R. V. TRUSSARDI. Impressive. As per our conversation Friday, Cy isn't wasting any time giving disclosure. Must have had Emily working all weekend. No doubt this is just the start. Supplementary megabytes will shortly flood our electronic networks.

It's three thirty on a sunny Tuesday. I've had a trying day in court wrangling over whether the police need a warrant to ransack the contents of my client's computer on a hunt for child pornography. *A man's computer is his castle* was my line. In pornography cases, it always seems to be a man. Between the inept posturing of the junior counsel for the attorney general and the technologically challenged judge—*What's an emoji?* he'd asked—today felt long.

"Bring them in," I tell Debbie.

"Sure," she replies without lifting her fingers from her keyboard. "We need a gopher around here. I haven't got time to do everything."

"Thanks." I pick up the top box, heft it under my arm, make a mental note to figure out how I can work a gopher into my office budget and how I can keep that person occupied for the remainder of the day after completing Debbie's requests. I dump the box in the corner of my office on the table that occupies a quirky alcove the architect forgot to eliminate. I pass Debbie on my way back for the second box; she drops her load on the table with an emphatic thump. When all the boxes are in, I buzz Alicia.

She arrives promptly, a bright smile pasted on her face. "We need to go through all these boxes and number the documents."

I watch her face fall. It's routine work. Jeff and I will need to peruse each document, looking for discrepancies, clues, but first everything needs to be catalogued. I push one of the boxes in Alicia's direction. "Start with the police reports. And I'll look at the transcripts of the police interview with Trussardi."

Alicia stares at the box. "We'll be here until midnight."

"Yeah, I know. Tedious. Plus they put some secret compound in them that destroys brain cells." She gives me a wide-eyed look and I smile. "Known fact."

Alicia settles in as I pull the other box of transcripts over to my desk. I slit my paper knife through the tape, and the box opens with a sigh. I'm about to find out what's been eating us since the first day of this case—what did Vincent Trussardi tell the police in the interview Joseph Quentin was naïve enough to let happen?

I reach for the top file. Bingo. The date is there, the time. VINCENT TRUSSARDI, INTERVIEW, the label reads.

The sheaf of paper inside is thick—page after page of double-spaced type. I feel my stomach turn. So much paper, so many chances to let slip what should be kept secret.

I scan, glossing over the trivial and searching for the vital. Corporal Beatty, an experienced detective, was by turns warm and comforting, probing and accusing. The whipsaw worked, like it always does, and before long, even stoic Vincent Trussardi was spilling out his anguish and his humiliation over the affair with the architect.

Beatty picked up on the revelation. "You were angry, weren't you, Mr. Trussardi? I mean you had a *right* to be angry—angry with Trevor Shore, angry with your wife."

Jump in, I mentally scream to the young lawyer Quentin sent along to hold Trussardi's hand. But he didn't.

"Clearly, it was difficult for me," Vincent Trussardi said. "But I loved my wife. It was my fault—I was not the husband that I should have been. So was I angry? Yes, but mainly at myself."

Nice move, blaming the affair on his failings as a husband. Still, it's not good. He's blabbed about an affair that might otherwise have remained hidden and given the police, who already have the means, the motive they need to complete the picture—jealous husband enraged over his wife's infidelity. I curse Joseph Quentin again. Then I remember Shore's grief-stricken face at the funeral. The affair may work in our favor, if we can paint the jilted architect as the killer.

I put the file down. Later I will go through it line by line. I pull out the folder with Carmelina's interview—Jeff's going to interview her tomorrow, so he needs to read it first. A glance tells me that Officer Denton is an experienced interrogator. He had

Carmelina sized up from page one—simple country girl who needs tender loving care.

"When did you come to Canada, Carmelina? It must be lonely sometimes. It's so lovely in Calabria—do you miss it?" he asked, edging into what he really wanted to discuss: Vincent and Laura's marriage. "Did the Trussardis treat you well?"

Soon enough, Carmelina was rambling on. "I loved Mrs. Trussardi. She was always so good to me. Mr. Trussardi, too, so considerate. They were such a lovely couple. Fighting? Never. Of course, I didn't see a lot—I was usually in the kitchen and went to my suite after dinner. So terrible what happened. It was such a shock—to come home and find Madam murdered."

At this point Carmelina appeared to break down sobbing, and Denton suggested a break. "I know this is hard."

Her best friend, her confidant. Beware, Carmelina. When they resumed, Denton, as expected, dug down for the dirt.

"Did you ever see anyone suspicious at the house? Do you have any idea who could have done this? Surely you must have seen Mr. and Mrs. Trussardi fighting? Only normal in a marriage."

Carmelina denied it. "No, no, never."

Brava, I think. *Maybe I've underestimated you.*

Denton zeroed in on her relationship to Mr. Trussardi. "Did you talk?"

"Oh, yes."

"Long discussions?"

"Yes, sometimes in Italian. He liked to talk with me about life in Calabria."

"Were you fond of him, Carmelina?"

"Yes, of course, such a fine man."

"*Very* fond?"

"What do you mean? No, no, no." Sobs, the transcript says in parentheses. Another break. Evidently Carmelina persisted in her tears—according to the time stamps, fifteen minutes later, Officer Denton concluded the interview.

Carmelina's strong, on our side, and wilier than I guessed. I set the file aside and look back to Alicia. "Anything interesting?"

Engrossed in her page, marker slashing across the lines, Alicia answers without looking up. "A motel manager named Emond Gates seems to think he saw Trevor Shore and someone who looked like Laura Trussardi the afternoon before the murder."

My heart plummets. "I see it now. Cy's going to say Trussardi learned that his wife and Trevor Shore met for a secret sexual rendezvous the day before the murder, imply that they had been meeting all along and that in his disappointment and rage, Vincent Trussardi killed the woman who had betrayed him." I survey the boxes. "Something's missing."

Alicia rechecks her box. "Just the pathologists' reports in here."

"Who's the pathologist?"

Alicia riffles the pages. "A Dr. Christine Moyer."

"A friend. Not that it will help. Anything else?"

"That's it."

Then it hits me. "Trevor Shore," I say. "That's what's missing. He was Laura's lover, and the police haven't interviewed him yet? His transcript should be here with the other major players."

Alicia looks puzzled. "If they've talked to him, they've kept it secret."

CHAPTER 16

TWO DAYS LATER, JEFF, ALICIA, and I convene a meeting to take stock. My boardroom has never felt so small. Cy's boxes line the east wall, lids askew, papers spewing in disorderly array. A number of the more critical police reports and photographs have earned a place of privilege at the center of the long table. By now, we've become inured to the graphic story they tell, and no one notices that Laura Trussardi's bruised breast peers out from under the banal report of a telephone interception.

I sit on one side of the table, absently thumbing the pathologist's report I have just picked up. The cause of Laura Trussardi's death—a bullet from the base of the neck to the temple—is not in doubt, but the fine print may yield tidbits that can help, like whether my client was telling the truth when he said she was pregnant.

Richard Beauvais comes through the open door and slides into the empty chair beside Alicia. "*Bonjour, tout le monde.*"

Richard—accent on the last syllable, no "d"—hails from Montreal. His face is handsome in the classic French-Canadian way—full lips, deep brown eyes—but not so striking you'd look more than twice, an asset in his line of business. He hears more than he says. When he listens, he has a way of tucking in his chin and rocking forward, which gives you the impression he is hanging on every word. As he is.

"What do you have on Trevor Shore?" I ask.

Richard runs a hand through his mop of wavy brown hair. "Short version or long?"

"Short, for now."

"Trevor is every designer's go-to boy. He's featured in glossy house magazines. Has a string of awards for innovative Pacific Rim architecture. Originality, artistic sensibility, that's his bag. Hasn't hit the really big time yet."

"Inference: creative genius," says Jeff.

"Creative yes, businessman no. He has a series of unsuccessful partnerships behind him."

"Inference: loner."

"What about his personal life?" I probe.

"Married briefly, long ago. A few affairs, no children." He shoots Jeff a look. "Inference: either can't commit or can't get along."

"Violent? Any brushes with the law?" I query.

"A couple of traffic tickets. Apparently likes to drive fast."

"That's it?"

"That's it."

"Let's cut to the chase then. Where is he?"

Richard spreads his hands. "No idea. I went to this little office on the sixth floor of a Homer Street refit. His name's on the door, along with a couple of other artist types, but the girl at the desk says she has no idea where he is. She guessed that he was taking a break. Apparently, he does that from time to time, disappears between projects to"—air quotes—" 'travel and recharge.' I did a preliminary check of airline rosters—no record of him flying out."

"Vanished from the face of the earth."

"So it seems."

"Maybe we can make something of that," Alicia chimes in. "Trevor Shore disappears after the murder. Looks suspicious. You might just translate that into reasonable doubt. He had motive and opportunity."

"What do you mean, opportunity?" Jeff asks.

"He designed the house, chances are he knew how to get in, how to get the gun," replies Alicia.

"Makes sense," I say. "With luck, we can twist the disappearance of Trevor Shore into an inference of guilt." I catch Jeff's unconvinced grimace. "What about Trussardi's alibi?"

"I've got my team checking out who ate at the yacht club that morning, who logged boats out, who might have seen him," Richard answers. "Assuming he was there. So far we've got him signing his boat out, but nothing on when it came in. Not great."

"We need a witness." Jeff leans back to toss a crumpled photocopy in the garbage. "Preferably someone who remembers seeing him late in the afternoon when the murder was being committed."

"Nice day, that Sunday," I muse. "Must have been lots of people around the yacht club."

"Most of them potted," inserts Jeff, ever the realist.

"Trussardi says there was a boy who used to hang around the house," I say. "Anything on him?"

Richard scrolls down his iPad, squints as he finds his note. "The gardener says he found a boy in the bushes at the edge of the garden a couple of times, sometime in February or March. Skinny guy, dirty blond hair, dirty clothes. Maybe eighteen or nineteen. Every time the gardener asked him what he was doing there, the boy would just run away. Finally, the gardener waggled his orange shears in his face and told him to get lost and never come back. Seems to have worked. Never saw the kid again."

"Did Carmelina see him?"

"She says Laura brought a boy back for supper one night, but he ran away. Same description as the gardener's. But Carmelina never saw anyone in the garden." Richard lets out a sigh. "No one knows the kid's name. There's no way to find him."

"What else do you have, Richard?"

"Laura. I need to track her activities in the days, weeks, and months before her death."

Alicia reaches for a pile of papers, pulls one out. "Disclosure documents say a blond woman meeting Laura's description rendezvoused with the architect Trevor Shore at a North Van hotel the day before the murder." She holds the paper up. "The Stay-A-While Motel."

"Maybe the affair wasn't over," I offer.

"Maybe Trussardi's lying about that, too," counters Jeff.

Richard ignores us. "I need to talk to her acquaintances, the ladies she lunched with, the women she met on her causes. Try to figure out what was going on with the street boy in her garden. I need to see what she was doing online, too. Her Facebook page looks innocuous, but I'll trace every contact and check them all out. And we need to find her cell phone. Maybe it will tell us if the lady at the motel was really her."

"Cops took it," I say. "They're getting a warrant to search the contents."

Richard raises his brow. "A warrant?"

"Yeah, Supreme Court just ruled you can't download from phones without a warrant. A woman's phone is private, even if she's dead. Don't worry—they'll get the warrant. Soon we'll get a transcript of all her calls for the past year or so." I look in Alicia's direction. "More scintillating reading, I'm afraid."

Richard smiles for the first time this morning. "If we're lucky, it will tell us whether she went to that motel."

"The chief coroner's a friend," I say, shifting gears. "I think I'll talk to her."

Richard eyes me skeptically. He knows what I'm thinking—more specificity on the pregnancy our client asserts, and if so, who the father is. Dangerous, if it turns out *not* to be our client.

I take a deep breath. "Okay, let's pull this together. What have we got?"

Jeff throws down his pencil. "Nothing, nada, *rien*. No Trevor Shore. No alibi backup. No kid. Just our crazy client, deep in denial. I can see it now. We put him on the stand. 'Ladies and gentlemen of the jury, my name is Vincent Trussardi and I'm innocent. My bed, my gun, my cheating wife. But trust me, I didn't do it. Really.'"

"It's early days, Jeff. We'll keep looking. Alicia's right, Trevor Shore is still a possibility. And the alibi may yet pan out. Maybe we can find someone who saw him that afternoon. We have to chase down every alternate possibility—Trevor Shore, the drugged-up kid—all we need is a reasonable doubt."

"I think Trussardi's making it up," Jeff persists. "Like the putative pregnancy. We need to find a way to convince Cy to take a plea to second degree. It's the only option."

"All right." I straighten in my chair. "I know I take chances from time to time, but I'm not suicidal." I look around the table. "Here's the plan. We continue the investigation. If we're still empty after we've overturned every stone, then we sit Mr. Trussardi down and tell him it's our considered advice that he should plead guilty to second degree, assuming we can cut a deal. If he refuses to accept our advice, I'll let him shop for some other lawyer who'll take his money and make a fool of himself in front of the jury. But we're not at that point. Not yet. Besides, getting a deal on a high-profile case like this may depend on coming up with something—anything—that makes a conviction less than an absolute certainty."

"Jilly's right," Richard says. "Something about the Crown's case is just too pat. We should investigate further. Then reassess."

I thumb the pathology report, start scanning the pages. "If we don't come up with something, we have a heart-to-heart with the client. Moment of truth."

"I just wish I could believe he was coming clean with us."

"I know—" I start to say, but stop. There, on page two, is the evidence staring me in the face.

Jeff spins his chair. "Got to get to court."

"Wait a sec." I shove the report across the table to him and watch his expression fall. *Pregnant, estimated time of gestation, nine weeks.*

CHAPTER 17

TREVOR SHORE FINDS ME BETWEEN the fruits and the salads, a half-laden basket over my arm. Much as I resent the intrusion of shopping on my billable hours, a girl has to eat.

"Ms. Truitt, may I have a word?"

I recognize him right away, his brown tam and Oxford scarf. He's tall and gaunt, but it's his eyes that hold me—thin rings of blue encircling enormous pupils that skitter as he tries to meet mine.

"Mr. Shore," I say. "What are you doing here?"

"I need to talk to you, Ms. Truitt."

There are ethical rules about this sort of thing. I should tell him it's a bad idea for us to be speaking alone, but I don't.

"There's a Starbucks next door," I say. I look at my shopping, set it down, and follow him out the door.

At the crowded coffee bar, I stand awkwardly beside him. "Go get a seat," he says. "What can I bring you?"

"Tall black," I reply and head to the plush chairs at the back.

A moment later he places two paper cups on the table between us and sinks into his chair. He looks like an origami doll—sweater hanging from angular shoulders, jeans falling in folds over his boots. He's lost weight since he bought these clothes. A lot. Laura's death has taken its toll, but if this is my one shot at Trevor Shore, I need to ask the tough questions.

I launch in. "Who killed Laura, Trevor?"

"Not me, if that's what you're implying."

"I'd say you're a prime candidate. You slept with her, then beat her when she wanted to go back to her husband. She's lucky she got away with just a black eye." I lean in. "You were jealous, weren't you? Furious that she'd leave you. You knew the house, knew where the gun was. Doesn't look good for you, Trevor."

"I loved her," he whispers hoarsely. "You have to believe me."

The ancient Othello theme, I loved her so much she had to die.

He's talking again. "She broke it off with me months ago. She and Vincent were reconciling, going to give it another go."

"She broke it off months ago," I repeat flatly. "Then explain why you went to the Stay-A-While Motel with her the day before she was killed."

He blanches. "I never—"

"Don't bullshit me, Trevor. "

"We never—it was over. I just wanted to talk to her, warn her."

"Warn her?" My heart sinks. "About Vincent?"

"No, no."

"Then who, Trevor?"

He shrugs.

"I get it. You wanted to warn her about yourself. Is that why you're here? To alleviate your guilt about Vincent taking the rap, Trevor?" I press on. "You were upset, not thinking straight. She told you she was back with her husband, pregnant by him, and you lost it. Part of you loved her, part of you hated her. You couldn't take it anymore. So you killed her."

"You've got it all wrong. I'm the one in danger now." His eyes dart wildly into the corners of the crowded room.

"Why?"

"I know too much."

"About?"

"The family, the business, the whole damned lot." He fixes his eyes on me. "And I know I'm being followed, Ms. Truitt. I can't stay long. Unless I get out of here, I'm dead."

"Who would want you dead? And why?" Our coffees cool on the table, untouched. "I'm getting tired of this, Trevor. Why are you here?"

"I loved Laura. I want to see her death avenged. And I want you to put the real killer behind bars so I can stop running."

"Then tell me who did it."

"If I tell you, I'm dead, no matter where I go. If I say nothing and leave town, they'll let me be. You have to figure it out yourself."

"Why can't you just tell me? Seriously, how would killing you help them, whoever they are?"

"Omertà," he whispers.

"Revenge?"

He nods.

"Revenge for you killing her?"

"No, Ms. Truitt. Revenge for telling."

My mind reels. *Who has that kind of power?* "You're afraid that if you tell me what you know, Vincent Trussardi will have you killed?"

He shakes his head. "No, no."

"Then who?"

Trevor's babbling. He can't talk sense, but he can't stop talking—it's irrational, but I've seen it before. A lot of things can drive a man crazy. Including guilt. I need to get back to what matters to my case.

"Have the police talked to you?"

"No, I've been hiding out. But they'll find me if I stay here any longer. I'm leaving the country."

I sit very still. I can't have anything to do with this. If Cy finds out, I'll be charged with obstructing justice—maybe worse.

"You shouldn't have come to me." I start to rise, but Shore's voice pulls me back down.

"I know what you're thinking: 'If he didn't kill her, why is he running?' Let's just leave it at this—if they find me or if the police talk to me, I'm done for."

"The police will give you protective custody. You need to talk to them."

"Protective custody can't save me."

"Then why did you come to *me*, Mr. Shore?"

"You're the only one who can set things right. For Laura, for myself."

"And how does that help my client?"

"If you figure it out—" He breaks off, gets to his feet. "I've told you this in confidence. A lawyer is bound to keep confidences—I read that somewhere. What I've said is between you and me. You must never tell anyone about this conversation."

If I wanted, I could give him a lecture on solicitor-client privilege, tell him you need a lawyer-client relationship for it to apply, tell him it can't be used to obstruct justice. But there's no point.

"The house, Ms. Truitt. You'll find the truth; it's all there." He swallows. "I've said too much. Goodbye."

He disappears into the crush of backpacks milling at the door.

CHAPTER 18

TREVOR SHORE'S VISIT GNAWS THROUGH my dreams, eats at my sleep. Of all the questions I put to him, there was one I forgot. Who was the father of Laura's baby? Was it Vincent, as he professes to believe? Trevor? Or someone else?

The next morning, bleary-eyed, coffee in hand, I settle into my office chair and fish out my phone. I scroll through the contacts and hit the call button. With luck, Christine, head pathologist at the downtown Vancouver morgue, can help with what I need to know about the baby. I'm just finishing my call when Debbie enters my office carrying an armload of files.

"Legal aids." She slaps the top of a hefty pile. "Only one you need to look at—that killing in a Gastown pub last week."

Used to live on legal aid, I think. *We're selective now.*

"Some telephone calls, one or two requests for appointments."

"Anything interesting?" I ask.

"Not really, but I never know what will interest you." Debbie sniffs and shifts through the documents. "A girl, Keltey's her name, was in here looking for a missing person. Apparently, this person once mentioned you." She peers at her notes. "Trulla James or something. Ring a bell?"

"Nope."

"Anyway, Keltey thinks Pickton and the pig farm may have got her. No money in it for us." Debbie makes a face.

I think back to the inquiry into the Robert Pickton killings, see the pain in the eyes of the families whose mothers and sisters and daughters were plucked from Vancouver's Downtown Eastside to be slaughtered at Pickton's pig farm. Worst serial killer in history, the newspapers said.

"Once in a while, we do one for charity, Debbie. Tell her we can't do anything without DNA."

"She knows. She left this." She sets a locket on a gold chain on my desk. "Open it."

I pry the locket open and see a lock of dark hair, then snap it shut. It lies in the palm of my hand, a gold oval set round with small rubies.

"This is exquisite," I murmur. "Old, valuable. I'll give Richard a call and ask him to take the sample to the investigatory team to see if the DNA matches any found on site."

"You're busy. I'll call for you." Debbie offers, scooping up the locket.

"No, there's something else I need to discuss with him."

She gives me a look, like I'm holding out, but I brush it off. This is personal. Maybe it's losing Mike, but all I know is that for the first time in thirty-four years, I need to know the truth.

"You can call Vincent Trussardi for me, though. We need him to come in. Today, if possible."

Debbie nods.

An hour later, Vincent Trussardi sits across from Jeff and me in our boardroom.

"We need to raise something with you," I start. "This may be difficult."

"Go ahead, I'm waiting."

"It's about your child. The coroner has preserved the fetus your late wife was carrying."

Vincent sits silent for a long moment. "What has that got to do with the case?"

"Not sure. She might be able to do a paternity test, find out if you're the father. If you're the dad, it supports your story and buttresses your case. The jury will have a hard time believing that a man could kill a woman pregnant with his only and long-awaited child."

"And if I'm not?"

"Then it would cut the other way," says Jeff.

"You think the baby wasn't mine." He looks at Jeff, then me.

"I think we need to weigh the risk of how an unfavorable result would play with a jury."

"I told you. I loved my wife, and we were making things work. Do the test."

"Mr. Trussardi, you should know that the prosecution has a witness whose testimony could be problematic."

Jeff continues. "A North Van motel clerk claims that a woman who looked like Laura Trussardi checked into the Stay-a-While Motel with Trevor Shore the afternoon before the murder."

Vincent's eyes widen briefly. *Shock? Anger? Fear at what the police have found?*

"We should still do it," he says, a gravelly certainty in his voice.

"Good." I give him an encouraging smile. "You need to visit Dr. Moyer at the City Morgue at ten a.m. tomorrow. Debbie will give you the address. Not much to it, just a mouth swab. I'll let you know when the results come in."

"And then?"

"We get you in for a war room chat. We have other questions arising from disclosure. And our detective has been digging. He'll have some questions, too." I fix my eyes on him. "Then at some point you and I will need to have a frank one-on-one, Mr. Trussardi."

I have questions of my own. Questions about his sister, about his marriage, about Trevor Shore and Edith Hole and the services she rendered him.

"What's wrong with now?" he asks. "Despite our visit at the house, I feel I hardly know you, Miss Truitt."

You don't need to know me, I think. *I'm your lawyer, not your confidante.*

"I'm afraid I don't have much time. I'm having lunch with my foster mother." I look at my watch. "In half an hour."

"So you have family, Miss Truitt?"

"A foster family. But yes, I have family."

Vincent clears his throat. "I'm moving out of the house," he says, apropos of nothing. "But we should have that one-on-one. Soon." He offers me his hand. "We'll find a day when the weather's right, take my boat out."

He makes it sound like a pleasure jaunt. His wife was unfaithful, his child—maybe—is in a jar in the morgue, and all he can think of is boating on a sunny day.

CHAPTER 19

MARTHA MAYNE, MY FOSTER MOTHER and friend, smiles as she weaves her way through the crowd of oyster chuggers milling around the bar at Earls on Hornby. I wave back. An hour ago, I was deep in Trussardi's case; now our meeting is just stored memory. *Compartmentalize—the criminal lawyer's key to sanity.*

"Happy belated birthday." I rise to offer a hug. Martha lets me go, and I motion to an icy glass opposite. "I ordered." Martha likes her drinks cold, dry, and preferably ready when she arrives.

"Thank you, Jilly," Martha says, her russet hair bobbing as we slide into our seats. "The boys came over to celebrate Sunday. You keep missing our weekend dinners."

I accept the reproach. "I always seem to be preparing a case Sunday night. Last-minute scramble before court in the morning."

"Either you're disorganized or you're working too hard." Martha's green eyes, only a few creases betraying her age, drill down into me. "And I know you're not disorganized, Jilly."

"You're probably right, Martha. But I love my work." I think of the long days I'm about to put in on a drug trial of stultifying tedium. "Most of the time."

"I'm glad you have Mike. He seems to be the only one who can tear you away from your beloved criminals. Quite a picture of you two on the front page of the *Sun* a while back."

"We'll get to that." I pick up my glass for a toast. "Meanwhile, here's to you. To us." Our glasses clink. "So, how are you?" I ask after we've both taken a sip.

"I'm great. Everybody's busy, Brock's immersed in the winery, Mathew's buried in running his trawler fleet, Mark's going gangbusters on his latest economic blog, Luke's got his clinic. John and Tristan—well, John and Tristan are John and Tristan." She lays her napkin over her lap. "They just bought a house together in Kitsilano. John's career is taking off. He's singing Figaro at Covent Garden next month."

"That's wonderful. I'll have to wish him good luck." My youngest foster brother is an opera singer. After years of struggle, he debuted at the Met last spring to respectable reviews.

"Just like your career, Jilly. You seem to be in the paper every second day with some win or other," Martha muses. "Remember how you used to agonize in second-year law about whether you'd ever find a job? If you had only known—"

"I would have quit right then," I laugh. "I wanted to save the world. That's why I went to law school, right? This life I've ended up with would have shocked me—fighting to get guilty people off, not to mention the condo, the extravagant car."

Martha smiles. "Let's order, then we can chat." She waves to the hovering waiter. "Sole and steamed spinach." Martha is perpetually watching her weight. Hungry from an early-morning run, I order pasta.

"So." Martha leans forward. "What are you wearing?"

"Wearing to what?"

"To the wedding. Ainsley Martin and Fred Telford. Remember, your old buddies in law school? I saw Ainsley's mother at the club yesterday. She can't believe it, after all this time." Martha frowns. "You mean you haven't been invited?"

It's coming back to me now, Mike mentioning it over microgreens at Bishop's a lifetime ago. Ainsley and Fred, big wedding in July—*We'll be invited, Jilly.* They must know we've split.

"No, it appears I haven't." I take a breath. "You should know, Martha. Mike and I are no longer an item. Awkward to invite both of us in the circumstances. Evidently, they've chosen him."

Martha looks at me with alarm. "Jilly."

"It's okay. I'll survive."

She covers my hand protectively. "Did Mike drop you? I can't believe it—"

"No, no, it wasn't like that," I protest. "More like a mutual parting of ways. Whatever it is—it's probably for the best for both of us."

"'Best for both of us.' Surely you can do better than that, Jilly."

"It's the truth," I say.

Martha puts her drink aside. "Tell me everything, Jilly."

So I do. Everything, or almost, like I've been doing ever since the Maynes took me in two decades ago.

When I'm finished, Martha leans back in the booth. "That's

sad, so sad. I mean, you and Mike have been there for each other forever. You've seen each other through some terrible times. Remember when you quit law school?"

"How could I forget?"

"Brock and I tried to get you back, but it was Mike who did it. You were doing stuff, Jilly—stuff that was stupid and dangerous—and Mike brought you back."

"I know," I stare at my fork as it puddles the pasta in rings of pink sludge.

"And in third year, when Mike's parents died in that car crash in Italy? He went crazy—sold all the furniture, refused to talk to anyone—just lay on the floor in that awful, empty house. It was you who helped him get back on track."

We sit quietly for a while. "You two were so *solid.* You were *family,*" Martha finally says.

"He wants more than I can give him, Martha." I'm startled by the bile I feel rising. "I tried to get back in touch. Texted, left messages, but not a word."

"Words aren't Mike's thing. You know that."

"A guy who doesn't talk and a girl who can't stop. What a match."

"Put yourself in his shoes. It probably took him months to work up the courage to do what he did. He put on the whole show, offered you everything—his love, his world. He was careful to mention your freedom, too—and you walked out without so much as a goodbye. You wounded him, Jilly. Humiliated him."

"No. I mean, I never meant to hurt him."

"Does this have anything to do with you taking on the Trussardi case? I mean, Laura Trussardi was his cousin . . ."

My foster mother, who knows me better than she knows

herself, has zeroed in on the tender truth that kills. *I would trade Mike for a case.*

"No," I say.

"Yes. I never met Vincent Trussardi—I think maybe Brock ran into him at some point—but I can tell you this: the Shaughnessy gossip machine has already convicted him." She looks at me anxiously. "This could be a loser, Jilly. A big loser."

I sigh. "I'm aware of that, Martha. But guilty or innocent, he's entitled to a trial and a competent defense. That's my job."

The waiter comes to claim our untouched plates. "Everything all right?" he asks nervously.

"Great," we say in unison. He smiles at our bleak faces and takes away the crockery.

CHAPTER 20

IT'S 8:00 P.M. THE NEXT day, and I'm on my way home from the office where I've been catching up on paperwork after a tedious day on my never-ending drug trial as I wait for news from Richard on Trussardi.

Instead of heading east to Yaletown, I take the long route through the dark streets that lie on the periphery of Hastings—that epicenter of vice where homeless mill, junkies shoot up, and prostitutes hook such fish as they can. In what I call my dark period, when despair temporarily unmoored me from the Maynes' embrace, I came here more often than was wise. I occasionally circle back—this time the catalyst is my lunch with Martha—to remind myself how close I came to being sucked into the vortex.

The streets are quiet tonight. Young people laugh in the warm evening air outside pubs; a few shove each other or detach and stroll into alleys. On every side, not-so-genteel hotels and rooming houses rise from the pavement. A face at the edge of a group catches my eye. I do a double take, feel a clutch in the pit of my stomach—Damon Cheskey. *We'll pick him up on something else before long,* Cy had said after the trial. I slow the car, follow Damon, see him stuff something into his backpack, then peel off from his group and head down the street. At the corner he turns and disappears beneath a sign that says INGLES HOTEL.

I pull over, idle for a while, but he does not come out. I sag, feel my forehead fall forward and hit the soft leather of the steering wheel. I'm naïve, stupid. I invested in Damon, believed in him. *You believed in your own fantasy, Jilly Truitt, the private myth of redemption that keeps you going.* I put the car into gear and head home.

I turn on the TV, pull up my orange chair, and plunk myself down, but I can't sit still. I'm up; I'm pacing. Damon's fate is not my problem, but it eats at me. My great victory reduced to this. A nice boy brought down again. I find myself rooting through a drawer for jeans and a sweater. I throw on a pair of low-cut boots and grab my leather jacket and keys.

I park the car on a side street and make my way around the corner to the Ingles Hotel—a sliver of blackened brick in a streetscape of sister establishments. The scratched wooden door and charcoal window promise privacy, no questions asked, for dark deeds and desperate trysts.

A man with a long, bony face straight from *The Scream* looks me over suspiciously from behind a battered counter. "Help ya?" he grunts.

"Damon Cheskey's room number."

"No idea."

I decide to get rough, nothing to lose. I pull out my ID, flash it too fast for him to see. "The law," I say. "Emergency." It's not quite a lie.

His eyes widen, and he reaches for a key on the board at his side, throws it on the counter. "Two-eight-seven."

I take the stairs two at a time—no elevators here—and find the room. At the end of the hall, a door opens and a man, pants undone, staggers out of what must be the communal bathroom. He sees me, clutches his crotch, and falls against the wall. I put my finger to my mouth, "Shhh . . ."

I insert the key, step inside two-eight-seven, and silently shut the door behind me. The room is small and sparsely furnished. A single bed, tightly made, hugs the wall, a table beside it. To my right is a metal dresser. The only light is a candle on the floor, behind which sits Damon, cross-legged in a Buddha squat. He is neatly dressed in jeans and a white button-down cotton shirt, open at the neck. His blond hair reflects the light of the candle as he bends his head to roll up the left sleeve of his shirt.

I flatten myself against the door and watch, trance-like, as he takes a rubber band from the pocket of his jeans, twists it around his upper arm with his right hand, pulls it with his teeth to tighten it. The muscles of his arm bunch. He takes the spoon, now heaped with white powder, and places it above the candle, contemplating as the drug melts. His left hand finds the syringe. With care, he tilts the spoon and fills the syringe, inserts the plunger.

I clear my throat. "Damon."

His head whips up. I read surprise, then anger in his face. "Go away," he hisses. The edge in his voice tells me he means it. I should go, but I don't. Instead, I slip to the floor and crouch across from him as he cradles the syringe in his hand.

"Damon," I say again. "I didn't put so much effort into your case only to have you end up like this."

He looks at me straight on. "I've done bad things. I fucked people over. I killed a man. I deserve to be in jail, *need* to be in jail."

"What happened when you went home, Damon?"

"They shunned me."

I do a double take at the archaic language, then realize this is exactly the word that a kid schooled in the Mennonite religion would use.

"Not my parents, the others. They took me to church, but no one would look at me. There's no place for me there." His eyes scan the middle distance. "No place here either. Kellen still wants me dead."

"Are you back on crystal meth?"

"No."

"So now you're on heroin?"

"I'm not on heroin."

"Then what's this?" I point to the syringe.

He doesn't answer and then I understand. He's going to overdose, kill himself.

"Damon," I say. "You have a choice."

"I have chosen." His voice is calm and settled.

"That choice is no longer available."

"Ms. Truitt, this is my business. You should not be here."

"You have two new choices. If I leave, I will call the police." I touch the cell phone at my hip. "They'll be here within minutes. They'll take you to St. Paul's and pump you out. It will be painful and cost the taxpayers about two hundred and fifty thousand dollars. But you will not die."

"And my other choice?"

"You come with me. We turn in your syringe at Insite—they'll keep it for you. Tomorrow we'll figure the rest out."

We sit in silence. His face tilts up to the ceiling, moves sideways to the wall, comes back down to mine. Teeth clenched, features contorted, he is pure, unalloyed anger. I remember that he's killed a man, and I feel the beat of my heart, louder than it should be. Then in a single motion, he throws down the syringe, tears the rubber from his arm, and rises. His eyes drill into mine, and he lunges toward me from his height. "Fucking bitch, just leave me alone!" he cries as he yanks me upright.

He's holding me up, gripping my arms hard. I hear my strangled cry, "Damon, don't do this."

Abruptly, his hands release me, and I fall back to the floor as he turns away. I watch his shoulder muscles bunch beneath the cotton of his shirt as he stares through the cracked window at the blackness outside. A minute passes, then another. His shoulders sag. He turns back to me, picks up his backpack, stuffs the syringe in its plastic bag and into the pack. "Okay, let's go," he says.

My knees are weak, but I try not to let it show. We walk to Insite, an inconspicuous place on the north side of Hastings where people who want to shoot up can do so in supervised safety. It lurches from court challenge to court challenge, persistently troubled by those who believe that addicts deserve to die. But tonight, by some good fortune, it's open. Damon fills out a form and drops the needle off, then walks with me to my car.

Back at my condo, I make up the couch in the den and ask

Damon if he wants anything. He shakes his head and closes the door of the den behind him. I wait in the living room. It's idiotic—I can do nothing to stop him from walking out of my apartment and back onto the street, if he wants to. Still, I wait. At half-past twelve I cross to the den, open the door a crack. His head, in the shaft of light from the living room, is back against the pillow. He looks so peaceful that, for a moment, I fear he has found some way to end it after all. Then I hear his deep, even breathing and, reassured, tell myself to go to bed.

WHEN I EMERGE FROM MY room the next morning, I find Damon sitting on a stool at the kitchen island, hair still wet from the shower. I set out orange juice, cereal, and milk. "Help yourself." Then I go to my newest toy—a gleaming gold-and-chrome coffee machine. I add the espresso, foam the milk, and present him with a steaming cappuccino. "Consider me your personal barista," I say.

He cradles the cup, then asks quietly. "Why did you do what you did?"

I feel my stomach constrict, like I always do when I think back to my dark place. "I was once in the same situation as you—on the floor of a room, with a candle and a spoonful of white powder beside me. I was scared, screwed up. I had been on the streets and done some stupid things. When I came to my senses, I was too ashamed to go forward, too sick to go back. So I decided to end it. Someone saved me, someone who wouldn't give up on me. For a dozen years, I've been looking for a way to repay the debt I owe."

Damon eyes me wearily. "Then you know it's not over."

"It's never over, but you've gained a day, Damon. That's good."

"I can't just stay here."

You're not going back to Insite to pick up your package, I think. Then I hear myself talking.

"Can you answer a phone?"

"Yeah."

"Drive?"

"Sure."

"Got basic computer skills?"

"Of course."

"Okay with lifting boxes?"

He raises his arm—a biceps flexes beneath his white shirt.

"You're my man, Damon. Let's go."

CHAPTER 21

"ARE YOU CRAZY, JILLY?"

"Shut the door, Jeff. And keep your voice down."

I introduced Damon to the team this morning—no explanation, just *This is Damon, our new gopher*. Debbie, picking up on the name, rolled her eyes. Jeff gave me an incredulous stare, but before he could open his mouth, Alicia dragged him off to deal with a pretend emergency. Now that Jeff's back from court, he's dressing me down.

"He's got to go, Jilly. What the hell were you thinking?" He stands on the other side of my desk, fists clenched into white-knuckled balls.

"I was thinking I was helping him out."

He rolls his eyes as he slumps to the chair. "He's our client. We can't hire our client."

"Was our client."

"Doesn't matter."

"It matters very much. Our relationship with Damon ended the moment the jury acquitted him. It's over. No reason we can't establish a new, different kind of relationship now."

"He's bad, Jilly. He hawked drugs, killed a man—who knows what other havoc he wreaked along the way. And you're inviting him into our office so he can liaise with our criminal clients? You're giving him the perfect platform for expanding his web of crime. Reputable law firms don't do that."

"What happened to the idea of a fresh start? *Rehabilitation* in the quaint language of the Criminal Code?"

"*Rehabilitation* is a pretty word. Makes the system feel better when they lock a bad guy up. But you know as well as I that they never change, our boys. It's the only world they know. Sooner or later they get sucked back in."

I put my hands on my desk, palms down. "I'm not going to argue with you, Jeff. I know the risks, but I am going to do this anyway. We'll watch him. Closely. Let him go if necessary. But I have to give him this chance."

Jeff grunts through gritted teeth. "Whatever you say, boss. But watch the till; watch your back." He turns to head out.

"Jeff, wait. I need your help."

He stops. "My *help*?"

"He needs a place to live."

"You're not suggesting Jessica and I take him in? My god, Jilly—"

"No, but you mentioned that your neighbor's in Europe for a few months. Maybe he'd be willing to sublet?"

"And let Damon trash the pad?"

"I'll pay for any damage."

Jeff pauses. "See what I can do," he mutters as he leaves.

I take a deep breath, decide to go find Damon. I don't need to look far—he's pacing outside my door, backpack over his shoulder. He pushes around me into my office.

"I'm leaving," he announces.

"Why?" I shut the door behind us.

"Jeff's right. It won't work."

"So you were eavesdropping."

"He was coming through the walls."

"And you agree with him? That rehabilitation's nonsense, a fresh start's a chimera?"

"No. Yes. I don't know what to believe."

"What about your family?"

He shifts his backpack uncomfortably.

"You owe it to yourself to give it a try, Damon. I believe you can make it." I look him straight in the eye. "Debbie is waiting at the front desk. Ready to put you to work."

He smiles faintly. "'Move that pile of boxes. After you get me a coffee,'" he mimics in a perfect Liverpool twang.

"Not bad, Damon. The accent, I mean. Just keep Debbie happy—that's your number one job."

"Tall order, Ms. Truitt." He lets the backpack slip from his shoulders. "But what the heck, I'll try."

CHAPTER 22

THE LATE-DAY SUN FILTERS FAINTLY through the arched window, the soft light making my boardroom seem larger than its diminutive dimensions. I have placed Vincent Trussardi on one side of the long table. Jeff, Alicia, Richard, and I take seats opposite. Alicia's laptop is open, her fingers poised to take notes. We are ready for our war room chat.

The door opens, and Damon shoulders through like he's been carrying trays of coffee his entire life. Against all the odds, in a few short weeks, he's acquired the air of a sophisticated go-to office hand cum paralegal. In black slacks, a pale blue shirt, and a tie, he's clean and groomed.

He goes straight to Vincent, halts. The tray wavers.

"Damon?" I say.

He recovers smoothly. "An espresso, Mr. Trussardi? Biscotti?"

He glances encouragingly at the drink and the cookie. Trussardi eyes him briefly and accepts with a gracious nod. Damon serves all round and exits, tray high on the palm of his right hand.

Richard looks at me—*Where did you find this guy, Jilly?*

I shake my head—*It's a long story.*

The shock at Damon's arrival has been supplanted by guarded acceptance as he makes himself useful doing whatever needs doing: answering the phone, roaming the net, politely convincing loiterers to leave the premises, and, yes, producing decent coffee on cue from our antiquated machine. When I finally told Jeff the details, he shook his head.

"He's bipolar," he opined. "Suicidal one day, our man Friday the next. Still say you're crazy, Jilly."

"Sure," I replied. "Anyway, thanks for getting him the sublet at your condo."

"Can't have the boss living in sin, Jilly."

I start the show-and-tell for Vincent by laying out the Crown's theory. "They're going to argue that you knew Laura had rekindled her affair with Trevor, that she was pregnant with his baby, and you killed her out of jealousy. We may be able to poke a hole in that argument, depending on the results of the paternity test, which should be in any day now."

"It will prove the child was mine," he says firmly.

I scan my notes. "They found residue of a sleeping drug in the body. Did your wife take sleeping pills, Mr. Trussardi?"

"Yes, sometimes she had insomnia."

"Might not mean much," I reply. "This particular drug has a half-life of eight or nine hours. If she took it late the night before, the traces would still be there. Otherwise, nothing noteworthy. She was strong, in the bloom of health." I turn to the police reports.

"We've been through all the statements from you, Carmelina, the gardener, the cleaning lady. The gardener talks about the boy who hung around the property. There's evidence of footprints on the outskirts of your property, but we can't prove much with that. Did Laura ever mention the boy after the evening she brought him to the house and he ran away?"

"No, we never discussed it."

"Did you ever see the boy, apart from that occasion?"

Trussardi hesitates. "Once. I told him to go away."

"What did he say?"

"He said—" He breaks off. "It was nonsensical babbling that doesn't matter. The boy may have had a fixation on Laura, but why would he kill her?"

I temper my rising frustration. "Mr. Trussardi, we're not looking for the killer; we're looking for a reasonable doubt."

"He had no way of knowing where the gun was, how to get it. He couldn't have done this thing the way it was done."

Jeff decides to move the conversation forward. "I interviewed your housekeeper, Mr. Trussardi. What she told me is consistent with her police interview. Mrs. Trussardi had given her the day off. She went to visit friends in Burnaby—her story checks out."

"And then there's the dishes," I say.

"The dishes?" Trussardi asks.

"It's a bit far-fetched," I reply. "But one of the police reports says there were two plates, two glasses, and two sets of cutlery in the kitchen sink. Maybe Laura had a final meal with someone—someone who killed her."

Jeff laughs. "Or maybe she had lunch alone, salad and omelet, a glass of water and a glass of white wine."

"Laura never drank alone," Trussardi responds. "And she was pregnant."

"Still," says Jeff. "Dishes in the sink? Could be any number of explanations."

"I agree. It's probably nothing." I put my papers down. "Richard, would you review your progress for us?" Progress—the overstatement of the week.

Richard straightens, goes into business mode. "The first task, Mr. Trussardi, is to back up that you were on your boat or at the club at the time of the murder. The waitress confirms you were there for breakfast and went down the pier in the direction of your boat about ten a.m. However, she has no further recollection of seeing you that day. We've talked to a number of people who took their boats out. Only one recalls seeing you—a man named Oliver Semple. He says he came up from his boat around five and thinks he saw you heading toward your car."

Trussardi looks up, eyes guarded. "I know Ollie. Is there a problem?"

"He may not be the best witness. He admits to drinking over the afternoon, so the Crown will try to discredit him. And he only saw your back. But it's a start. We'll keep looking." Richard continues. "Our next line of inquiry concerns your late wife. We've been over everything—her diary, her cell phone, the landline to the house—and re-created, as best we can, a picture of her last week or so. With some success—there is nothing in her calls or comings and goings that suggests she was in touch with Trevor Shore, much less met him at the Stay-A-While Motel."

I unpack what this means. "With luck, we can convince the jury that the blonde Mr. Shore saw that afternoon was someone else—at the very least, we can raise a doubt."

"The affair was over," Trussardi says as much to himself as to us.

I don't tell him that I've seen Trevor, that he didn't deny meeting Laura at the motel. I've locked the memory of our supermarket encounter deep in the confidential casket every lawyer keeps. No one knows. Not even Richard.

Richard circles back to the boy. "I know you don't think this homeless boy could have done it, Mr. Trussardi, but finding him could answer a lot of questions. Can you tell us more about him? Anything that might single him out from the horde of kids that drifts through the streets of this city every day?"

"I didn't pay much attention. As I told you, he was thin, sick looking, matted blond hair. I remember his eyes, though—skittering around one minute, staring off at who knows what the next. It was unsettling."

"He was on drugs." Richard nods. "Maybe he's the one who delivered them to the house."

We all look up.

"What drugs?" Trussardi asks, echoing everyone's thoughts.

"I picked up a street rumor of a cocaine delivery to your residence shortly before your wife's murder. Could be nothing." He glances at me. *Trust me, I'm onto something.*

"That's impossible," Trussardi says. "Laura abhorred drugs."

Richard leans back before moving on. "That leaves Trevor Shore. Who, it seems, has vanished from the face of the earth."

"The Crown has a bigger problem with Trevor Shore," I say. "They'll have to explain why the police failed to interview him and get a statement. Right now, his disappearance is the only thing going for your defense, Mr. Trussardi."

Trussardi shifts his gaze to the middle distance, like it's

someone else's life we're talking about. I nod to Richard—*Thank you*—and he gathers his iPad and papers. Alicia closes her laptop and follows Richard out. Jeff and I are alone with our client.

"Mr. Trussardi, there's one more thing we'd like to discuss," I say.

"Yes?"

"We would like to explore the possibility that the Crown might agree to a plea to second degree." I think of the photos—the public would never accept manslaughter.

"And what would a plea to second degree get me?"

"Fifteen fewer years in the penitentiary," I reply.

He draws himself up. His words come out like bullets. "I did not do this. I will never plead guilty."

Jeff winces.

"Twenty-five years without parole is a long time, Mr. Trussardi." I lower my voice. "Very likely the rest of your life."

"I am prepared for that, should we lose."

"Life imprisonment," I persist. "Easy to say, hard to live."

"Would you take this deal if you were innocent, Miss Truitt?"

"Maybe," I say, momentarily taken aback—I'm not used to clients questioning me. "The jails are full of lifers who may be innocent."

"Miss Truitt, I admire you, but I don't believe you. You are intelligent and determined. And proud, if I'm not mistaken. You would not say you were guilty of killing someone if you were innocent. You would fight it to the end." He pauses. "And so will I."

"You're right, Mr. Trussardi, I would. But what *I* would do is not the issue. As your lawyer, it's my duty to advise you what *you* should do."

He rises with a small smile and nods. “I appreciate your counsel. But my answer is the same one you would give to yourself—no plea bargain.” He buttons his suit jacket. “Is this meeting concluded?”

“Evidently.”

“When will we meet again, Miss Truitt?”

I stand up. “May I remind you, Mr. Trussardi, that I am your lawyer. We will meet if and when we need to meet for the purposes of your defense.”

“Of course,” he says.

I suddenly realize how silly I sound. *No need to be rude, Jilly, just because the client’s a gentleman.*

“I’m taking a family holiday in the Okanagan next week. When I’m back, we’ll have that one-on-one we talked about.”

He bows ever so slightly. “I look forward to it, Miss Truitt.”

CHAPTER 23

A FEW HOURS LATER, RICHARD calls. "Jilly, can I come by? News on Trussardi."

It's 8:00 p.m., mid-July, and hot. Martha's just texted me with a long list of things to bring to the lake, and I'm packing. Cradling my phone, I look out my window to the waters of False Creek, where the boats rock gently in the evening breeze. "Sure, Richard, come on by."

Ten minutes and he's on my threshold, wearing jeans and a beige shirt. Tonight it's his *fade into the woodwork* look.

"You're working late, Richard." I go to the fridge, open a beer for him, pour myself a cold glass of Riesling. "So what's new on Trussardi?"

He takes a deep breath. "I know where Trevor Shore is."

"Where?"

"Somewhere in Brazil, it seems. He copped a flight to Rio the other day."

"If you could find out, so could the police."

"Not necessarily."

I let it lie. It's an understanding we have, Richard and I—he gives me the info, I don't touch the sources. Still, checking on airline records isn't rocket science. Unless—my mind races—Trevor Shore scored a fake passport and used a false name.

"If we know what they know—fine. If we know what they don't know—even better. We can present the court with the flight records, make them look like they trained their sights on Trussardi and overlooked the real killer. Or, if they tried and failed, we make them look incompetent. Win-win."

Richard nods, takes a drink.

"Keep digging into what he did in Vancouver before he left, Richard. Anything you can find that shows Trevor Shore was right under their nose and they let him get away. We need to beef up our *cops had tunnel vision* defense."

"Gotcha."

"Let me tell you *my* news," I say, setting down my glass. "The paternity test results came back just as I was leaving the office. Our man's the dad."

"More good tidings. Could it be he's telling the truth about the murder?"

"As I keep saying, Richard, all we need is a reasonable doubt."

I stretch out on my orange chair and survey the sneakers at the end of my jeans. The world is looking slightly brighter.

"I appreciate this, Richard. You've done an amazing job. But I should let you go. Your family awaits."

"I know." He puts down his half-finished beer and moves toward the door. "By the way, Keltey, the girl with the locket?"

I look up. "I'd forgotten."

"Bad news. Turns out her friend died on Pickton's pig farm. I checked out the victim's background. She lived in a bed-sit on Main, cheap but respectable. Did some desperate things from time to time to feed her addiction. But it seems she got Keltey off the street and straightened her out."

Yet another victim, I think. *What's the tally now, forty-three? Forty-four? He bragged in jail he was shooting for fifty. Almost made it.*

"Did you contact Keltey?"

"Yes, she'll be okay. One more thing, Jilly." He shunts his shoulder against the doorframe. "You know what you mentioned—about your parents?"

"Forget it, Richard. I wasn't serious."

"Sure. Still, I did a search. Girls born in the Vancouver General Hospital, October 3, 1983. Just to be sure, I looked a month ahead and a month back."

"What are you telling me?"

"There's no record. It's like you were never born, like you don't exist."

"Richard, I have a SIN. I have a passport. I exist."

"I can see that. And at some point the records must have been there. It's just that now, they're gone."

My stomach clutches.

"Probably just a clerical error," Richard says. "But clearly the parent thing has been bothering you, Jilly. Enough that you asked me to look into it."

"I wasn't serious," I repeat.

"I worry about you, Jilly."

"But you shouldn't. I'm okay. I should never have mentioned it. We have enough mystery on our hands with Trussardi."

Richard gives me a fierce one-armed hug, and I feel the stubble on his cheek against my hair. "Take care, Jilly."

CHAPTER 24

FAR FROM MY WORLD OF courtrooms and cases, I lounge with Martha at the end of the dock in Lake Okanagan. I feel the tension seep out of my bones, as I ponder the wake of the retreating boat. My foster brothers and their father, after a desultory lunch, have decided that a thirty-mile trip to Kelowna is an absolute necessity. John halloos from the stern of the boat. I raise my hand in a lazy wave.

"Hope they have enough gas," says Martha.

"They could power that boat to Kelowna and back on testosterone," I reply. Martha smiles and returns to her book.

It's a tradition we have, Martha and I, to choose something from the current bestseller list and bring it on vacation. She's picked a book by Rachman, someone she knew when he lived in Vancouver, with the ominous title *The Rise & Fall of Great Powers.* I've got Donna Tartt's *The Goldfinch.*

As she nears the end of her book, I ask, "What's it about, World War Two?"

"No, a girl—a young woman—finding out who her parents are, who *she* is."

"Funny—mine, too. Sort of. It's a boy, though. He loses his mother in a terrorist attack and falls in love with a portrait of a yellow bird instead. I'm not joking. All while discovering he hates his wretch of a natural father, who, thank God, has just died"—I pat the book—"and finding a new father."

"The paternity theme. Or can we now say *maternity*?"

"Nope. Different meaning. Some things just aren't fair, including the English language. French is better—some really important things get to be feminine."

We lapse back into our books for a while longer, then put them down and swim out to the sandbar, where we can just stand on tiptoe. It's pleasant—bobbing in the water, lifting and paddling when a wave comes in. Damon and Trussardi and all the petty woes of my working world melt away.

"Do you ever think about your parents, Jilly—I mean your *real* parents?" Martha asks unexpectedly.

"No, not much," I lie.

"I mean, so many people nowadays are trying to find their natural parents. I just wondered."

"You're my parents, you and Brock. Besides," I tease, "no way I could ever trade up."

Martha laughs. "Thanks, Jilly."

We languidly swim back to the dock, where I see William, caretaker cum butler, standing on the terrace, waving. "Miss Truitt, telephone. A Mr. Solosky. Shall I tell him to call later?"

I want to say yes, but I can't. I make my way into the house, perch at the granite kitchen bar as Alfred hands me the phone, disapproval at the intrusion of business into paradise written all over his face.

"Jeff?"

"Sorry to bother you on your holiday, Jilly, but I thought you'd want to know. Carmelina's in hospital. Took an overdose."

I digest the news with difficulty. *Carmelina, wily, resolute, and strong, trying to end it all? Doesn't make sense.*

"Jilly? Are you there?"

"Yeah. An overdose? Will she be all right?"

"I think so."

"Do you know why she did it?"

"No, but it seems Cy paid her a visit."

"Shit, what did she tell him?"

"No idea."

"How's Trussardi taking it?"

"Not sure. He waited at the hospital until she came around. Now he's just sitting in his penthouse looking at his bentwood boxes. And a photo of a young woman with black hair in a flowing white dress. I'll have Richard keep an eye on him, make sure he keeps it together."

"His sister, maybe? In the photo, I mean."

"No, someone else."

"Should I come back to Vancouver?"

"Nothing you can do here. I realize now I shouldn't have bothered you. Sorry, Jilly."

"No, you were right to call. I would have been ticked if you hadn't. Get Alicia. Tell her to tell Cy I'm seriously pissed off that he didn't go through me and that I need the statement *now.* And ask Richard to find out who the woman in the photo is."

"Sure." The line hums for a long moment. "Jilly, remember, it's just a case."

THE DAY BEFORE I'M DUE to leave for Vancouver, Brock announces over luncheon hamburgers that he wants to show me the grapes. Though he's in his fifties, Brock swings lithely into the driver's seat of a little Kubota RTV—not the noisy kind with big wheels, more like a tiny truck—his cropped salt-and-pepper hair catching the afternoon sun. I slide in beside his angular frame, and we climb the slope to his vineyards. "These are Chardonnay grapes, just put in three years ago," he tells me as we scan the acreage. "We're hoping to make a decent bubbly."

"As in champagne?"

"Yes, but you lawyers won't let us call it that." He chides me about being a lawyer, but I know he's secretly pleased with where I've ended up. He needs to win, like me.

The plants march in neatly trellised rows to the top of the hill. As we pass between them, Brock points to the clusters of small green grapes that nestle between the leaves. "Bunching out nicely," he says. "Bad year for forest fires—hot and dry—but good for the grapes." He stops, plucks two tiny orbs from a cluster, hands one to me and bites into the other.

I follow suit, make a face. "Sour."

"Good. The sugar will develop with the late-summer sun. Like life, wine is all about the balance between the acid and the sugar. This year should be good."

We move on to a vineyard of Riesling grapes, head down a lane and up another hill to a field of what he tells me is Cabernet Franc. Every once in a while he stops the Kubota and explains how the terroir and the slope and the way the sun strikes the vineyard work together with the plants to make fine wine, and how he helps the process along the way—pruning, dusting, irrigating, and finally, in October, an intense month of harvesting.

"So much work. I had no idea," I say.

"Yes, I'm hoping to make my mark with a vintage Riesling. I've hired a new and very expensive vintner from Germany, just to make sure. Or try to."

In the shortening rays of the sun, we start back to the house. The boys and their significant others have taken the Suburban to Osoyoos for dinner at the Burrowing Owl. Martha's BMW is gone, too.

"It's a crazy business," Brock says over glasses of chilled Riesling on the west terrace. The phrase *house wine* takes on a new meaning when you own the vineyard. "You spend a fortune, invest every bit of love and care and intelligence you can muster, and you still may fail. The wine will be drinkable, but not the special, unique elixir that you dream about. The weather, the heat, the je ne sais quoi—or luck—will make the difference between okay and exceptional. You do your best, but the result is out of your control."

"Sounds a lot like raising kids," I comment wryly.

"I got lucky in that department." He stares out over the lake. "With all five of you."

I give him a side look.

"Yes, Jilly. You know I count you as ours. No escaping. In fact, Martha and I wanted to adopt you legally all along. But there were impediments. Doesn't matter."

What impediments? I wonder. It's not like eligible families were clamoring to adopt me. Nobody ever wanted me, except maybe the Maynes. And why is Brock raising this now, after all these years? I'm about to ask, but something in the set of his jaw tells me not to pursue it. Instead I say, "The imprimatur of the law can be overrated."

"You're right, Jilly. Sometimes the law doesn't matter a damn."

I consider touching his hand where it lies on the arm of his chair, then decide against it. Brock has never touched me—initially, a relief to a girl whose previous foster fathers took the view that the ideal paternal greeting was a close clutch and a kiss; later, a comfortably distanced stance that I came to accept without thought.

"Speaking of the law, how's your work going, Jilly?"

"Fine. In fact, better than I could ever have expected. I'm building a nice little firm with people I like. Making a bit of money. Had some good wins lately; getting some high-profile cases."

"Like the murder charge against my old friend Vincent Trussardi."

I choke on my wine. "I didn't know you were close," I manage.

"Not close. I knew him in university."

I clear my throat. "It's a difficult case. He seems a fine person—courtly and polite on the surface, broody and melancholy beneath. But then I hear things, and I can't get a handle on him."

"He's not a bad person. He's just lived an inauthentic life."

An inauthentic life? I let it go. "Well, it's my job to provide him the best defense the evidence and the law allows. Like your wine, I can't control the outcome."

Brock gives a laugh. "Nice work, Jilly, if you can get it."

CHAPTER 25

BACK IN VANCOUVER, JEFF AND I survey Carmelina across the table of our boardroom. She is wan and thin. The vital sexuality of our initial encounter is gone, sucked out by the pills and the detox, or maybe something else.

We've walked through her statement and learned that Cy called her at Vincent's penthouse where she was unpacking boxes, invited her down to the Second Cup for a coffee, and the truth came out—yes, she had slept with Vincent Trussardi.

"Never before Madam's death, never," she protested to Jeff and me, as she had to Cy. "But later, yes—once, the night of her death. He was so sad; he needed comfort." *The frailty of human nature*, I think sadly.

Once Cy had what he wanted, he left—*Thank you, Ms. Cappelli, very helpful, that will be all.* Later, as the fact of her betrayal sank in, Carmelina went to the box she had packed with the contents of Laura's medicine cabinet, took the bottle she used to bring to Laura when she could not sleep, and swallowed the lot. Vincent, returning late from a meeting with Hildegard, found her amid the packing crates, prone and near death.

"Carmelina." I take her hand. "You shouldn't blame yourself. You only told the truth, and it's not so terrible. What happened between you and Mr. Trussardi after Laura's death has nothing to do with how she died or who killed her."

What I refrain from saying is that a grieving husband who takes solace in the arms of the housekeeper while his wife's body is still cooling is hardly a sympathetic figure.

"Where are you living, Carmelina?" Jeff asks.

"With my friend Emilia and her family in Burnaby." She senses what we're getting at. "I can't go back to work for Mr. Trussardi. He rented a small apartment for me near Emilia's house. I'll move there next week."

I show her out the door and down the stairs, put her in a cab, and hand the driver two twenties.

Jeff is prowling in the reception area when I return. "This case just keeps getting sweeter and sweeter. Trussardi leaves a hell of a lot of female suffering in his wake."

"You got that right."

Damon, manning the front desk while Debbie's on holiday, looks up from the phone. "Cy Kenge," he says, covering the mouthpiece, "for you."

"I'll take it." I shut the door to my office and pick up the receiver.

"Yes, Cy?"

"Male receptionist, Jilly?"

If he only knew which male. "Cy, in case you hadn't noticed, the age of equality has arrived."

He chuckles. "If you say so, Jilly."

He's in a good mood—no doubt still high on his coup with Carmelina. I let him hang a while.

"Jilly, I'll get right to the point. Alicia conveyed your message. If it's an apology you want, you won't get it. I have the right to question any witness who agrees."

"And I suppose you have the right to break another human being, get what you want from her, and walk away?" I sigh. "If you had let me know what you were planning, I'd have delivered her to you and then been there to pick up the pieces. As it was, we almost lost her. I just saw her a few minutes ago. She's a shell of the woman she once was. And all that for an irrelevant revelation."

"Hardly irrelevant."

"You know as well as I do that whether she slept with him after the murder has no bearing on who killed Laura Trussardi or why."

"We'll let the jury decide that."

"Maybe. But before you get to the jury, you've got to convince the judge. The judge will look at the relevance—zilch—and balance it against the potential prejudice, just like the law says, and it won't go in."

"It will go in, Jilly, and you know it. Subsequent conduct. Always relevant."

He's got a point, not that I'm about to let him know. "Whether it goes in or not, I can make sure the judge understands how you seduced a naïve woman from the accused's apartment, got what you wanted, then left her alone. Maybe I'll find myself moved to add a little more about what happened next. You won't look so sweet in the jury's eyes. Hate to do that to you, Cy."

He snorts. "Spare me your pity, Jilly. You don't seem to understand something. I've cut you slack from time to time in the past. This time I'm playing hardball."

"Is that a threat, Cy? "

"No. It's a fact."

He shifts gears abruptly. "Lois and I are having our usual beginning-of-term party, Jilly. Saturday, September twenty-seventh. Lois instructed me to make sure you came."

What's he up to? "I'll check my calendar," I say noncommittally. "How is Lois, by the way?"

"She's in hospital being prepped for a transplant as we speak. By the time of the party, she should be home and back to her old self."

"Give her my best, Cy." I hang up.

Piles of paper mound my desk. Police reports on a manslaughter I just took on. Transcripts on my never-ending drug conspiracy. Richard's formal report on the missing woman: *We regret to confirm that that DNA matching the sample was found at the site of Robert Pickton's farm.* I put the file down as Damon walks in.

He scans the papers on my desk. "You all right, Ms. Truitt?"

"Just busy." I thumb the report. "You might as well call me Jilly, Damon. Everyone else does."

I take a moment to study him. He would be in prison now but for a sympathetic barista and me. Fighting off rape, scrambling for drugs—the desperate survival of the condemned. But here he is, by some miracle, sitting in the chair opposite me, shining with force and intelligence. Still, his smile is tight. He's worried about something. Kellen?

"You're doing well, Damon. Been here a month now."

"Thanks, Jilly."

"Not just at the telephone and the coffee," I say. "Jeff tells me you bailed him out yesterday. He was heading for the Court of Appeal, no precedent, and you sat down at the computer and found him a case. A case he could win with. Impressive."

Damon leans forward. "I like it here, Jilly. I mean, for the first time in my life, I've found something I like. The people—you're real. The work—it's real, too. I know it's stupid, with my past, but this is what I want to do with my life."

"Do what, Damon?"

"The law."

You've killed a man, I think. *You're here by a fluke of luck and mercy, and you want to be a lawyer.* My head tells me it's crazy, but my heart tells me I'd move the earth to help him succeed.

He shifts in his chair. "Jilly, I need to tell you something."

"Sure."

"You can throw me out if you want. But I have to tell you."

"Tell me what?"

"I knew Laura Trussardi."

"What?"

"I delivered drugs to her. Cocaine. More than once."

I skip a breath. *So Richard's rumor was right. Laura, working at Eastside charities. Laura, rescuing sick and addled boys. Laura on cocaine. Something doesn't add up.*

"Damon, did Laura tell you why she needed the drugs?"

"No, I couldn't figure it out. And whenever I went to the house, I had to call ahead to make sure her husband wasn't there." He searches for something that makes sense. "Maybe the coke was for the maid?"

"Carmelina? I doubt it."

I remember what Trussardi said about the boy. "You went *into* the house, didn't you, Damon?"

He bows his head. "She invited me in one night. She said he wasn't there. I said no, but she transfixed me, she was so lovely, so pure. She gave me tea, poured me a bath, laid out clean clothes. I know it sounds crazy, but it wasn't crazy then. Not in my mind. My brain was all over the place—part of me was scared, part of me didn't know how to say no, part of me was writing poetry. That's how it was. In my head. At the time." He looks up bleakly, palms on his knees. "I shouldn't be telling you this."

I can't believe what I'm hearing. Every meeting we asked the questions: *Who's the boy? How can we find him?* And the whole time he was here, sitting at my reception, moving my boxes, making my coffee. This case keeps looping back to me in ways it shouldn't.

"What happened next, Damon?"

"Her husband came in. Mr. Trussardi. He just looked at us. She said, 'This is my friend.' He walked out on the terrace. When I came down after my bath, the table was set for dinner. I suppose I ate, suppose I talked. I don't remember much. After dinner, she said I should stay, sleep well for one night. Then she led me to the couch by the fire and disappeared. I sat there on that white couch, but my mind wouldn't be still—I was having scared, paranoid thoughts. Amphetamines do that to you, even when you think you're sober."

"And then?"

"I don't remember, exactly, except that at some point, the man—Mr. Trussardi—wasn't there. There seemed to be a hallway leading off behind the fireplace wall." Damon swallows. "I must have got up because I saw him, in his office. He was at a paneled wall. He pushed a door and a safe appeared, then he pushed a section below and a compartment slid out. He took out a piece of paper and looked at it as he punched numbers into the safe. When it opened, he took a revolver out—a black, shiny revolver like I'd never seen before—and began polishing it with a cloth, polishing like it was a rite. Once he was satisfied, he put the bullets in—*click, click, click*, one for each chamber. He took the gun in his hand and moved farther into the house, until I couldn't see him anymore."

I sit back in my chair, stunned. Damon has described the house, the room, *the gun*. He was there, he *remembers.*

"Suddenly, I understood—it was a plot. Their plot. Her job to lure me in, his job to kill me. So I turned and ran. Up the steps and out the door. I found my van, gunned it out the driveway." He halts. "I know now the amphetamines were messing up my thinking. There wasn't a plot, and he wasn't going to kill me. But that's what I thought then." He pauses. "But what if Mr. Trussardi really did kill his wife?"

"That's not for us to decide." I take a breath. "Damon, who have you told about this?"

"No one. I wasn't even going to tell you. But it's been eating at me ever since I saw Mr. Trussardi that day with the coffee. I thought he might recognize me and put two and two together."

"If he did, he never said anything."

"I wanted you to hear it from me. I'm sorry, Ms. Truitt, I know I've messed up your case."

"Maybe."

"I'll go now. Pack my things."

"No, Damon, you'll stay." *Better here than on the outside.* "I need to ask: Did you ever see Laura Trussardi again?"

"No."

I want to believe him, but I can't help thinking that he's not telling me everything, not telling me the worst. He saw the safe, saw where the code was hidden. Damon knew. My case has gone from no suspects to too many. It's one thing to tell the jury it was Trevor Shore, safely hidden in Brazil; it's easy to suggest it could have been a nameless street kid. But Damon? I feel sick. Damon, Laura, drugs, what the hell was going on? The more I find out, the less I understand. Weariness sweeps over me. This case is getting deep into me, too deep.

CHAPTER 26

ON MONDAY, STILL RECOVERING FROM Damon's revelations, I hit the office early. I want to tell Damon to keep his distance—he knows too much about the case and Chinese walls are in order. At the same time I need to keep him close—the last thing I want is him talking to Cy. I'm still working on how to combine these conflicting objectives at ten o'clock when I stroll to Debbie's station.

"Where's Damon?"

Debbie shrugs. "How should I know?"

Jeff has just arrived, Starbucks latte in hand. I turn to him. "What does Damon do on weekends, anyway?"

"I am not my brother's keeper, lo though I dwell in the same condo." Seeing my scowl, Jeff gets serious. "He runs, pushes weights in the gym, takes classes in Tae Kwon Do. Seems intent on building muscle and modes of self-defense."

"I hope it's just recreational." I think of Kellen, unhappy that the kid who shot his enforcer is out scot-free. I tell myself that it's been over a month—if Kellen wanted to get Damon, he would have made his move by now. *Or maybe it's something else.* My gut tells me Damon didn't give me the whole story on Laura.

I muddle through the rest of the day and the next, pretending to work up background on a new drug conspiracy, but when Damon fails to show on Wednesday, I start making calls. No response on his cell, no answer at his condo. I try to focus on the police reports in front of me, but it's not working. I pick up the phone and call Richard.

"Damon's gone missing," I blurt when he comes on the line. I fill him in on Damon's Friday night confession.

"*Merde,*" Richard breathes. I don't need to say more; he understands the implications. For some reason, like everyone, he cares about Damon. "I'm on it," he says, and hangs up.

I pull another report out of the pile and slog on. All I can do is wait.

JEFF WALKS IN AT FIVE, sagging from a hot afternoon in the Court of Appeal. He's been there all week, and I need to tell him about Damon's connection to Laura. I close down my Mac. "Let's go for a drink."

We walk up the street toward the Pan Pacific Hotel, take the escalators to the lobby floor, and head for a table on the patio beyond the lofty walls of glass. Below us, tiny figures lean over the rails of a cruise ship; across the harbor the slopes of West Van merge with the mountains. Over glasses of Pinot Grigio, I catch Jeff up on the latest.

"We found the boy," I say, and take a long sip. "And now he's gone AWOL."

Jeff's long fingers tap the table. "We need to get a grip on this case. Way too many mysteries."

I note that Jeff's no longer talking about a plea bargain—he's resigned to the fact that Trussardi won't cut a deal, even if we could get an offer. Nor does he mention bowing out of the case; it's too late for that.

He pulls the napkin from under his glass and starts writing. *Questions.* He double underlines the word.

"Number one," I say, "who was doing the drugs?"

Jeff writes it down, then lists the names. "Laura? Carmelina? Vincent?"

"Don't forget Raquella."

"Why would drugs for Raquella be delivered to Laura? Her apartment has a separate entrance."

"I don't know. Question number two," I continue, "what's going on between Raquella and Vincent?"

"What do you mean? We know they're not overly fond of each other. But why does that matter?"

"Not sure. But my instinct tells me there may be more. She'd love to take over the family business, for starters. Vincent in prison might suit her. Maybe I should talk to Hildegard, try to suss out any takeover intentions."

Jeff looks skeptical. "You won't get anything out of Hildegard. Besides, it doesn't make sense. Why kill Laura to get Vincent out of the way? Apart from the fact that Raquella's in a wheelchair and couldn't physically manage it."

I sigh and move on. "Question number three: Why didn't the cops make a serious effort to find Trevor Shore and talk to him?

And why, if Trevor's innocent, did he flee to Brazil? Do the cops know something we don't?"

"Never underestimate incompetence, Jilly. They had settled on Vincent. No need to look further. Tunnel vision."

"Question number four: Damon."

"As in, did he do it?"

"I don't want to go there. But he knew where the gun was, knew how to get it. He was high, paranoid, and infatuated with Laura. It's possible something happened between them that set him off."

"He killed Lippert," says Jeff. "Maybe he killed Laura, too. He was out on bail at the time of her murder, after all."

"I don't want to believe that."

"This does put us in an awkward position. We can tell the jury there was a crazy boy in the picture, hope it helps to raise a reasonable doubt. But now we know who the boy was, do we have an ethical problem?"

"As in misleading the court? I don't see how, Jeff. We lead with evidence that some boy hung around. It's not our job to identify him."

"What about calling him to testify?"

"And have him prattle on about Trussardi polishing his gun? Have him deny he killed Laura? Better to leave the boy as a mysterious possibility." I trace the rim of my wineglass. "There's another question. Something that's been bothering me. People keep warning me off this case, and I don't know why."

"Like who?"

"Like Edith Hole, my social worker."

Jeff's left eyebrow spikes up. "What the hell's your social worker got to do with the case?"

"That's just it. Nothing."

"Have you asked Edith why?"

"I tried to, but she ran away. Literally." I spread my hands. "She also said something about Trussardi's sister. I need to bear down on that."

"Good," Jeff says. "One more thing."

"What's that?"

"The picture."

"What picture?"

"The photo Trussardi stares at in his condo. The dark-haired woman in a white dress. Pretty, young. The photo's faded, looks old."

"An old flame? Or old regrets stirred up by the prospect of prison?"

"That's what Richard thought. But something tells me it could be important. I'll circle back to Richard on his progress."

A seaplane takes off, interrupting our conversation. We follow its arc as it curves to the west.

"So we have a plan," I say, as the plane recedes from view. "I talk to Edith, maybe Hildegard. Richard gets more info on the photo. And we keep our eye on Damon."

"'Ring out the false, ring in the true,'" Jeff says, downing the last of his drink.

CHAPTER 27

I RETURN TO MY CONDO, throw tuna and lettuce on a plate. Fine dining and the single girl. My evening looms bleakly before me. I consider TV, debate checking out Facebook. I'm coiled like a spring. I finish eating, then go down to start my car. This is as good a time as any to accost Edith. Find out why she warned me off the case. Find out why Vital Statistics says I don't exist and why the only living person who knows where I came from won't talk.

I park across from Edith's townhouse. The street is empty, except for a dark van that sits at the corner. The wall of windows behind the screen of cherry trees is black. *Maybe she's out.* I jog up to the door, push the bell, wait, push again.

The door opens on the chain. Through the chink, Edith peers at me.

"Edith, I need to talk to you."

"Go away, Jilly."

Go away? She's never spoken to me like this before. "Edith, what's wrong? Let me in?"

She slams the door shut in my face.

I should walk away, but I can't. I go round the house to the glass door in the dining area, give it a push. It slides open and I step inside. I find her standing near the front door, body rigid against the wall. "Edith, tell me what's going on."

"I can't," she whispers.

"Are you sick?"

A fat tear slips down her pale cheek. "Jilly, please, you need to go."

I take her shoulders in my hands. "This is about Trussardi, isn't it?"

"That's absurd."

"What's your connection with him?" I persist. "His sister told me you did something for him—'rendered him certain services' was how she put it." She sinks into the sofa and I take a seat next to her. "Edith, you can't hide from me."

"If you must know, I came into contact with him in the course of my work. I did my job. That was it."

"If that's it, why did you tell me not to take his case, Edith?"

"Because he didn't do the right thing." The bitterness in her tone rocks me. "A long time ago, I had a file. Vincent Trussardi was the father involved. I didn't like how he behaved. In fact, I developed a deep dislike for him. I haven't seen him in years, but I'll never forget how he treated his child. That's why I begged you not to act for him."

Trussardi had a child? What other secrets does he keep stashed in his past?

Edith goes on. "But now, someone's sent me a warning. Not Vincent Trussardi. I've worked with a lot of lost kids and families, poor and rich, and I've come to know things. Someone doesn't want me to reveal the details of their case. Of course, I never would, but they don't understand that. They're unreasonable." She looks at me, fear in her eyes. "This has nothing to do with Laura Trussardi's murder. Believe me."

I do. I've seen how ugly child protection cases can get, and not just in the courtroom.

"You should contact the police, get protection."

"Perhaps. But maybe I'm exaggerating this thing, this threat, if that's what it is." She manages a laugh. "Chalk it up to middle age. Menopausal moods." New tears well up. "I tried to live my life in a way that helped others, Jilly. But sometimes I feel it's all been for nothing."

I reach out my arm, and she falls limply against my shoulder.

"You helped me, Edith. You got me through. I was headed straight for the correction center, maybe worse, but you found me a home. You found me the Maynes."

"No, I didn't—"

"Hush, Edith." I hold her at arm's length, survey her face. "I don't want to get you into trouble, so I'll go. But I'll call you tomorrow."

"No, Jilly, don't call me. Don't come to visit me. If they see me with a lawyer, they might—" She breaks off. "Please."

Something's not right here, but I can't help her if she won't let me. "Okay, Edith, but I'm here if you need me." I turn and go.

Not much, but at least it's something, I think, as I rev my car into gear. I still don't know anything about my own parentage, but I now understand why Edith didn't want me to act for Trussardi.

He's a man with a past he's hiding, a man who did wrong and left the detritus of suffering in his wake. But that doesn't make him a murderer.

As I round the corner to Burrard, I glance into my rearview mirror. The traffic is steady. Three cars back a break opens, and a dark van glides into the space behind me. It follows me all the way home.

CHAPTER 28

I CAB IT TO HILDEGARD. I would have taken my Mercedes, but my current go-to mode is caution. Since my visit with Edith, paranoia has moved out of my dreams and into my days. *Get real, Jilly, you're losing it,* I tell myself, but my self isn't listening.

The tower looms over me as I step out of the cab—not the tallest building on the block, but the most beautiful, as befits my aesthete client. Officially it's the TEC Tower—Trussardi Enterprises Corp.—but locals simply call it the Trussardi Tower. I cast my eye to the top, glimpse terraces and trees—the penthouse where my client broods on a photo of a dark lady.

"Waste of a sunny Thursday morning," Jeff opined as I headed out. "I tried to pry something out of Hildegard when I saw her about the bail. No chance. Consiglieri to the godfather, mouth welded permanently shut."

But I have questions, and I'm determined to at least try to get some answers.

The waiting room on the twenty-ninth floor is modestly elegant. A Tom Thompson and an A. Y. Jackson grace the wall where a young woman in a tailored suit and black pumps waits behind a Louis XIV desk. She lifts her groomed head as I enter. "Miss Truitt, I presume." There is neither warmth nor chill in her manner. She leads me down a short hall, opens a door, and steps inside. "Miss Bremner, Miss Truitt has arrived." She retreats and shuts the door softly behind her.

It's not an office, but a sitting room, filled with pieces straight from the antique catalogues Martha Mayne used to keep on her coffee table—Aubusson carpet, damask drapery, silken fauteuils flanking a marble fireplace. Hildegard Bremner looks up from a delicate escritoire, puts down her Montblanc pen, and rises to greet me. Her face is blandly regal—powdered skin, bright lips, delicate nose—surmounted by a halo of gleaming white hair. Her piercing blue eyes record all there is to see about me in a single glance as she extends her pale hand. A simple dress of pale blue skims her matronly figure, and a diamond brooch worth half my condo glimmers discreetly on her left shoulder. *The Queen*, I think. *Or at least Helen Mirren.*

"Miss Truitt, we meet at last. Do sit down." Her voice is high and clear, with just a suggestion of a Germanic accent. She motions to one of the fauteuils by the fireplace, perches on the other. I park my battered briefcase, forlornly out of place in this elegant room, beside my chair. "Thank you for agreeing to see me—"

"This is a terrible business," Hildegard cuts in, shaking her head at me like I'm part of the problem. "Of course, Vincent is innocent of this crime. I fear, however, that I can be of little help in furthering his defense."

The door opens, and the young lady from the front desk enters. She places a silver tray on the small table between us, stoops to pour tea into Meissen cups. I shake my head as she proffers milk and sugar, and she leaves us once more. I spent the better part of last night pondering how to put my question on the future of Trussardi Enterprises Corp. to this woman, but to my surprise, she preempts me.

"What are the chances of Mr. Trussardi being convicted?" she asks.

"I can't give you a precise figure. At this point, it could go either way." I pick up my tea and take a delicate sip. "Why do you ask, Miss Bremner?"

"Corporate succession planning. Don't misunderstand me, Miss Truitt. I am utterly loyal to Vincent, and I very much hope he will be acquitted. But my duty is to ensure the continuance of the family business. In the event—"

"In the event Vincent goes to prison you will need to make arrangements," I finish. "Such as putting Raquella in charge?"

"That would be an option." Her eyes survey me with steely contempt. "I would have expected his lawyer to have been of greater assistance on the prospects of his case."

"Then help me," I say. "I take it you have been associated with the Trussardi family for some time, Miss Bremner?"

"Yes. I was born in Munich. My family had close business and family associations with the Trussardi family. My parents were killed in the war. When Vincent Trussardi Sr. immigrated to Canada in 1945, he brought me along. I was just a child. And I have been with the family ever since."

"You knew the children—Raquella, later Vincent?"

"Of course." She ripples the surface of her tea with a tiny silver spoon before settling it back on the saucer.

"You know them well?"

"What do you think?"

"Then tell me, how was their marriage, Vincent and Laura's?"

"I did not pry into their private life. As far as I could tell, they were happy."

"Mrs. Trussardi had an affair," I persist. "Did you know anything about that?"

Hildegard sets her cup down, takes her time before answering. "Vincent discussed it with me."

"What did he say?"

"He was distressed about it, as you might imagine. I advised him to be patient—suggested that she would tire of the man in question. As she did."

"Did you discuss the cost of a divorce with him, what the consequences might be for the family fortune?"

"If you are implying that Vincent might have killed his wife to avoid an expensive divorce, Miss Truitt, you are wrong."

"I am implying nothing, Miss Bremner. I am merely exploring matters that the prosecution may wish to explore. We need to know everything. We cannot afford surprises. You know this family better than anyone else. That is why I am here. Are there any enemies of the family that I should know about?"

"No, none."

I repress the impulse to tell this woman, who purports to care for my client, that she is proving perversely unhelpful. Jeff was right—questioning Hildegard is futile.

"Tell me about Vincent," I say, taking a flier. "His dalliances in love. There was someone from long ago whom he loved deeply."

Hildegard's cup rattles in its saucer. "Why do you muck about in ancient history? Yes, he had relationships in his youth, with a variety of women. Nothing unusual in that or wrong by today's standards. And there was nothing after his marriage. He was devoted to Laura."

"But there was someone special who stood out from all the rest," I press. "A dark woman in a white dress. He keeps looking at her picture. Do you know who she was?" I don't tell her that Richard snapped a photo of the picture, that I've propped it on my desk, that I keep looking at it like I should know who she is.

"Ask *him*," Hildegard spits out angrily. "I know nothing about a picture of a dark woman."

Was Hildegard this nasty with Jeff? Or does she just dislike me? I have a few more questions, none of which will help endear her to me.

"Did Vincent have any children? I have information that Vincent had a child out of wedlock."

"Your audacity astounds me, Miss Truitt." Hildegard stands, a tide of red creeping upward from her neck to her face. "You're wasting your time and Vincent's money prying into gossip, Miss Truitt. I must ask you to leave."

"What you call gossip may be vital to Mr. Trussardi's case," I say, rising. "My job is to provide him with the best defense the law allows. If you think of anything that might help, please let me know." I pause. "This is about him, not me."

We stare at each other in cold defiance.

"You should know that I advised him not to engage you. I told him it was a mistake. And you should also know that this encounter has done nothing to alter my view."

I take it in stride. It's not the first time I've been told I'm not up to the job—it comes with being a woman.

Hildegard moves to the door, opens it. "Goodbye, Miss Truitt."

CHAPTER 29

EIGHT P.M., THURSDAY NIGHT. RICHARD is sitting in my living room, denim-clad leg propped on denim-clad knee. "It's about Damon. Prepare yourself, Jilly."

Damon has been missing for six days. I know, I have counted each one. *He's just decided to move on*, I've kept telling myself. Hopped a boat for Asia, headed east to Alberta. Now I know it's not so. The lateness of the hour, the words—*Prepare yourself, Jilly*—tell me the worst.

"Go ahead."

"Word on the street is Kellen put out a contract on Damon. The guy who killed his enforcer was out, free and clear. Sent a bad message to other guys eyeing his turf. Damon went underground for a while and was getting ready to head east, but he didn't make it. Early this morning, a garbage truck operator emptying his

Dumpster saw what he thought was meat, decided it might be human, and called the police. They found blond hair. No one else has been reported missing. No one with blond hair, at least. I saw the photo, Jilly. Same color, thick like Damon's."

"No," I whisper. I bow my head between my knees and slump toward the floor, sobbing. *Don't get too close to the client*, they say. They're right. I've broken the cardinal rule in the criminal defense lexicon—*Do your job and move on*. But I had to try and rescue him. Now he's just another dead street kid, another statistic. Better I had lost his case, left him safe in his prison cell.

Richard is beside me, arm around my shoulder. "You did your best, Jilly. You did what you could."

The bromides of sympathy should bring comfort, but instead they revolt me. "I did too much. I prolonged the agony."

We sit for a while in silence. A new guilt assails me. "Richard, can you believe I actually entertained the possibility that Damon killed Laura Trussardi? I feel sick."

Richard shrugs uncomfortably. "Just because Kellen got him doesn't mean Damon didn't kill Laura."

"No, I don't buy it. Laura wasn't part of the picture. He loved her."

Richard looks at me, his brow furrowed. "The coroner will confirm the identity of the body next week. If she can."

I can't stand pity. I let out a deep breath, refocus on Trussardi. "I went to see Edith."

"And?"

"It seems Trussardi had a love child in his youth. She says it's irrelevant, but you might want to check it out. Cy might try to raise it in cross-exam. Forewarned is forearmed."

Richard gives me a small smile. "I'll poke around. But don't get your hopes up, Jilly. If the child was adopted out, the birth parents' identities go into limbo. And so what? It's a stretch that Cy would even have that information. What has it got to do with Laura's death?"

"You've got a point," I say. "That's what Hildegard said. Edith, too. Still, something in me tells me this matters." To the case, to me.

"You're the boss."

"Another thing. Edith's worried about an old child protection case of hers, says someone threatened her. I know your resources are finite, but could you look into it?"

"Of course. That's what I'm here for."

"Thanks." I think of Kellen's revenge and decide I can't keep the latest development to myself. "And that's not all. Richard, I think someone followed me from Edith's. A dark van. I've seen it a few times in my rearview mirror since."

"Jilly, why didn't you tell me sooner? Did you get the license number?"

"Never gets close enough. It could just be coincidence. Jeff tells me I'm getting paranoid."

I stand up, signaling it's time for him to go. It's almost nine, and I still need to swing by the office to check out details for tomorrow's dangerous driving trial.

"I'll look into the van. Be careful, Jilly."

I nod. "Sometimes I wonder why I do it, Richard. Why I care." I sigh. "Damn the presumption of innocence. They're all bad; they're all guilty. The odd acquittal is a miscarriage of justice."

"I wouldn't go that far, Jilly."

I force a laugh. "Just how I feel sometimes. Goodnight, Richard. And thanks."

Richard leaves. I sit on my couch, my head in my hands. Visions of madness mingle in my mind. Damon in the Dumpster. Trussardi caressing his gun. Dark vans pursuing me. I lift my head, try to clear it. I'm in too deep. I'm losing the thread. I look at my watch. *You can handle this, Jilly,* I tell myself. *All will be well in the morning.* I shut the door behind me, find the elevator, and push the button marked *P*. A woman's work is never done.

It's cold down here, and the freshness of the late-summer evening has coated the car windshields with condensation. I reach for the door of my car, step back for a second, look at what I see on the glass. Marks in the condensation, jagged, irregular blotches. They're starting to run, and in the dim light of the parking garage I can barely make them out. Still, I see enough to send me reeling.

Jilly Truitt, the lines say. *Stop digging.*

CHAPTER 30

I FALL SICK. THE YOUNG doctor who orders me to the hospital says it's the latest strain of Asian bird flu, but I know better. I have fallen sick of mind, of spirit, of the enigma of what I do and who I am. I drift in and out of consciousness. I wake and dream, dream again. My dreams are stories—the stories I want, the stories I have made myself believe, the stories of my life. Of innocence, of abuse, of neglect. Never stories of guilt; no, never guilt. The people in my dreams are deprived perhaps, confused maybe, but never guilty. I will prove it. I lie back on my pillow. So many stories. The past mingles nonsensically with the present—Edith, Vincent, Raquella, Laura alive, Damon reprieved. Now both are dead.

They come to see me, those few who, against all good sense, have loved me—shapes drifting in and out of my dreams. Martha and Brock, tall forms with masks over their mouths; my brothers, too; and Richard for a few minutes. Each evening—it is always evening in my dreams—an old friend named Diane reads me poems as she did when we were young and too fresh to fall asleep. She reads a poem of a tree that changes colors with the seasons, from green to yellow to deep red.

"Where did you find it?" I murmur.

"In the *New Yorker*," she replies.

"It's about death," I say, and see her eyes grow wide with fear. "It's all right. It's lovely." I fall back into my dreams.

Michael St. John does not come.

On what they later tell me is the eighth day, I wake and sense a presence in the room.

"Ms. Truitt," a voice says. A voice I know. Used to know.

I look up. *Not a real voice, a dream.*

A figure is standing in the doorway. The light glints on a thick shock of yellow hair. I struggle for words, hear them, thin, far away. "You're dead, dead in a Dumpster."

The figure moves slowly toward the end of the bed, and the dream becomes reality. Damon's face. I hear my cry. I'm alive, awake. "Damon? You—here? You're—"

"Jeff said you were sick."

"But you—you're dead. The body in the Dumpster."

"Somebody else."

My drugged and addled mind races. "Kellen."

"Jilly. It's over."

"How do you know?"

The muscle in his throat quivers. "I don't want to lie to you, Jilly. Don't make me." He moves to my side, finds the chair by the bed.

"What are you going to do now?"

"Get my life back."

"What?" My hands feel for the bed, find the railing. I look around the room. *How long have I been here?*

He looks down. "I'll understand if you don't want me at the office."

"Damon," I say. "You disappeared. The undertow, the street, it's pulling you back, pulling you under."

His jaw clenches. "It's over, Jilly."

"It's never over." I feel weak. My arm slips from the sheet and falls.

I feel his hand on my forehead, feel him lift my hand and slip it back under the sheet.

I sink into a deep and dreamless sleep.

CHAPTER 31

IT TAKES ME TWO WEEKS to recover.

"What did you expect?" asks Dr. Khan when he comes to call at my condo. He watches me force myself from my bed, struggle to walk a little farther than the day before. "A less healthy person would have died."

My little family welcomes me to the office with looks and lectures and much tut-tutting. In my absence, they've made it through. A few cases adjourned, others handled thanks to double duty by Jeff and Alicia.

"Alicia's coming along," Jeff says. "Picked up some difficult stuff, pulled it off with aplomb. Every cloud has a silver lining, or at least some of them."

We're back to normal. Qualification—the new normal. Damon and I have developed an understanding. We don't speak of the body found in the Dumpster. We don't speak of that night at the Trussardi home. Who knows, I might need to call him to develop the *boy defense* or to take the gloss off Laura's virtue by showing she bought drugs, although the possibility of Cy cross-examining Damon on the safe and the gun sends shivers up my spine.

I've resumed driving, although occasionally I still think I see a dark van behind me. So far, no other warnings have appeared on my windshield. I've decided to keep digging—to hell with the consequences.

Any doubt that it's not business as usual is dispelled by Debbie's shout down the hall, "Cy Kenge for you, Jilly. Line 2." No *ifs, buts,* or *would-you-like-to-take-the-calls,* just *you're on.*

I pick up the phone. "Cy, what can I do for you?"

"Heard you were away, Jilly." Something in Cy's tone puts me on edge.

"If you think I went off for a tummy tuck, Cy, you've got the wrong girl. Just a mundane case of H7N9, I'm afraid. Now that we're through the gracious preliminaries, what's your book of business?"

"Two things," he says. "One business, one pleasure."

"Let's start with the pleasure."

"No way, Jilly."

I sigh. "Okay, Cy, the business."

"I'm prepared to accept a plea to second degree in Trussardi, release on parole after ten years if he behaves himself. Against my better judgment, might I add. It seems someone upstairs has your guy's back."

No preamble, no negotiation, just the offer, one I would have jumped at a month ago.

"Sorry, Cy," I reply. "To be frank, I discussed this possibility with my client, but he refuses to plead to anything. I'll convey your offer, of course."

"No accounting for stupidity." He moves on to the pleasure part of the call. "Lois and I still hope you can come to our party. This Saturday."

"Thanks. How's Lois recovering?"

"Splendidly, Jilly. She's got her new liver, has been out of the hospital for a week now and feeling better every day. You'll see on Saturday."

"I'll try to make it." I'm about to hang up when I hear his voice again.

"Jilly, while I have you, there's something I should tell you. On Trussardi."

Now we're getting down to the real business.

"Yes?"

"News about Trevor Shore."

My stomach clenches.

"He's been killed in a little town near São Paulo. Shot. Looks like gang violence—a case of being in the wrong place at the right time. Although you never know: it could have been targeted. Maybe he knew too much. Maybe your man fingered him."

Stupid me, assuming the cops didn't know where Trevor Shore was, when all along they were watching him. A game has been playing out, a game I do not understand. Why is Cy offering me a plea if he thinks Trevor Shore's disappearance is my problem? Was it his plan to get Trevor back and have him testify? Viewed objectively, the Crown's case is thin—the gun, the bed, a wisp of a motive that I hope to blow out of the water. Trevor on the stand would have strengthened the motive, maybe provided some juicy detail that would have clinched the conviction.

"I'll send you the police reports as we get them," Cy says crisply. "See you at the party." The line goes dead.

I look up. Jeff is hovering in the doorway. "So?"

"Eavesdropping?"

He slides into the chair across my desk.

"Trevor Shore's been shot dead. Brazilian police are investigating. Cy's hinting that Trussardi is behind it."

"Crazy."

"What's with this man we call our client, Jeff? Do you think he could have hired someone to kill Shore? Why would he do that?"

"Who knows what goes through his head? He just sits there brooding over the photo of the dark lady."

"And at the same time he's conspiring how to take out Trevor Shore? Doesn't figure. Maybe our police told the Brazilian cops to keep Shore away so they could convict Trussardi, and the Brazil boys went overboard."

Jeff raises an eyebrow.

"Or maybe somebody we don't know about yet killed him." I change tacks. "Cy just offered to reduce the charge to second degree. Ten years to parole. Our duty to tell the client."

Jeff's up, pacing to the window. "Our *duty*, Jilly, our *duty*? It's our lifeline. We're going down, and you talk like you'd rather not throw it to the client? It's a case, not the bloody Holy Grail. You've lost perspective on this one, Jilly."

"Calm down, Jeff. The Crown's case isn't all that strong."

He laughs. "If you forget the matrimonial bed and the gun. Trussardi's crazy if he doesn't accept this offer. This isn't like Damon's case—good kid scared out of his wits—where we had a real chance at second, maybe manslaughter. The person who committed this crime meant it." He leans toward me over the paper-strewn table. “Please tell me you’re going to tell him to take it, Jilly.”

“I’ll recommend it.”

Jeff slumps into his chair. “Thank god. This case is a high-speed train about to go off the tracks. Whoever said speedy justice was good was a fool.”

CHAPTER 32

VINCENT TRUSSARDI SITS ON THE white leather bench in the stern of the boat. *We'll take the sloop*, he said when I called to ask to have a one-on-one. I wonder how many boats he owns.

His binoculars train the horizon where orcas cavort. The late sun shadows his profile, and I understand why so many women have fallen for him. He lowers the binoculars and offers me a regretful smile. "Gone."

I lean forward, elbows on my knees. "We need to talk." *I failed with Edith and Hildegard*, I think. *Today, with luck, I'll figure things out. Or at least get closer.*

I decide to open with the plea. I may be floundering on this case, but you can't fault my due diligence. If Vincent says okay, we can clink our glasses and head back to harbor.

"Mr. Trussardi, the prosecution is offering a plea bargain. You plead guilty to second degree, and you're out on parole in ten years. First degree, which is what you're facing, is a life sentence with no possibility of parole for twenty-five years. Our case isn't looking great. It's my considered opinion you should accept the offer."

He gives me a kindly look. "I respect your opinion, Miss Truitt. But as I told you before, I will not plead guilty to any charge involving the death of my wife."

I could tell him I'm quitting, but I'd be lying. Despite all the secrets, at the back of my mind the voice of Trevor Shore lurks: *Put the real killer behind bars, so I can stop running.*

"I'm sorry I asked again," I say, and I mean it.

"I have a question for you, Miss Truitt."

"Yes?"

"Are you—how shall I put this—are you entirely well?"

I bristle. "Of course I'm well. I had a bout with the flu a few weeks back, but I'm better now."

"You've lost weight."

"Are you worried I won't have the strength to win your case, Mr. Trussardi? If so, I would be happy to find you another lawyer."

"No, I'm not worried about that. Not in the least. And you will do quite well as my lawyer."

"Then what's this about, Mr. Trussardi?"

He faces the wind, turns back with a shrug. "I've come to care about you, Miss Truitt."

I stiffen. "You shouldn't. I'm your lawyer; you're my client. In another world we might have been friends. But we can't be friends in this one. It gets in the way."

"I understand, Miss Truitt. But life is complicated. More complicated than you can imagine." He clears his throat. "Never mind. Let's get down to business. Lawyer. Client."

"Shall we start with Raquella? I know you haven't always gotten along. And I know that Laura was close to her."

"Why do you need to get into the mess of my family affairs, Miss Truitt?" he asks defensively. "It's painful for me and has nothing to do with the case."

"Let me be the judge of that," I say, steering him back on track.

"If you insist," he replies, his voice tight. "Laura was good to Raquella. Too good."

"Did Raquella try to undermine your relationship with Laura? Did you feel left out? Jealous perhaps?"

He looks out to sea.

"Mr. Trussardi."

He whirls back. "What can it matter, how I felt?"

It might matter a lot, I want to say.

"Raquella was lonely. Laura befriended her, helped her out of her depression. Raquella became dependent on her, infatuated with her," he says bitterly. "But it passed. Laura and I were back together, expecting a child."

"Raquella can't have liked that."

"No, she didn't like that, but she wouldn't kill Laura for it."

"She was jealous of you running the family business," I persist. "It might have suited her to have you in prison."

"I know you've talked to Hildegard about the business. But if you're thinking Raquella killed Laura, for this or any other reason, you're wrong. She adored Laura and had long reconciled with the idea that she had no place in the business."

I try to put the pieces together. Even if he knew, he wouldn't say anything against Raquella. Some ancient code of family loyalty.

I regroup. "We've confirmed that Laura was, in fact, buying drugs. If not for herself, then for whom?"

"I don't know, but thousands of people buy drugs. They don't get killed for it—at least, not the way she was killed."

"What about Carmelina?" I ask. "You and she were intimate. Perhaps she was jealous, wanted Laura out of the way."

His face colors. "Carmelina and I were not intimate," he spits out. "Yes, we were together the night of the murder. It was a desperate, stupid act of confused sorrow. Carmelina worshiped Laura. As did I."

If everybody loved Laura, I want to yell, *then who the hell killed her?*

Instead, I step toward him, locking my eyes on his. "Trevor Shore is dead," I say. "Shot in the head in Rio."

I see the shock on his face. So he did not know.

"Do you think Trevor could have killed Laura?" I ask.

"Maybe. Perhaps she had told him about the pregnancy, that the baby was mine, and he lost his mind and killed her." He breaks off. "I don't know. I just don't know."

I read the pain and exhaustion in his face. He's not a bad man; he may well be innocent of the crime they have pinned on him. I steel myself to carry on.

"There's a photo of a woman in your condo, Mr. Trussardi. Can you tell me about her?"

"You pry too much, Miss Truitt." The line of his brows belies his even tone. "The woman in the photo was someone I loved deeply, someone I betrayed. Lately, I've taken to reflecting on my life. Perhaps the bleakness of my future allows me to look back on the past now and realize I wronged her terribly."

"Who was she?" I say, as softly as I can.

He looks away to the ocean. "She was my first love. Let it go."

"Does she have anything to do with a woman named Edith Hole?"

"I know no one by that name."

"I know you had a child. Edith Hole looked after the adoption."

His voice is hoarse when he next speaks. "Yes, I did have a child. Her mother and I agreed on adoption. And yes, Edith Hole was the social worker they assigned to the file." He swallows. "If I could live my life again, I would keep the child, cherish it, hold it to me forever. But I was young and foolish and weak."

No man who feels so deeply about having lost one child would kill the woman carrying his second.

"I'm sorry," he whispers, coughing and collecting himself. He sinks back to the bench, head bowed. A profound sense of sadness sweeps over me.

"He said you lived an inauthentic life."

He lifts his head. "Who said that?"

"Brock Mayne," I say. "My father. Foster father."

"I heard he and Martha took on a foster child."

Took on, such cold words. I stare out over the western sea. The lowering sun streaks the horizon with red and gold. His eye follows mine.

"Beauty," he says. "*Sic transit gloria mundi.* Thus passes the glory of the world."

"*Tempus fugit,*" I reply. *Time slips away.*

"Whatever happens, Miss Truitt, I want you to know this. I admire you. It has been a pleasure—a great pleasure—to have spent this time with you."

I could say I don't think he's come clean with me. I could say I still don't trust him, but for once I skip the scolding. "Thank you, Mr. Trussardi."

"Thank you, Miss Truitt. You cannot know how much this means to me."

He starts the motor and we head back to harbor.

CHAPTER 33

THE NEXT AFTERNOON, I'M BACK at Trussardi's house. Today's episode of my never-ending drug trial broke off early, and there are things I need to check out before we go to court with Trussardi—a looming date. My resolution to de-obsess myself has fallen flat. *Face it, you're out of control*, I tell myself as I compulsively pull at every tangled thread this case spins off.

The furniture is still there—the long glass table where Damon dined and the white banquette where he sat—but the room is empty of life. No people, no paintings, no bentwood boxes. A barren abandoned stage. I sit on the banquette and cast my eye to the fireplace and beyond. I see what Damon saw: walls of ash. I move toward them.

I find myself in a study with nothing more than a desk, a sofa, and pale wood panels. I push on one, and it slides back to reveal the safe. The door is ajar, so I peer inside, but it's empty. I slide my hand into a crack that opens between the shelves beneath. No paper, the code is gone. *The house, Ms. Truitt. You'll find the truth; it's all there,* Trevor said. Is this what he meant?

I go back to the living room, turn at the banquette. Yes, Damon could have seen Trussardi retrieve the code, could have watched him open the safe and take out the gun. But how can I use Damon's testimony to create doubt without damning my client? Or without damning Damon? One of them did it, the jury would reason. I don't like either result.

I sense a presence in the room and swivel. "Raquella."

"This is fortuitous," she says. "I was about to summon you." She wheels to a corridor behind the dining area. I follow her to the elevator.

Back in her apartment, she gets right to the point. "Stop your inquiries into matters that are not your business, Miss Truitt."

I think of the words I saw on my windshield the night I fell ill: *Stop digging.*

She leans forward. "Some things are best left in the past, Miss Truitt. I understand that, *he* understands that."

"Did he talk to you last night?" Are brother and sister in some secret conspiracy?

"You ask too many questions, Miss Truitt. You need to learn to let some things go."

"Is that a threat?"

"Make of it what you will."

"You're afraid I'll discover something that would absolve your brother, lead to his acquittal. It would suit you just fine if he were sent to prison, wouldn't it, Raquella?"

"Absurd," she hisses.

"Do you know anything about the drugs that were delivered to Laura?"

Raquella sniffs. "How would I know?"

I look at her, hunched sideways in her chair, and suddenly I understand. "So many years in a wheelchair. It must be painful."

She makes no reply.

"Perhaps Laura got the drugs for you, Raquella? A little cocaine to ease the pain."

"Leave!" she shouts, arm raised. "Now."

I turn at the door. "This is the second time you've thrown me out, Raquella. I won't return for a third. But I want you to remember this: before this case is over, I will know everything."

A flash of fear crosses her features. *Good*, I think.

In the garden, Botero's sculpture looms before me, enormous of thigh, pendulous of breast, vacuous stare malevolent. Once she made me laugh. Now, for some reason, I feel revulsion.

CHAPTER 34

IN THE END, I DECIDE to go to Cy's party. I need a break from the mess my office calls "Jilly's Trussardi Obsession," and I need to scotch the rumors that I've suffered a near-mortal blow. I've regained most of the weight I lost and booked into the spa this morning to get my hair cut and my nails painted in my new signature black. Before my bathroom mirror, I dab a spot of blush on my still-pale cheeks, put on bright lipstick, and tell myself I don't look bad in my low-cut black dress and heels.

I wedge my Mercedes between a Bentley and a Ford, and stride across the gravel of the parking area and up Cy's crumbling walk in the long rays of the dying sun. I pull my shoulders back and toss my hair as I push the bell. I'm back and here to stay.

Lois greets me at the door. She's a new woman—jaundice gone, face shining, decked out in a chic red-linen shift and sandals. "Jilly, we were so hoping you'd come," she says brightly. "How *are* you? Cy says you've suffered a tiny contretemps. Obviously, you're over it—you look wonderful." As she speaks, she draws me into the crowded great room and through to the back terrace.

Cy's house is old by Vancouver standards. It's big barn of a place with a two-story living room from which all the other rooms radiate. An eccentric house; nothing but a few pieces of plumbing have changed since his father built it half a century ago. The land upon which the house sits, however, is spectacular—two acres of prime real estate descending down the cliff to the Pacific Ocean. Cy jokes that the land is his retirement plan. He'll need it. They don't pay prosecutors a lot, even the best of them.

People call to me, smile, lean over for a buss. Whatever they've heard, most seem genuinely pleased to see me. The prosecutors I spar with in court, the lawyers I share the defense bench with, a smattering of judges—it's good to see them again.

Outside on the terrace, Cy, surrounded by a coterie of admirers, mans the barbecue. I know his secret—he has the beef tenderloins prepped by a caterer so all he needs to do is warm them up—but I would never tell. I watch him hobble to a table draped in white linen and lined with salads, one arm in its brace, the other holding a platter bearing a huge slab of meat. He sets the dish down neatly beside the salads without a tremor. I marvel at the performance.

He sees me and comes over, braced leg swinging, butcher knife in hand.

"You wouldn't stab me in the back, Cy, would you?" I ask with a laugh as he reaches behind to hug me.

"Never, Jilly, never. Good to see you. I told Lois you'd come." His round face beams down at me as though he means it. "Smashing, Jilly, smashing." He looks over at the man behind the bar, single-handedly fighting off the crush of people demanding drinks. "A glass of white wine for Ms. Truitt," he yells. The bartender shakes his head like Cy's an idiot.

"I'm fine," I say. "Nice evening—lots of people. I'll just wander for a while."

I drift from cluster to cluster. At some point, Ben, a prosecutor from up-country, decides to do the gracious thing and finds me a drink. I accept it with a smile and chat with him for a polite interval. At a break in our conversation, I look around. That's when I see him.

He stands near the terrace door, engaged in conversation. I scan for a woman on his arm, find none. Just guys. *What the hell is he doing here? Is this Cy being cheeky?* He sees me, takes a step toward me, then stops as if thinking better of it. I decide to take matters in my own hands. As I approach, he detaches himself from the group. I move into an alcove near the door, and he follows.

"Hi, Mike," I say. He looks good to me, like he's always looked. What a fool I was to walk out on him.

"Jilly. How have you been?"

"Rumors of my demise are greatly exaggerated."

His face breaks into the beaky grin I remember. "We should have lunch or something, Jilly. For old times' sake." He looks at me thoughtfully. "How's your case coming?"

"Trussardi? Between us, not as well as I would like. But it will soon be over. We go to trial in a couple of weeks."

"So I've heard. My various aunts keep me in the loop."

"Yeah." I angle back to where I want to be. "I'd like to do lunch, Mike. I miss you."

I feel a touch on my arm, but it's not Mike. It's one of the men

I saw standing at the barbecue with Cy—an undercover cop working in Oregon, I overheard someone say—high forehead, sharp chin, trendy leather jacket.

I move back to Mike, but before I can, the cop takes my hand, closes my fingers around the stem of a glass of white wine, and gives me an intimate smile, his eye following the line of my dress. *Is this from Cy?* He's about to tell me, but I'm not interested, not now. "Thanks," I say, cutting him off, and turn to Mike. But Mike's gone, weaving through the crowd toward the front door. I whirl back to the cop, ready to give him a piece of my mind, but he's no longer there either. "What the hell?" He must hear me because he turns and gives a lazy wave before continuing toward Cy at the barbecue. I hear his low laughter as he shares something with Cy. What kind of game are they playing?

The party has gone sour, and I have no appetite for more. I deposit the glass the man forced on me on a small table and head inside. Halfway across the room, I stop. I should at least thank Lois, wish her a speedy recovery. I scan the crowd. "Looking for Lois?" someone asks. "Try the kitchen."

As befits an old-fashioned house of pretension, the only way to the kitchen is through the butler's pantry. I push open the swinging door. What I see stops me dead in my tracks. Lois stands at the kitchen counter, her back to me. Her head is tilted back and her right hand holds a bottle to her lips. Sensing someone, she spins around with an accusing stare—*So what?* My hand leaves the door, and it starts to swing shut.

Then I hear her voice from the other side. "Come in, Jilly."

I step inside. The bottle is on the counter.

"I know, I know," she says, moving toward me. "Just a few nips; tomorrow I'm back on the wagon. I've done all the counseling, all the never-another-drop stuff. But recovery—it's hard, Jilly, so hard."

"Lois, no." I reach for the bottle, throw it in a trashcan that's been set up for the party.

"You're a good person, Jilly. I can't let him do it to you."

Who? Cy? I must have misheard. "Lois, what are you talking about?"

"Cy. He's got something up his sleeve. The Trussardi case."

"Like what?"

"A police report, an occurrence report, I think he called it."

I feel a chill. "What does it say?"

"I can't be certain—I overheard one of his calls. Just the other day. Something about Laura Trussardi crying in the street outside her house a couple of days before the murder."

Why would Laura be crying in the street just before the murder? How many secrets can one woman take to her grave?

I take a deep breath and give Lois a hug. "Thanks. I appreciate the heads-up. But I'm not too worried. Cy can't use the report in evidence unless he gives me disclosure." I force a smile. "I have to leave, Lois. Why don't you see me out?"

"Yes, of course." She takes my hand. "Let's go." And then she lurches to the side, stumbling.

"Lois, you're not well," I say. "Let me take you upstairs."

She nods sickly, leans against me as we walk up the servants' stairs, out of sight of the party. I lay her on the big bed in the room at the end of the hall and cover her with a throw.

"Jilly, don't tell anyone what happened downstairs. And don't tell Cy what I said about the report. Please. He'd kill me."

"Don't worry, Lois. Not a word." It's not the first time I've run into women who are scared of their husbands. Still, she's shaken me. Sure she's drunk, but why tell me about some phantom report? Why double-cross her husband? I pat her arm. "Get some rest." I take the stairs and push through the crowd below and outside.

I slump behind the wheel of my car. Mike's crooked smile fills my mind.

Lois is right. Recovery is harder than they say.

ACT THREE

CHAPTER 35

THE FIRST DAY OF THE trial dawns bright and clear, and the crisp smell of autumn hangs in the air. I rise early from a fitful sleep, pull on my Adidas and Lycra, and head down to the seawall for a run before I meet Trussardi. Already I feel the adrenaline rush that accompanies each new trial. It's my only remaining addiction—the addiction to risk. Despite all the disclosure, all the rules, there are always surprises, and this case will be no exception. Witnesses who say more than they should. The push in cross-examination, always calculated, but sometimes going further than safe. "The play's the thing," Hamlet said. The play I am about to enter—its acts, its scenes, its climax, its ultimate denouement—stretches before me in all its incertitude. Running takes off the crazy edge, leaves just enough behind.

At precisely nine fifteen, Vincent Trussardi meets me at the office, dressed in a dark suit, crisp white shirt, and understated black silk tie. At a casual glance, he looks confidently distinguished, but there are deep shadows under his eyes. I shrug a coat over my black suit and join him in the limo that waits on the street. Jeff has gone ahead in his van with the books. My job is to deliver the client safely into the hands of the waiting sheriff and hence into the prisoner's box.

"Keep your eyes straight ahead and don't blink," I advise in the back seat of the limo. "Remember, you're presumed innocent."

He pulls his face into a look of haughty reserve. Not great either.

I've warned him, but the crowd outside 800 Smithe Street still hits him like a tsunami. He flinches, then, remembering my instructions, forces his chin up. Curious court watchers press between cameras and the clamoring press. "Wife killer!" someone shouts. In the background, crudely painted signs wobble in the wind: ANOTHER WOMAN KILLED. END THE SLAUGHTER. His shoulders stiffen as he steps out of the car and onto the curb.

The crowd parts to allow us through. Lights flash on every side, and reporters thrust mics in our faces. We ignore them and push through the glass doors and into the building where two uniformed men await us. I nod and watch as they escort my client through the locked doors to the cells.

I find Jeff in courtroom twenty neatly stacking files on our counsel table. It's a big room in the bowels of the courthouse, kitted out with technology and screens and bulletproof glass. Just in case. I hear Cy's step in the aisle and turn to greet him. Lois's warning at the party comes back to me, but the rules of civility must be maintained.

"So we do battle, Jilly," says Cy, swiveling his bulk to view the mass of potential jurors in the well of the courtroom.

"So it seems, Cy. 'Once more unto the breach.' "

He has barely settled himself when the court clerk—a genial blond lady named Marion—puts down her phone, rises from her desk, and approaches us. "Justice Moulton would like to see you in his chambers before the arraignment and jury selection," she tells us.

We hitch up our gowns and follow her out the door behind the bench, up the elevator, and down an inner corridor carpeted in red. On our right, a long row of pale wooden doors stretch as far as we can see. Marion pauses before one of them, raps on the door. From deep within comes a low grunt, "Open." Marion pushes on the door and bids us follow her in.

Mr. Justice Albert Moulton sits behind his blond beech desk, leaning back in a high red leather chair. A lordly swath of white hair waves back from his handsome face. Although he exudes self-satisfaction, there is an air of malaise about him—the down-turned lip, the complexion blotched with choleric spots, the deep creases on either side of the mouth that now settle into a scowl. He motions vaguely in our direction. Cy and I take the chairs on the other side of his desk, leaving Jeff and Emily to settle uncomfortably on the red leather couch against the wall.

No greetings, no courtly exchanges. Justice Moulton gets right to the point. "Regrettably, we do not have the benefit of a pretrial conference in this matter." He glares at us like it's our fault when he's the one who cancelled it. *The judge sees this as a straightforward case,* Marion had intoned on the telephone. "Even more regrettably," he now continues, "this appears to be a trial that will attract a certain amount of media attention. These two circumstances place a heavy duty on counsel. Respect for the administration of justice must be preserved. I feel it only right to inform you that I will not tolerate sending the jury out for long periods while we haggle over fine points of evidentiary admissibility."

Was that last comment aimed at me, or is it just my imagination?

"As you may be aware, my practice is to err on the side of admitting everything—let the jury see it all and then sort it out." He singles me out for a glare. "If you insist on challenging evidence tendered by the Crown, Ms. Truitt, the objections will be dealt with outside regular sitting times."

"Yes, my Lord," I reply.

"Good. Now I expect my opening address to the jury to consume the afternoon. We'll start motions at nine tomorrow. I will tolerate no grandstanding for the press. Do I make myself clear?" Another glance my way.

I nod. *Any other insinuations you'd like to hurl my way?*

Justice Moulton plants both hands on his desktop and frowns at Cy and me indiscriminately. "Counsel, you have my point. Now let's get on with this trial."

THE BOOM OF THE HEAVY door brings me to attention. I watch the sheriffs lead Vincent Trussardi to the prisoner's box. There's nowhere to go once the gate slams shut. A foretaste, should things not go his way, of the rest of his life. I give him an encouraging smile.

The gallery behind us is full: reporters in the front benches; family, friends, and court followers jammed in the benches behind. I glimpse Lois on the far side, here to witness Cy's big win. She catches my eye and nods. In the aisle, Raquella sits in her chair, her face an inscrutable mask. The world thinks she's here to support her brother, but I know she's here to see him go down.

"Order in the court," Marion calls. The door from the inner sanctum opens, and Justice Moulton ascends the bench. Marion announces the case. It's jury selection time.

The game is complex, ruled by stand-asides and preemptory challenges. From a pool of sixty good citizens—give or take a few—we must choose twelve jurors. One by one the candidates come forward, give their names and occupations. We question a few. Many say they've read about the case or have an opinion about it or think they may know someone who knew someone involved in it. The judge recognizes this for what it usually is: an attempt to get out of jury duty. Others are avid, their smiles telling us that they're dying to be picked. We're wary of them, too.

Jeff and I are prepared. We've studied their occupations, searched for online chatter and blogs. We want a sympathetic jury, youngish, on the liberal side, university professors, social workers, teachers—these are our cup of tea. Cy, on the other hand, wants jurors from the angry right who rant about law and order and the crimes that the six o'clock news tells them lie around every corner. Throughout the morning, Cy and I do what we can to nix each other's choices. We stand up; we stand down; we tussle. But in the end we get pretty much what we usually get—a mix that does not fully please either of us.

We manage to secure a school librarian (formerly married to a wealthy businessman), a commerce professor, a portrait artist with a shop in Granville Island, a real estate executive, an accountant, and a magazine publisher. The prosecution ends up with a mill worker, a cab driver, a nurse, a turbaned grocer, and the ubiquitous dockworker. Six men and six women, six from the right, six from the putative left. Except no one owns anyone.

It's late morning by the time the grocer takes the final oath.

Justice Moulton looks at the clock, then at the jury in their box. "I will now ask you to retire, ladies and gentlemen of the jury, and to choose one among you as your foreperson."

When they return after a fifteen-minute break—true to his word, Justice Moulton runs the trial precisely to time—Janus Kasmirsky, the woodworking artist, stands up and announces that the jurors have chosen him as their leader.

Good, I think, nodding at Jeff.

Janus Kasmirsky, angular of face and gaunt of body. He emigrated from Latvia to Montreal with his mother when his parents separated. Immigrant roots, artistic, just like Vincent Trussardi. I scan the research Damon compiled, and my initial enthusiasm sags. Further investigation shows a Jewish father who ranked high in the Communist Party in postwar Poland.

At two o'clock, we return to face the tedium of Justice Moulton's opening instructions to the jury. The press that occupied the backbenches in the morning has fled, having better things to do than listen to judicial boilerplate. Moulton advises the jurors of their duties, reminds them of their oath.

"The onus is on the prosecution to prove that Vincent Trussardi is guilty beyond a reasonable doubt," he tells them. "Any doubt must be resolved in favor of the accused."

Reasonable doubt, our best and only hope.

CHAPTER 36

IT'S 9:00 A.M. ON TUESDAY, day two of the trial of Vincent Trussardi, and we're in the empty courtroom for preliminary motions on evidence. We need to settle what goes in and what stays out. Cy and I both know that the outcome of this case may well depend on what the jury gets to hear. The process is governed by a complicated and sometimes opaque area of the law known simply as *Evidence*, the bane of every second-year law student. In his old mentoring mode, Cy taught me to fight hard to keep damaging evidence out; I've learned the lesson well.

At stake are two critical pieces of evidence—the motel clerk Emond Gates's identification of Laura Trussardi from the photo lineup, and whether Cy can ask Carmelina if she slept with Vincent Trussardi after the murder. Justice Moulton listens as I talk, interjecting here and there to interrupt my submissions. Then, just when I think all is lost, he surprises us by announcing that he will reserve his decisions until tomorrow morning.

"That's a good sign," I tell Jeff as we organize our papers.

"He's just scared of botching the trial. He's not on our side, this judge."

Precisely at ten o'clock, the door to the inside corridor opens, Marion calls for order, and Justice Moulton strides up the steps to his chair, flips open his bench book, and runs the heel of his hand down the pristine page.

"Mr. Kenge," he says, raising his square jaw. "Let this trial begin."

The press, back in full force, hushes. The jurors, arrayed in their box, shift expectantly. Vincent Trussardi straightens in his seat. The real action is about to start. Cy pushes himself up from his chair and moves toward the jury, leg swinging wide, head lowered as though in pain—which he may well be. I see the jury's wonderment at this strange hulk of a man, watch sympathy pass over their faces. Cy hasn't uttered a word yet, and he has them in the palm of his hand. I know all his tricks from friendlier days. Now I can only sit back and admire.

It doesn't get better for Trussardi as Cy works his way through his opening address. Cy is sad; Cy is grieved; Cy is overcome by the horror of the crime that will occupy us for the next ten days or so. He tells the jurors they are in for terrible shocks and difficult experiences. The testimony they will hear will disturb them; the photographs of the crime scene will expose them to more brutality than they have ever imagined. Yet it is their duty as citizens to study the evidence, consider what kind of a person could have done this.

So far, so good, I think. Vincent Trussardi, a civilized man with no history of violence, could not have committed this crime in the way it was committed.

But Cy moves on. "You will hear evidence that the deceased, Laura St. John Trussardi, was having an affair with the architect who had designed the Trussardi residence and that she was pregnant." The jurors take note. *A baby, a life unborn. The ante is upped.* "Indeed, the Crown will prove that Laura visited her lover the day before the murder. It is the Crown's contention that the accused, enraged at learning that the affair was not over and that his wife was carrying another man's child, killed his wife—and did so intentionally and in the most punitive fashion imaginable. Sadly," he tells the jurors, "you will not hear from the architect, who was killed under mysterious circumstances after fleeing to Brazil."

Cy swivels his massive head and stares at Vincent Trussardi, who sits stonelike in the prisoner's box. He does not say the words, nothing on the record for an appeal court to see, but the invitation is clear—*Draw your own inferences as to who might have benefited from the architect's death.* The power of silent suggestion, another thing Cy taught me.

"What you will hear," Cy picks up a new theme, "is that the deceased was killed by a bullet fired by a gun registered to the accused, Vincent Trussardi. You will hear evidence that the gun was required by law to be kept locked in a safe in Mr. Trussardi's residence and that the police found the safe locked. And you will hear"—Cy pauses for effect—"that the revolver was missing and that despite a minute search of the property, it has never been found."

Cy moves on. "You may find yourselves wondering, ladies and gentlemen of the jury, how a civilized man with no formal record of violence could commit this crime in such a brutal and sadistic manner."

So that's how he's going to play this. Seize the weakest link in the chain that leads to guilt and forge it into iron.

"I would only urge this caution upon you—do not be too quick to conclude that only a man with a history of violence is capable of the evil you will see revealed in the evidence of this case. Evil wears many faces."

I stand. The judge sees me and jumps in. "Mr. Kenge, some latitude may be allowed in addresses to the jury, but please confine yourself to the evidence and avoid speculation about the accused's character."

"Yes, my Lord." But the seed has been planted. He turns back to the jury. "Ladies and gentlemen, the state has placed a profound responsibility on your collective shoulders—to do justice in the matter of the brutal killing of a beautiful and vibrant woman, Laura St. John Trussardi. I am confident you will not fail in your duty to the state and the people of Canada."

The librarian nods, the nurse leans sympathetically forward. From my place at the counsel table I look across to the prisoner's box to see how the client is wearing the proceedings. If he's concerned, he's hiding it well; Vincent Trussardi surveys courtroom twenty with equanimity. He inclines his head as I take my seat and our eyes briefly meet. He smiles, or maybe he doesn't. Then he resumes his remote and distant pose.

"I call Constable Burns," Cy says, and a stout man in a black suit that bulges at the buttons strides to the box. "Please state your role in the murder investigation, Constable."

"I was in charge of the CSU," Burns replies proudly.

"Can you tell the jury what CSU stands for?"

"Crime Scene Unit, the house, the room, the body."

"Carry on please."

In the passionless voice of an airport security guard unpacking a traveler's bag—messy maybe, but all in a day's work—Burns gives us the details with scientific precision.

"The body showed signs of multiple assaults," he says, absently stroking his clipped orange beard. "A bruise to the face, beneath the left eye, bruises on both forearms, and a large bruise to the right buttock. Note the lesion below the left breast, and the lesions at the wrists and ankles caused by the bonds." He goes on in excruciating detail—death reduced to horrific data.

Forty-eight graphic photos—each described, stamped, and placed in the record—deliver the final punch. Forty-eight times, I watch the jurors' eyes widen in shock, close in horror. The modern murder trial is a technical affair. Fingernail scrapings, hair, blood, blood, and more blood—all must be collected, stored, analyzed, and then, when the trial finally arrives, explained in meticulous detail to yawning jurors. Chemists to explain the composition of blood, and ballistics experts to link gun to bullet. Usually, the process takes weeks, but in this case we've consented to the experts' reports going into the evidence immediately.

"Maybe I taught you something after all," Cy had grudgingly chuffed as we'd tied up the arrangements a week earlier.

"Maybe, or maybe I figured that one out on my own." Prosecutors like to wallow in bad facts; defense lawyers need to shut them down.

Despite our concessions, the process of identifying, marking, and explaining the reports to the jury consumes the rest of the day. In the late afternoon, I watch the jurors file out, exhausted from a day of yawing between shock and tedium. We will have only a few questions for Constable Burns when the time comes tomorrow—the evidence speaks for itself, and our defense, such as it is, lies elsewhere—but I have listened to his testimony with growing apprehension.

"Not good, not good at all," I say to Jeff as we gather our things. "Horror breeds blame. Outrage needs its outlet, and the jurors are going to direct theirs against Vincent Trussardi."

"The judge will tell them to consider the evidence calmly," Jeff assures me. "He'll remind them they shouldn't be swayed by emotion."

"Easier to say than do," I say. "But I love your uncharacteristic optimism."

CHAPTER 37

MY OFFICE DOOR IS SHUT; my screen is off. I'm going over Alicia's draft for the examination in chief of Vincent Trussardi. In the next room, Jeff is working on questions for the mock cross-examination he will conduct to prepare Trussardi for the real thing. That's if we call him. Outside the sky is darkening. So much for an early evening.

I push Alicia's notes aside. Words, words, words. Evil deeds dressed up in words. The trial's barely started, but already I feel it spiraling toward disaster. Vincent Trussardi, who I have convinced myself is innocent, stands to be convicted. And all I can offer are words.

Cy's list of witnesses looms up at me. It's what we expected, except he's put in the possibility of calling a surprise witness, depending on circumstances, at the end. I stifle apprehension. *Nice try, Cy, but sorry, we need the name.*

I'm relieved to find no mention of the occurrence report about Laura Trussardi crying in the street shortly before her murder. Maybe Lois was just babbling, drunk and confused.

Jeff pokes his head in the door. "I'm off."

"Night, Jeff," I call.

Alone now, I realize how tired I am. It looks easy, what lawyers do—sitting in soft chairs, making notes and noises from time to time—but that's an illusion. Tension, concentration, the uncertain interval between question and answer all take their toll.

The static in the back of my mind doesn't help either. The dark van is gone, but since my visit to Raquella, a beige Toyota has been popping up in my rearview mirror more often than I like. There are thousands of beige Toyotas in Vancouver, but it still bothers me. And I'm worried about Edith, who no longer answers her phone. I asked Richard to check on her townhouse. Her car was there, but she didn't answer the door. Maybe I should send the police in.

The red light on my desk phone blinks, my private line. I hesitate, pick it up.

"Jilly Truitt speaking."

Silence. Five seconds pass on my big watch. I hear a click, then the buzz of a vacant line.

Another crank call. The third this week. *Don't be crazy*, my mind tells me, *it's just a wrong number.* But my gut sends a different message: *Someone's out to get you. He's here, she's here, waiting, biding their time.* My fingers grip the edge of my desk. My familiar chair, my glass worktop are suddenly foreign, unsafe. I need to go; I need to flee.

The parking garage is deserted, except for my car, sitting exactly where I left it, shining, clean, no messages on the windshield. This time.

On the way home, I assess the possibilities.

One: I'm paranoid.

Two: someone wants me to stop investigating.

Three: someone is trying to mess up my mind so I lose the trial.

If I'm paranoid, there's nothing to worry about. If someone wants me to stop investigating, too bad, I won't. If someone is trying to mess with my mind, I sure as hell won't let them succeed.

CHAPTER 38

WEDNESDAY, DAY THREE OF THE Trussardi trial, eight fifty-six in the morning. Jeff and I are seated at the defense table. At the back of the room the usual audience—the press, the gawkers, Lois, Raquella—waits for the show to start. Across the aisle Cy and Emily confer in whispers. We're all in our places, just in case Justice Moulton's watch is fast and he comes in with his rulings on the evidence three minutes early.

"You okay?" Jeff queries as I open my tablet.

"Yeah, fine," I say.

It's a lie, and Jeff senses it. He's about to pursue the issue, but Cy leans over the aisle and says sotto voce, "You look tired, Jilly. Working too hard." There's an edge in his voice that belies the sympathetic words. Does Cy have something to do with those calls? No, he would never stoop to unprofessional gambits. Maybe the case really has gotten to me.

Marion's cry—"Order in the court!"—saves me from further speculation. Justice Moulton mounts the stairs and opens his red leather bench book.

"The first matter," he starts, "concerns the exclusion of evidence that a certain Carmelina Cappelli and the accused had sexual relations after the murder." He outlines my arguments, refers to Cy's. But, as usual, all that matters is the bottom line. "Ms. Truitt submits that this evidence has no probative value. Mr. Kenge argues that post-crime conduct is always relevant and that any prejudice to the accused is negligible in an age when casual sex is common."

Cy shoots me a knowing smile, but I ignore it.

"I accept Mr. Kenge's argument," Moulton finishes. "The evidence will be admitted."

We're done, I think. As I feared, this judge is against us. An arcane piece of defense lore comes to mind: you can win over a skeptical jury, but if the judge is against you, you're lost.

"The second matter," Justice Moulton drones on, "is the admissibility of the evidence of the motel clerk, Emond Gates, purporting to identify the woman who came to the Stay-A-While Motel the afternoon before the murder as the deceased, Laura St. John Trussardi. It is well-settled law that identification by photo lineup is inadmissible if the persons shown in the photos are unlike the person in question." He digs out the photo lineup. "Here the witness was shown twelve photos of women. Three might be described as blond, like the victim. However, the two blond comparators are unlike the deceased—one has a plump round face, the other, while somewhat resembling the victim, shows signs of acne. None of the other photos remotely resemble the late Laura St. John Trussardi. It follows that the photo lineup is unfair and that the identification evidence based on it is inadmissible."

Cy shows no sign of dismay, but I see Emily's lips part momentarily before she flattens her face back to impassivity. I survey Justice Moulton with new respect. It's a gutsy ruling on important evidence. On balance, we've come out ahead.

"We'll take a short break," he announces. "The trial will recommence promptly at ten o'clock." He exits the courtroom in a swirl of red robe.

BY LUNCH, THE LAST OF the crime scene experts wraps up her description of the bed, the body, and the house. We sit and listen, no choice but to accept the evidence and what flows from it. It's not good that the only blood in the room is Laura Trussardi's, not good that there's no sign of a struggle as she was being tied up—*She consented to this,* we're meant to infer—not good that these indisputable facts point squarely to her husband. Jeff makes a few forays in cross-examination—even has a go at the coincidence of two plates in the sink—but he can't draw the connections and nothing comes of it. In due course, we will suggest alternative scenarios, but for now, we can only listen, taking care to keep our faces serenely unperturbed.

In the afternoon, Cy moves on to Officer Kostash, who headed up the perimeter search team. Kostash is broad of beam and balding, smugly erect in a cheap suit that hangs like a smock. Beetle eyes dart beneath bushy brows as he explains the meticulous search he and his men (a phrase that includes two women) conducted. They searched the house and grounds inch by inch, he tells the jury, producing elaborate site plans marked with "X"s and lines to prove the point. They found a number of things—broken pottery, garden shears, three decaying condoms, but no gun. In subsequent days, they extended the search to neighboring properties—still no gun.

Jeff leaves this evidence—more accurately lack of evidence—alone, but zones in on another tack. "Did you check for footprints in the garden or on the adjoining property, Officer?" he asks, rising from his seat, rearranging his gown across his shoulders.

"It's a matter of routine. If we had seen any footprints, we would have noted them."

"Would you check your notes, Officer, to see whether any are mentioned?"

The officer's beefy forehead wrinkles in a frown as he licks his fat thumb and applies it to the first of the sheets on the thick stack before him. Jeff rolls his eyes to the ceiling, all patience.

"Officer, perhaps I can help you," he says at last. "Could you go to the page numbered one twenty-six, near the bottom of the pile?"

Laboriously, Kostash thumbs through the pages, finds 126.

"Would you read the second-to-last paragraph to the jury, Officer?"

Officer Kostash begins to read. "'Approximately five feet to the west of the eastern boundary of the property.'"

"Precisely, Officer. Tell us what was found there, according to the notes?"

"It says, 'Footprints, two, man's treaded shoe.'"

"Did you measure these footprints, Officer?" Jeff moves to the center of the courtroom. *This is just the beginning*, I think.

"No."

"Did you take a photograph of them?"

"No."

"Why not, Officer?"

"We couldn't see what relevance they could have. I mean, lots of people might have walked in that area. It was wooded, and it wasn't even on the subject's property." Kostash exhales heavily. "We were looking for a *gun.*"

"Did it occur to you that it might be useful to ask who could have accessed the property? Not to put too fine a point on it, the *person* who might have used the gun you were looking for?"

"We knew—"

"You *thought* you knew," Jeff says contemptuously.

I catch a few jurors taking notes.

"You do agree, Officer, that the footprint could have been made by someone entering the Trussardi property on the day of the murder?"

"I suppose, but it's highly unlikely."

"Just answer the question. Yes or no."

"Yes," Officer Kostash says, his voice barely audible.

"And that person might have gone on to enter the house and kill Laura Trussardi?"

Cy is on his feet. "Objection—counsel is asking the witness to speculate."

"Objection overruled," Justice Moulton intones, and I suppress a smile. We need all the minor victories we can get.

"I suppose it's conceivable that a person making those prints might have entered the house," Kostash finally answers.

"Yet you didn't bother to check the footprint for details, Officer. You didn't even take a photo?"

The answer takes a long time coming. "No."

"No further questions," says Jeff and sits down. I give him a quick nod—*Well done.* From his perch in the prisoner's box Vincent Trussardi inclines his head and catches Jeff's eye—a gracious thank-you.

CHAPTER 39

"I CALL DR. CHRISTINE MOYER," Cy informs the court when we resume on Friday morning.

Christine Moyer, bobbed hair shining, moves confidently down the aisle and into the witness box, her athletic figure sheathed in a blue pantsuit. She looks around the courtroom, acknowledges the jury, glances up at Justice Moulton. She is careful not to let her eye catch mine. She is a professional.

Cy takes her through her report, line by line, confirms the cause of death. Then, swiveling back to his table, he picks up the sheaf of photos of the body, nods to the clerk to hand identical piles to each juror. I know his game. He's going to horrify the jurors with the details of the killing, stoking their anger against the only available target, Vincent Trussardi.

"You examined the body of the deceased carefully, I presume, Dr. Moyer?" he asks.

"I did, Mr. Kenge."

I decide to let him go on for a while. If I object too soon, Justice Moulton will just wave me down. Besides, too much graphic detail may backfire on Cy. As he works through the first photograph, a process that takes five minutes, I watch the reactions of the jurors. Most are disgusted. Some try to look away. The nurse and the dock-worker are fascinated. But Mr. Kasmirsky, our foreman, has put the photos down—*You can't force me to keep looking at this stuff.*

As Cy starts in on the second photo, a flicker of annoyance passes over Moulton's face, and he looks at the clock.

I rise. "My Lord, I would usually not presume to interrupt my learned friend's examination of this witness. But may I respectfully submit that not much will be gained by dwelling on the injuries inflicted on Laura Trussardi's body? The nature of these injuries is plain from the photographs, and the defense accepts them." If Cy has his way, we will still be looking at these photos at noon tomorrow.

"Ms. Truitt has a point, Mr. Kenge. What do you say?"

"I take the point, my Lord. However, there are two photographs to which I feel I must direct the jury's attention."

"Very well. Just two."

"Dr. Moyer, would you be so good as to find photographs forty-six and forty-seven?" Cy requests.

Jeff has pulled them out, but I do not need to see them. Each shade, each gradation, is indelibly imprinted on my mind.

"Would you describe for the jury what part of the body we are looking at in photo forty-six, and the nature of the wound?"

"We are looking at a woman's breast," Christine answers.

"And the nature of the wound?"

The broad hand of Justice Moulton rises and hits the desk like a thunderclap. "Mr. Kenge," he nearly shouts, "I take it you have completed your questions of this witness."

Brilliant. Cy shut down and nothing on the record to complain to the Court of Appeal about. Still, the brutal images have taken their toll. Across the room, Vincent Trussardi slumps, head to the side. Out of the corner of my eye, I glimpse Raquella Trussardi in her chair, stiff as a statue, her face white, her gaze fixed. She knew Laura, loved her; I feel her anguish as I watch her whirl her chair toward the door, but I have my own preoccupations.

The beige Toyota still lurks in the periphery. The late-night hang-ups haven't stopped. And Edith is still missing. The police have checked her townhouse and found nothing suspicious—*She's probably just away on vacation.* They sent a junior officer over to tell me in person—*Read: we're taking you seriously, but you're losing it.* But that hasn't stopped the rampages of my overwrought imagination. I'm on edge, overworrying, overreacting. I need a break from this case. I make a decision. Damn the trial. This weekend I'm going home to Martha.

Cy's up, interrupting my reverie. "I do have a few further questions of this witness, my Lord. On a different matter." He turns to Christine. "You did a thorough autopsy, Dr. Moyer?"

"I did."

"Including an internal examination of the abdominal area?"

"Yes."

"Would you please tell the jury what you found?"

"The deceased was pregnant." Dr. Moyer consults her notes. "About two months."

"Thank you, Doctor," says Cy.

I rise. "Dr. Moyer, did you have occasion to conduct a paternity test to determine the father of the unborn child?"

"I did."

"Would you tell us about it?"

I hear the click of Cy's artificial limb as he stands. "I have had no notice of this," he protests.

"My Lord, when I last checked, the defense is not obliged to give the prosecution notice of what questions it will put to its witnesses in cross-examination," I retort.

"Ms. Truitt is right," Moulton intones. "Witness may answer the question."

"I took a buccal swab from a man whom I identified as Vincent Trussardi," Christine says.

"The same man you see in here today?" I motion to the prisoner's box.

"Yes. I then compared the DNA on the swab with the DNA of the fetus that I had earlier removed from the deceased and preserved."

"Please tell the jury the results of your test, Dr. Moyer."

"The test results showed that Vincent Trussardi was the father of the unborn child."

I sit down.

The buzz is welling up from the back again, the doors whooshing in and out. *What man would murder the woman who is carrying his only child?*

Score one for the defense.

CHAPTER 40

FRIDAY AFTERNOON. FROM THE WITNESS box, Carmelina looks at Vincent Trussardi where he sits across the courtroom. He has not seen her since her suicide attempt, and his eyes momentarily widen at the diminished person before him. He gives the smallest of nods, and she turns her face away, raising a tissue to wipe the corner of her eye.

Cy opens his examination gently, inviting Carmelina to tell the jury how she came to the Trussardi household and what she did there, before launching into the laborious exercise of exploring the activities of the deceased in the days leading up to the murder. Carmelina sits a little easier as she recounts the mundane events of the Trussardi household. It takes a long time but the takeaway is simple—nothing out of the ordinary.

The court learns that the day before the murder, Mrs. Trussardi had gone shopping and come home with a lavender gown and new shoes for an upcoming gala. "*Bella, regalia,* Prada. Madam was happy," Carmelina tells the jurors in response to Cy's probing.

That night, Mr. and Mrs. Trussardi had gone out to a party—Carmelina doesn't know where, just that they came home before ten and shared a glass of Prosecco by the fire before going to bed.

"And the morning of the murder?" asks Cy.

"Mr. Trussardi was already gone before I got up. He had told us the day before that he was going sailing, so I wasn't surprised. Madam came into the kitchen where I was rolling out pasta."

"What time was that?"

"About nine, I think. She said it was my day off. Usually, I took the bus to visit friends in Burnaby. But Mrs. Trussardi offered to drive me." Carmelina wipes her eye. "She was very good to me."

"Did you notice anything different about her, about her mood?"

"She was like usual. Only more relaxed than sometimes. *Contenta.*"

Cy cranes his neck to look at the clock on the back wall, which says two fifty-three. Justice Moulton nods, happy to take the afternoon break. A small smile flickers over Cy's face before he settles his features into studied indifference. My fist tightens around my pen; Cy has something up his sleeve.

"WERE YOU AWARE THAT MRS. Trussardi was having an affair with the architect Trevor Shore, Ms. Cappelli?" Cy asks Carmelina when we're all back in courtroom twenty.

I could object to leading but I know what Carmelina will say.

"No, no," she replies. "I mean, Mr. Shore came to the house a few times—he was the architect and had the door code so he could check on details. I served them lunch once, but they were always very proper."

"Let's go back to the day of the murder. When did you return to the house?"

Carmelina is tired. The circles under her eyes are dark, and she slumps in the witness box. But she has her pride, and she pulls herself erect to answer Cy's question.

"About seven o'clock, Emilia's father drove me back, and Emilia came along. They let me out in the street outside the Trussardi house. I came down the drive and saw the police cars. I knew something was wrong."

"Did you go in?"

"Yes. There was a policeman by the door, but when I told him I was the housekeeper, he let me by."

"What did you see when you entered the house?"

"Police, everywhere. I went past them to the living room. Mr. Trussardi was sitting there on a sofa. He just looked at me for a while, like he couldn't get up. Then he spoke. His voice was all broken; I could hardly understand. 'A terrible thing has happened, Carmelina,' he said. 'Mrs. Trussardi has been killed.' I must have screamed and cried. I don't remember. The next thing I knew, they were carrying a bag—a long, lumpy, black bag. I knew it was Mrs. Trussardi. I must have screamed again."

"Laura Trussardi, the kind woman you admired and loved, carried out in a lumpy black bag." He leans toward Carmelina sympathetically. "Terrible for you."

Carmelina dabs at her eye.

"But the horror for you wasn't over, was it, Miss Cappelli? What happened when the police eventually left?"

I glance up at the clock—half past three. *He's stretching this out*, I think, my stomach tightening.

"Well, they didn't all go right away—two of them stayed to guard the room because they hadn't finished what they needed to do. Mr. Trussardi still was sitting on the couch in the living room in shock. I went to the policewoman they had left and said that I needed to get some things for Mr. Trussardi so he could go to bed in another room. She said okay. So she lifted the tape, and I got his pajamas and robe and some things from his bathroom and brought them to a guest room. Then I went back to the living room and told Mr. Trussardi he needed to get some sleep. He didn't seem to understand, but when I pulled him up, he followed me. I left him in the guest room, and I went to my own apartment."

"What happened next, Ms. Cappelli?"

Carmelina falters. "Nothing."

"Come, come, Miss Cappelli. That's not what you told us in the course of the investigation, is it?"

"I—I . . ." Carmelina convulses. We wait while she mops up her own tears. I stifle an inward groan. This is terrible—she should be getting through the bad part quickly and smoothly; instead she's marking it—underlining and emphasizing and adding an exclamation mark to boot.

I catch Carmelina's eye, and she pulls herself together. "I couldn't sleep," she finally says. "I started thinking about Mr. Trussardi and how he looked. I got worried he might do something stupid, something to himself. So I put my robe on and went to the guest room."

"What did you see, Carmelina?" Cy's voice is low, for the first time addressing the witness by her first name.

"He was lying on the bed in his robe, crying. Big cries, like—

how do you say it?—sobs. I went over to him." She wipes her eyes again. "I put my arms around him."

"Was that all, Ms. Cappelli?"

"No."

"Let's get to the point," says Cy, abruptly aggressive. "Tell the jury. Did you have sex with Mr. Trussardi?"

"Yes," she whispers, "we had sex."

The jurors stare at Carmelina, then at Trussardi in the prisoner's box, disgust on the faces of the librarian and the nurse. Vincent Trussardi gives no sign that he has heard what Carmelina has said, nor that every eye in the courtroom is upon him. Cy's narrative of a crazed and immoral man is taking shape.

"Your witness." Cy concludes, swinging back to his chair.

"Court will retire for the day," Justice Moulton says.

I look at my big round watch. Four thirty on the dot. Precisely as planned, Cy's left the jury hanging with the image of Vincent Trussardi in Carmelina's arms four hours after the murder. The jury will spend the weekend with a bad taste in their mouth. By the time we get to cross-examine Carmelina on Monday, they'll have made up their minds. I give Cy a pointed look. He responds with the fleetest of smiles before heaving his heavy body up to mark the judge's exit. A game, and he plays it well.

I check my iPhone, pull up a message from Richard: **Got some info on Trevor Shore. Cops had him and blew right by. Think you'll be interested.**

I text back. **See you at the south entrance in five.**

CHAPTER 41

IT'S FIVE THIRTY, AND I'M back at my desk. Below, in the street, the evening traffic thickens. Cabs halt, arm-linked couples cross the cobblestones beneath the mock gaslights to meet friends over a drink. I've sent Jeff home, this time for real. "Take Jessica out to dinner," I told him. I sit alone and ponder the street scene.

"I'm going now," Debbie yells. I tell her to lock the door after her. I resume reading—research for my drug trial—but the words won't jell. I shove the pages aside and grab my bag to go, when I hear the lock click on the outer door. I freeze.

It wasn't just my imagination—they've come for me. I reach for my lamp, turn off the light. In the dark, my hand finds my Inuit bear sculpture, heavy, substantial. I wait in breathless silence. Nothing. Then a squeak. The door easing open. I instinctively start to dive, then straighten. Come and get me. If I must go down, it won't be cringing on the floor.

The light clicks on.

"Damon." Relief washes over me. "You startled me." I put down my stone bear.

"Sorry, Ms. Truitt. I didn't mean to scare you. Jeff asked me to do some research on a robbery case."

"Of course." I feel myself recovering.

He angles into the chair opposite. "How's the Trussardi case going?"

So that's why he's here. "Damon, we can't talk about the case. In fact, you shouldn't be here at all."

He picks at a loose thread on his shirt. Unease, guilt maybe?

"Damon, you didn't tell me everything, did you? You told me about the night you saw Vincent Trussardi take out his gun. You didn't tell me you went back."

"What do you mean?"

"The gardener says the boy—you—kept coming back to the house."

He pulls on the thread harder. "I was so crazy, so drugged up, and she was kind and lovely. So I went back, once or twice, hoping she might walk out onto the terrace. But she never did."

I take a wild intuitive leap. "You were there the night of the murder, weren't you?"

He starts to shake his head, then stops. "Cy subpoenaed me."

So Damon is Cy's mystery witness. How the hell did he find out about the drugs, about Damon?

"You're not on the witness list," I say. "And with this visit, you've made sure I can't claim surprise."

"Sorry, I didn't think of that, Jilly."

"I tried to keep you out of this." I drum my fingers on my desk, thinking. Cy wants Damon to talk about the drug deliveries. I'm not sure why. Maybe he wants to imply Trussardi had a second reason to kill her. It wasn't just the adultery; it was the drugs, the causes, everything—building up until he couldn't take it anymore and killed her.

Damon rises, miserable. "I'm sorry, Jilly."

I take in his contrite face. I believe him, but I'm not about to let him ruin my case. "One more thing, Damon."

He turns in the doorway.

"You should know. When you testify, I will cross-examine the hell out of you. And not just about the drugs."

I watch the color drain from his face before he shuts the door behind him.

CHAPTER 42

GRAYING SKIES, IMPULSIVE GUSTS. MARTHA and I spend the weekend outside, tidying up the planters for the winter. As we work, we talk, desultory snatches of conversation on family doings. For hours at a time I'm able to forget about Trussardi and his trial.

"John and Tristan are getting married," Martha says.

"I'm happy for him," I say, meaning it. "It's a lonely life, being an artist. Tristan will ground him. Be there for him."

Martha puts her trowel down, looks at me. "Have you talked to Mike at all? Have you thought about getting back together with him?"

"Yeah," I say. "A couple of problems there."

Martha's garden-gloved hand dismisses my excuse. "The only real problem is you, Jilly." She smiles a sad smile. "All those years bumping from foster home to foster home. Deep down, you're too scared to commit. Deep down, you still can't trust."

"Look how I trust you," I say in my defense. *And sometimes others*, I think. Like Damon.

Martha puts down her trowel and folds her arms around me. She's right. Deep down, I am afraid. Afraid of hurting and being hurt.

"You may just have a point," I whisper.

CHAPTER 43

ON MONDAY, I SLIDE INTO my seat in courtroom twenty. Cy and his ceaseless wiles, Damon lurking in the shadows, and now, before me, Carmelina in the witness box, fighting for her dignity, what's left of it, and maybe her survival. I approach, offer a smile. *You're in good hands. We're on your side.*

"Ms. Cappelli, I know this is hard for you. I have only a few questions. I'd like you to cast your mind back to the time before the murder. Did you see Mr. and Mrs. Trussardi together often?"

"Yes, most nights, when Mr. Trussardi wasn't traveling or at some late meeting. When he was away, Mrs. Trussardi would go down to Raquella's apartment, have dinner with her, sometimes spend the night." Carmelina turns to the jury. "Raquella is Mr. Trussardi's sister." She's warming to this, recovering a little of her old élan.

"Tell us about how it was between Mr. and Mrs. Trussardi on those nights—most nights, as you put it—when they had dinner together. Would they talk over dinner?"

"Yes, always."

"What did they talk about?"

"I didn't really listen, but ordinary things, like how their day had been, the food, that sort of thing."

"Did they ever argue?"

"Not that I saw."

"Did Mr. Trussardi ever threaten her or speak badly to her?"

"Never."

"Did they laugh together, share stories or jokes?"

"Sometimes."

"So as far as you could tell, Mr. and Mrs. Trussardi got along well?"

"Yes, very well. No opera, like we Italians say."

"Did they sleep together?"

I half expect Cy to jump up and object that the witness has not been qualified as an expert in this particular subject, but he only scowls at me from his seat. Carmelina blushes but answers the question. "Yes. Housekeepers can tell, you know."

"They were comfortable together." Carmelina searches for the right words. "Not kissing all the time, you know, but liking each other."

Good enough, I think. I change tacks. "I want to ask you, Ms. Cappelli, if you ever saw Mrs. Trussardi crying or upset?"

"Only once."

"Will you tell us about that?"

"One night—I don't know when, maybe last fall, Mr. Trussardi was at home. Mrs. Trussardi was out and didn't come home like we expected. We couldn't figure it out—her car was there. Mr.

Trussardi said she must have gone out with someone and got delayed. Finally, I served him his dinner alone. He had almost finished his coffee when she came in the front door. There's a little window in the door to the kitchen, and I watched from in there. She had a black eye and blood smeared under her nose. It looked like someone had hit her. She was crying."

"How did Mr. Trussardi react?" I sneak a glance at the jury. They're leaning forward, on the edge of their seats.

"He put his arms around her, tilted her face up to look at it. I heard him say, 'My god.' Then he yelled to me to get a cold compress. I brought ice and some towels to him, and he wiped her face and held the ice to her eye. Then I took her to their room and put her to bed. Mr. Trussardi came in and sat beside her, and I left."

"Did he seem concerned?"

"Very concerned, a little angry maybe. Not with her—he was gentle with her—but still he was upset."

"Did anyone ever tell you who had attacked her?"

"Hearsay," calls Cy, standing.

But Moulton seems interested. "Let's hear what the witness says," he replies.

"No, no one said who hit her. But it could not have been Mr. Trussardi because he was at home."

A rustle of paper as Kasmirsky makes a note of Carmelina's answer.

Brava, I want to say. "Ms. Cappelli, you told Mr. Kenge that Trevor Shore would come to the house sometimes."

"Yes."

"Do you remember the last time he came to the house?"

"It was a long time ago. Maybe six months before she died." *Inference: Trevor Shore could have hit Laura.*

"One more thing, Ms. Cappelli. You told Mr. Kenge that you

went to Mr. Trussardi to see if he was all right the night following the murder. Do you remember that?"

"Yes."

"And you said you ended up having sexual relations."

"Yes."

"How did that happen?"

Cy smirks and in a voice loud enough for the jury to hear says, "I expect the usual way." I ignore him, wait for Carmelina's answer.

"I never—he never—meant it to happen. He was always so proper with me. But he was upset, and I was trying to comfort him. I think we both felt terrible afterward. It never happened again. It was two days before the police came to arrest him, and it was like we just went around the house trying not to run into each other."

"You were ashamed, Carmelina. Did that lead you to do something you might not otherwise have done?"

"Irrelevant," Cy shouts.

Moulton waves him down. "Objection overruled."

Karma, Cy.

Carmelina wipes her eye with a delicately embroidered handkerchief, looks at Cy. "Mr. Kenge came to ask me about my relationship with Mr. Trussardi. I didn't understand. I thought it was the law that I had to answer him. So I told him everything. I felt so guilty. I went home and took pills, too many pills." Her voice drops. "I wanted to kill myself. I woke up in the hospital, and I was angry. I wanted to die."

The jury is leaning forward, captivated by the story of the simple girl gulled by the wily prosecutor. Moulton frowns at Cy. Perfect.

"Thank you, Ms. Cappelli. You have been most helpful. I have no further questions."

Justice Moulton glances at the clock. "Court will rise for the morning adjournment."

"I CALL EMOND GATES," CY intones.

On day two of the trial, a young homicide detective explained how he went out on a limb to find anything that might help solve Laura Trussardi's murder.

"I combed the records of all the motels and hotels in West and North Van to see whether anyone related to the case had checked in recently," he testified proudly. "That's how I found out that Trevor Shore had used his credit card at the Stay-A-While Motel just days before the murder."

Now, days later, Emond Gates steps smartly into the witness box to finish the detective's story. His dark skull shines in the overhead lighting, and his eyes beam like twin flashlights. He looks about the courtroom with interest, noting how things are arranged. At Cy's prodding, he takes us through what he can.

"The man—Trevor Shore—paid in advance for room 208. A half hour later, I saw a blond woman in a trench coat go straight to the room without checking at the desk. She was pretty; elegant, even; and wore expensive clothes." He wants to say it was Laura Trussardi, but Cy and Emily have told him he can't. "Two hours later they left the room together," he says. "I saw them kissing goodbye in the parking lot before she got in her car."

Vincent Trussardi's mouth sets in a hard, unforgiving line, before he rights himself and recovers his usual composure. Jeff takes the cross and he's good. He doesn't touch the evidence that the man who registered at the desk was Trevor Shore—a credit card is a credit card. Instead, he homes in on the blonde. "Lots of blondes come by the motel?"

"Yeah, every day."

"A lot of them look alike?"

"I guess you could say so. You know, with peroxide hair and face-lifts and Botox, you don't know what you've got anymore when it comes to a woman."

Jeff gives the witness a conspiratorial smile—*I know what you mean*—and then closes in for the kill. "All you know, then, is that one of the thousands of blond women wandering North Vancouver that day may have—and we're not even sure about that—spent two hours with Trevor Shore?"

"Uh," Gates stammers. "I guess that about sums it up."

"Thank you, Mr. Gates." Jeff sits down with an elegant furl of his gown. Across the aisle, Cy stares stonily ahead.

TWO O'CLOCK AND WE ARE back and waiting. The jury is in place. I sneak a surreptitious glance in their direction. The angry mood of the day before has lightened. Our foreman, Kasmirsky, is focused on the far wall inscrutably, but a couple of jurors in the second row—the dockworker and the accountant—are whispering. A grin cuts the accountant's face, and he gives the dockworker a knowing wink.

They're discussing motel trysts. Emond Gates may have shored up the motive Cy needs, but Laura Trussardi—to the extent the jury believes she was the woman at the Stay-A-While Motel—has come off tarnished.

Emily comes down the aisle in an anxious flurry of black, leans to whisper something to Cy. I can't hear what they're saying, but I know something's wrong.

"Bring the judge in," Cy tells Marion. The clock on the back wall stands at precisely two twenty.

Cy pushes himself to his feet as Justice Moulton mounts the low stairs and takes his place behind the glowing ash bench. "Mr. Kenge?"

"My Lord, the prosecution's next witness is a police officer. I regret to inform you that although he was subpoenaed for this afternoon, he has not arrived. He's on his way from Seattle as we speak. He was there on police duties."

Seattle? Then I remember Cy's party and the undercover cop who gave me a drink. What's Cy up to?

Justice Moulton's fist hits the leather surface of the bench with a soft thud. "Mr. Kenge, did I hear right? It costs a great deal of money to run this court, and you are asking me to stand it down for the better part of an afternoon. Surely you have another witness you can call."

"I regret I do not, my Lord."

"Very well, you leave me no alternative but to adjourn." He swivels to the jury box. "Ladies and gentlemen of the jury, you stand dismissed."

"It's a show," says Jeff as we head for the basement. "Did you see Cy's smile? Gave the judge a chance to dump all over him, nix any suggestion of pro-Crown bias. They understand each other, the judge and Cy."

I should tell him he's crazy, but it makes sense. Cy's out to win. Just like me.

CHAPTER 44

WE ARE ALL IN OUR places on Tuesday morning, and the gallery is full. Reporters, supplemented by a smattering of court watchers, cram every corner. Lois and Raquella stare at our backs from their usual seats. In the last row, I glimpse Hildegard's gleaming white coif. Has she been here the whole trial?

Justice Moulton, still seething about losing yesterday afternoon, scowls at Cy. But it's Emily who gets up. Either Cy is scared of the judge—not likely—or he's decided it's time for Emily's trial debut.

"I call Detective Sergeant Sydney Evans to the stand," Emily says in a clear, firm voice.

Sergeant Evans does a languid march to the witness box. He leans back and stretches his legs before catching the judge's glare and straightening up. I recognize the narrow face, the high forehead—no leather jacket today. In his trendy narrow suit, he's all business.

Evans brings back bad memories, and I feel my paranoia kicking in. Did Cy put him up to accosting me at the party knowing he'd be a witness? Is this part of a plot to rattle me?

Emily puts Evans through the preliminary paces of what he does—international liaison; and his relevance to the case—Trevor Shore.

"Trevor's death is a great loss to the investigation—no doubt he could have shed important light on who killed Laura Trussardi." Evans shifts his gaze to Vincent Trussardi in the prisoner's box. *Inference: Who else would have wanted Trevor Shore out of the way?*

Satisfied, Emily sits down. "Your witness."

"I suggest we take the morning adjournment now," I say as I stand. "I expect to be some time in the cross-examination of this witness."

Justice Moulton nods, but I am aware of the jury's curious stare—*What can she do with this?* I shoot them an enigmatic smile as we rise. *Just wait.*

"YOU HAVE MADE PRELIMINARY INVESTIGATIONS into Trevor Shore's death, Sergeant Evans?" I ask when we return.

"Yes, based on what the Brazilian police have told us." His eyes narrow, and his lip twists imperceptibly. I remember his swagger the night of Cy's party, how his eye traced the line of my black dress. *Today I'm in my robes, Sergeant, watch out.*

"Have his killer or killers been found?"

"No, it appears not."

"The homicide rate is high in Brazil?"

"Yes."

"Lots of crime?"

"You could say that."

"Random shootings are not uncommon?"

"Not in Brazil."

I step out from behind my table and move deeper into the well of the courtroom. "Something puzzles me about all this, Sergeant. Trevor Shore was a person of interest in the investigation of Laura Trussardi, correct? I mean, you had been told he was her lover?"

"Yes, he was a person of interest."

"A suspect, a prime suspect, you might say?"

"A person of interest."

"The lover of a murdered woman, who disappears immediately after her death, would be a prime suspect in any competent homicide officer's books, wouldn't he?"

"I suppose so."

"No supposition, officer. Just the facts."

Evans blinks. "Yes."

"And I think you've just agreed, Sergeant, that if a woman is murdered, it would be important to interview the man you were told was her lover?"

"Yes, I suppose so."

"But you never bothered to contact Mr. Shore?"

"We tried. We investigated. We put out a BOLO—be on the lookout—notice. Nothing turned up. We couldn't find him."

"Surely Vancouver's finest did not simply allow a prime suspect to escape the jurisdiction right under their nose?"

"We put out an INTERPOL alert. Normally he shouldn't have got out of the country."

"Yet we know he did, Sergeant. How did that happen?"

Evans leans back, closes his eyes.

"Sergeant Evans, are you still with us?"

He looks at me, his smugness morphing into irritation. "It seems he obtained a false passport and traveled under an assumed name. Arne Jacobs was the name on the passport the Brazilian police found in his room. They advised us, and we checked it out, found the real Arne Jacobs in Richmond. We sent blood work and dental records to Brazil. They checked out: Trevor Shore."

I turn to Justice Moulton. "My Lord, the defense has had no disclosure of any of this. It comes as a total surprise."

Cy stands. "We advised the defense of Trevor Shore's death as soon as we confirmed it. These are mere details—elicited in cross-examination, may I add."

I let it go. "When did Arne Jacobs, who we now know to be Trevor Shore, fly to Brazil?"

Evans shuffles his papers. "Air Canada records show that he departed Vancouver for Toronto on July ninth and connected through Toronto to Rio de Janeiro the same day."

"July ninth, almost three months after Laura Trussardi's death? Three months, and you couldn't find him." I retrieve a paper from the defense table, cross to the witness box, and hand it to him. "Let me show you a document, Sergeant Evans."

Cy nudges Emily. Out of the corner of my eye, I see her stand. "My Lord, we have not seen this so-called document."

"Since when is the defense obliged to give the prosecution disclosure of Vancouver Police Department records?" I shoot back, and Emily's face goes white.

"Proceed," Moulton says with a withering glare at Emily, which sends her shrinking into her seat.

"Sergeant, what is the document I have handed you?"

"It looks like a traffic ticket." He squints, trying to make out the printing.

"I suppose you've seen a lot of traffic tickets in your work as a police officer?"

"Quite a few, in the early years."

"Would you tell the jury the name of the police force that issued the ticket?"

"Vancouver Police Department."

"And what is the date of this ticket issued by the Vancouver Police Department, Sergeant?"

"July first of this year."

"Would you tell the jury what this ticket is for?"

"It's for running a red light."

"And would you tell the jury the location of the red light that was allegedly run?"

Evans studies the form. "Granville and Forty-First."

"Thank you, Sergeant. One more thing. Please read the jury the name of the person the ticket says ran the red light at Forty-First and Granville in the city of Vancouver on July first."

Cy sees what's coming, and this time he's not leaving it to Emily. "Hearsay!" he shouts.

"Read the name," Justice Moulton tells Evans.

Evans replies, his voice faltering, "It says, 'Trevor Shore.' "

The jury gasps audibly. I let the answer sink in.

"So tell me if you agree with this summary of the situation, Sergeant. The Vancouver Police Department Homicide Unit is trying to find Trevor Shore in connection with a murder case in which he is a potential suspect—indeed, a prime suspect. Some three months after the murder, the same police force issues a traffic ticket to the very same Trevor Shore they say they are trying to find."

"I don't understand." Evans shakes the ticket. "There was a BOLO. It would have come up on the CPIC—the electronic record attached to his license—and the police would have brought him in for questioning. Standard procedure."

"Except it appears they didn't bring him in. Or, if they did, they let him go without asking him about Laura Trussardi's murder." Arms crossed, I wait for Evans's response.

"Yes, so it seems."

"Would you call that effective police work, Sergeant?"

"Something went wrong. That happens sometimes despite our best efforts."

Half turning, I catch Richard's eye in the public gallery. He gives me a thumbs-up. I resist the urge to smile back. Raquella, from her chair on the aisle, wraps us both in a glare of contempt. Time to finish up. "The picture I'm getting is this: the Vancouver police did all the routine things to locate Trevor Shore, but they did not put out red alerts as you have suggested. Why wasn't Trevor Shore an urgent priority, Sergeant?"

"We assumed that because the victim was killed in the matrimonial home—"

"You assumed, Sergeant? What kind of police work is that?"

"Sometimes we have to assume things to do our jobs."

"You knew Mr. Shore had designed the Trussardi residence?"

"Yes."

"And you knew he had the code to the front door that would have allowed him to get in?"

"I didn't know that, don't know that."

"You never checked, did you, Sergeant?"

"Not personally."

"But you did know Trevor Shore had designed the cabinet where the combination to the safe that held the gun was kept?"

"No, I didn't know that."

"Did you check?"

"No. Maybe somebody else did."

"If they did, they never told you or anyone else on the investigative team."

"No, I suppose not."

"I suppose not," I repeat, letting the words sink in for the jury. "All those months, weren't you concerned that Trevor Shore might be hiding, Sergeant? Trying to avoid arrest for the crime he committed?"

"No, as I say, we had arrested Vincent Trussardi."

"Tell the jury the truth, Sergeant. Your department, early on in its investigation, focused on Vincent Trussardi and made him its prime suspect on purely circumstantial evidence. Didn't they?"

"Yes, we did. And with good reason."

"So you thought. But having done so, you failed to effectively investigate other possibilities."

"I deny that." But there's a quiver in his voice that belies the bravado of the words.

"We'll let the jury decide what you did and, more to the point, did not do. There's a name for this in police work, isn't there, Sergeant?"

"I don't know what you mean."

"Have you heard of tunnel vision?"

"Of course."

"And do you know what tunnel vision refers to in the context of homicide investigation work?"

Evans looks at Cy, but Cy just stares at the wall. Finally, he answers. "Tunnel vision refers to the possibility that investigators develop a theory early in the case and then don't investigate other possible suspects."

"And would you agree, Sergeant Evans, that the term *tunnel vision* has recently been cited in studies as a leading cause of wrongful convictions?"

Cy rises. "Counsel knows better than to give evidence," he bellows.

"Careful, Ms. Truitt," Justice Moulton warns.

I keep my eyes trained on Evans. "We await your answer, Sergeant."

"Yes, I've read something to that effect."

"*You* let him get away, Sergeant; *your* police force is responsible. And now we will never know what Trevor Shore might have been able to tell us about who killed Laura Trussardi." I enunciate each word, as I eye the jury. "We will never know if Trevor Shore killed her."

"I don't believe he did—"

"No further questions," I say, and return to my seat.

CHAPTER 45

WE REGROUP AT TWO. WE know what's coming. Cy, as required by the rules, has told us that his penultimate witness is an inmate from the penitentiary up valley—a drug dealer by the name of Regie Coop. After that, the surprise witness. At least, a surprise to some.

The sheriffs bring Regie Coop through the side door. They've taken the shackles off, but he still wears his prison jumpsuit. He settles his muscular frame into the witness box, greases his black hair with the palm of his tattooed hand, and shoots a smirk in the direction of the defense bench. Nice manners.

"Your name?" Cy asks.

"Regie Coop."

"You are currently in custody, serving a sentence for drug dealing, Mr. Coop?"

I rise. "Objection. As far as I have been able to glean from the

Crown's disclosure, drug dealing has nothing to do with this case." Richard dug the drug evidence up, Alicia confirmed it: nothing in the Crown's records mentions drugs.

Cy shifts. "The defense has had ample notice of this witness's appearance. The relevance of his evidence will become clear in due course."

"Objection overruled," says Judge Moulton.

Cy repeats the question. "You are in custody for drug dealing, Mr. Coop?"

"Yes, sir," Regie answers proudly.

Cy takes him through the details, and we learn that Regie Coop is a biker. During his decade and a half on the street, he ran whatever the bosses wanted—booze, drugs, women. Reliable and efficient, he always got the job done. Not that he actually sold the drugs or women. Regie works at the "executive level," he informs us. Present tense.

"Do you recall the names of your clients, Mr. Coop?"

"Of course, man. That is my job. Not like you can write them down or put them on your iPhone." He laughs. "Keep 'em in your head or you're dead."

Cy proffers a piece of paper. "I'm going to show you a list of names and ask you to tell the jury if any of them are among the names of clients you kept in your head, Mr. Coop. Can you do that?"

Regie nods, all business now.

Emily slips a copy of the paper across the aisle. Regie's finger runs down the twenty or so names, forehead creased. "This one—a woman named Trussardi. Used to place an order once a week or so."

"And you made sure she got the drugs she wanted?"

"Sure, mostly coke."

"And how did you deliver the drugs, Mr. Coop?"

"Kids, runners with a habit. Of course I had to check everything out first. There were only certain times she could receive. Afraid of her husband, maybe."

"Objection," I call. "Pure conjecture." But Moulton, captivated by Regie's street swagger, ignores me.

Cy decides not to take it further. "Give us some of the runners' names."

"Rob Fink, Tuffy Leon, kid named Damon Cheskey." A grin twists the corner of Regie's mouth. "I remember Damon telling me she was a real looker, this Mrs. Trussardi."

"Hearsay, my Lord," I cry, but it doesn't matter. Cy got what he wanted.

"Over to you, Ms. Truitt."

"Content," I reply, and I take my seat. Cross-examination will only make this worse.

Cy hefts himself to his feet. "The Crown has one more witness. I call Damon Cheskey."

The jury follows Damon's figure as he strides down the aisle and into the witness box. He's dressed in a dark jacket, gray roll-neck sweater, slim gray slacks, shining shoes. Styled blond hair falls artfully over his forehead. The women in the jury box lean forward.

"If only they could have seen him six months ago," Jeff whispers. We sculpted him, Pygmalion style, and now he has returned to haunt us. I could object, argue that we haven't had notice of this witness, but we have, from the young man himself, no less. Cy's doing, I'm sure of it.

"Mr. Cheskey, did you deliver cocaine to the Trussardi residence?" Cy begins.

"Yes, to Laura Trussardi," answers Damon, his voice deep and clear.

"How did you know she was Laura Trussardi?"

"I didn't. Except on one rainy evening, after I had been delivering for a while, she invited me in. She told me her name was Laura."

"So Laura Trussardi was doing cocaine?"

"Objection." I rise. "Mr. Kenge is both leading and giving evidence."

"You know better, Mr. Kenge," Justice Moulton admonishes.

Cy nods in mock contrition.

"Can you describe how she looked when you saw her that time? Was she happy? Sad?" Cy asks.

"Usually she seemed anxious, trying to hustle me out as fast as she could. Except the time she invited me in."

"Did you stay the night?"

"No. At some point, Mr. Trussardi came home. She looked surprised. She told him I was a friend. I was scared, but he just nodded. He didn't say much. She asked the maid to set a third place at the table, and we had something to eat. When supper was done, Mr. Trussardi left the room. I could tell something wasn't right, so I got up and left."

Hope surges briefly. Maybe Damon didn't tell Cy what came next; maybe he's going to leave out the part about Trussardi caressing the gun. But Cy isn't finished.

"Something wasn't right . . . between Laura and her husband?"

Damon hesitates. "I can't say that."

"Did he kiss her when he came in, say 'hi, dear,' or something like that?"

"No kiss. He just said hello."

"Did he seem angry?"

"Objection," I interrupt. "Mr. Kenge is leading. Again."

Cy rolls his eyes to the ceiling. "How did Mr. Trussardi seem as he greeted his wife who was standing there with you?"

"He seemed upset."

"Did he talk during dinner?"

"No. Not much."

"And as soon as dinner was over, he left the table?"

"Yes."

"Did you see where he went?"

"Behind the fireplace. There seemed to be rooms there, another wing of the house."

"When did you decide to leave?"

"She—Laura—told me to sit on a couch in the living room, to wait while she fixed the bed. I got to thinking. Maybe . . ."

"Maybe what, Damon?"

"Maybe he would do something to me."

"You were afraid Mr. Trussardi would harm you, Damon?"

"Yes."

"Afraid he might kill you?"

"Leading and speculative." I stand, but Damon's already speaking.

"Yes."

Cy lets that lethal *yes* sink in. Damon looks at me with the same wild expression I saw that night in the hotel, tries feebly to make amends. "You have to understand, I wasn't thinking straight because—"

Cy cuts him off. "Who do you think was doing the drugs?"

"Objection!" I shout, but it's too late.

"I didn't know, I assumed—"

"You assumed it was Laura," Cy finishes.

"Yes," Damon whispers.

"Can you tell us approximately when that evening was, the evening she invited you in?"

"I don't know, but it was winter, a few months before her death maybe. You have to understand, I was doing a lot of drugs then—I was a little crazy."

"So let's sum up, Mr. Cheskey," says Cy, brushing over Damon's attempt to qualify his evidence. "Laura seemed sad; she seemed lonely."

"Leading again," I say. "My Lord, I'm getting tired of jumping up to object. Mr. Kenge knows better than to give evidence."

"I retract the question." Cy shrugs. "Let's put it in your words, Damon. Laura wanted the drugs. Laura wanted to talk to you. Laura on one occasion invited you in to stay overnight." He turns to the jury. "The jury will draw the inferences as to whether Laura Trussardi was sad and lonely."

Damon nods.

"On the one occasion you saw her husband, he seemed upset with her."

"No, I couldn't—"

"Mr. Cheskey, don't play games. You've told us how Mr. Trussardi was hardly the picture of a pleased husband. In fact, you were terrified of him. He scared you so much you ran away."

"Yes," Damon says faintly.

"Thank you. That's all. Your witness." Cy slumps down.

I stand, move toward Damon, keeping a neutral expression on my face.

"Mr. Cheskey, did you ever see Laura Trussardi take drugs?"

"No."

"She might have been buying them for someone else, then?"

"I suppose so."

"There were other people in the house?"

"I don't know. The maid, maybe. And I recall her saying something about a sister in a separate suite when she was showing me the house."

I glance back to the gallery. Raquella's face is unreadable.

"The night Mrs. Trussardi invited you into her house, Mr. Trussardi came home and said hello to his wife. And to you?"

"Yes."

"He didn't raise his voice? Tell you to get out? Threaten you?"

"Never. He was polite."

This is the hard part, the choice I've been agonizing over. Leave Damon alone or take a risk? No choice but to go for it, or we're lost.

"You were high on drugs, doing amphetamines?"

"Lots."

"How did the amphetamines affect you?"

"I saw things, but differently from normal. I was scared, more suspicious, paranoid maybe, but I still saw clearly."

I circle back. "After dinner you said Mr. Trussardi went somewhere."

"Yes, there was a corridor behind the fireplace."

"At some point, did you walk over and look down that corridor?"

"Yes. I did."

"And did you see Mr. Trussardi?"

"Yes."

"What did you see him do?"

Damon gives me a confused look, but he answers. "He went to a panel and pushed it. There was a safe."

"And then?"

He searches my face—*Are you sure?*

I remain expressionless.

"He pushed a panel below and a little drawer came out—a drawer with a piece of paper. He looked at the paper and punched in some numbers. The safe opened. He took out a gun."

"And that's when you got scared and ran out of the house?"

"Yes."

"But you had no real reason to be scared of Vincent Trussardi. It was just the drugs, right?"

"Right," he says at last. "Looking back now, I know my reaction was irrational."

I move on. "You were infatuated with Laura Trussardi, weren't you, Damon?"

"Infatuated? I don't know about that. I delivered drugs to her."

"But it was more than that, wasn't it? You were entranced by her; you *loved* her."

He grows pale. "I thought about her a lot. I—"

"You kept going back to her house, hanging around the garden, waiting for her to come out, to ask you in again, didn't you?"

"I may have," he whispers. "I can't remember everything clearly."

"But you remember that you kept going back to her place, hoping desperately to see her."

"Yes."

I buckle down for the kill.

"You were there the night she died, weren't you?"

He bows his head mutely. We wait for him to speak, but he cannot. I let him hang, his silence more eloquent than any words. "Yes, I was there," he whispers.

The jurors sit transfixed. Out of the corner of my eye, I see Cy turn to Emily. *Where did this come from?* his face asks.

"You were there the night she died. You knew where the code to the safe was, where the gun was. And you were crazy. High on drugs."

"Yes." A tear trembles on his lower lash.

Cy is on his feet. "Objection!" he roars.

"I thought this was cross-examination." I turn to sit. No need to give Damon the chance to deny the deed. But Moulton, caught up in the moment, jumps in.

"What did you do while you were there the night of the murder, Mr. Cheskey?"

Damon's face is white as he turns it to the judge. "Nothing," he whispers, "nothing."

"My Lord." I leap up angrily. Moulton, by intervening at a critical moment in cross-examination, has given Damon the opportunity to deny killing Laura Trussardi.

Justice Moulton sees my glare and attempts a mop-up. "Nothing you want to tell the jury," he adds with a twinge of sarcasm.

"No further questions." I sit, offer Damon a small, sad smile as silence descends upon the courtroom. *I didn't want to do this to you.*

Justice Moulton is looking at Cy. He rises. "No reexamination. That concludes the case for the Crown."

"Order in the court," the clerk cries and court breaks.

I catch Raquella wheeling away in disgust, but Jeff is grinning. We've made it through the worst, and everything's more or less on track. So why do I feel so empty?

CHAPTER 46

WE HUDDLE IN OUR ANTEROOM. The Crown's case is closed; ours is about to begin. Jeff and I convened late the night before, debating whether to rest with what we have or to call evidence.

Jeff stated the obvious. "The jury will wonder why Vincent Trussardi wouldn't testify if he's innocent. Moulton will tell them he's presumed innocent, doesn't have to testify, but they'll still wonder."

In the end, we decided that the risks of not calling evidence were greater than the risks of doing so. But I still have my doubts.

"I think we should reconsider," I tell Jeff now. "We've got our tunnel vision; we've got our reasonable doubt. Cy could get to Trussardi in cross." I think of Lois's drunken babbling about an occurrence report. "Who knows, he could even scrounge up rebuttal that could hurt us. Why give him the chance?"

"Too risky. Way too risky."

"Okay, okay." I go to the door. "Bring Mr. Trussardi in."

Minutes later, the guard pushes our client through the door, and he slumps into the seat opposite me. Fatigue lines his face. His eyes are still proud, but the shadows beneath them grow darker every day.

"How are you doing, Mr. Trussardi?" I ask.

"Well enough, under the circumstances. I long for this trial to be over."

Jeff shoots me a look. He's talking like a man who's given up—not a good sign.

"We open the defense tomorrow morning, Mr. Trussardi. First thing, I address the jury."

"I see."

"The prosecution bears the burden of proving guilt, and we've thrown the jury the possibility that someone else did it, whether that's Trevor Shore or Damon Cheskey. Still, it's our considered opinion that we need to call evidence. More precisely, we need to call you. We need you to tell the jury that you were sailing when your wife died, need you to tell them that you and she had reconciled and were happy together, that you believed she was carrying your child, that there is no way you would have killed her."

"I agree," he says. "I'll testify."

"You need to prepare for some tough cross-examination. They might try to suggest that you fought with your wife, maybe even assaulted her."

"I never laid a hand on my wife. Ever," he protests angrily. "Not on any woman. I am not that sort of man."

"She had no reason to fear you?"

"None."

"So if someone suggested that she was seen running from your house, cowering in fear in the street—that would be false?"

"Laura never feared me. She had no cause to run from me."

Jeff gives me a confused look—*Where did that come from?* I shake my head. *Not now.* I haven't told him what Lois told me at the party, my promise to Lois niggling at in the back of my mind.

"Let's order in coffee and sandwiches, and go over what you're going to say tomorrow," I suggest.

Vincent Trussardi shrugs. "It cannot be so difficult to tell the truth."

"The truth can sometimes be complicated. Before we get started, is there anything else you need to tell us?"

"There is one thing," he says. "I'd repressed it, maybe thought it didn't matter."

"Tell us, Vincent. Now."

CHAPTER 47

IT'S 10:00 A.M. ON WEDNESDAY, and I'm on my feet, outlining the theory of the defense.

"Ladies and gentlemen of the jury," I begin, moving close to the jury box, engaging each member as I speak—Mr. Kasmirsky, the nurse, the dockworker, the accountant. My friends, my confidants. "You have heard a great deal over the past eight days about the death of Laura Trussardi. You've heard a great about Laura Trussardi—the kind of person she was, who she saw, who she met. And you've heard about other people who had opportunities to kill Laura Trussardi. What you have not heard anything about is the accused, Vincent Trussardi. That, in the defense's submission, is because he is innocent."

I had prepared my opening an eon ago, revised it over the weekend at Martha's. After bidding Vincent Trussardi farewell late last night, I went over it yet again, tweaking, adjusting. In the jury business, every word and intonation counts. At least, that's what we lawyers like to think.

"The Crown's case," I go on, "rests entirely on what the law calls circumstantial evidence. Great caution is required before convicting on circumstantial evidence, which has been the source of countless wrongful convictions. For this reason, the law places a special obligation on the prosecution in such cases. The prosecution must establish beyond a reasonable doubt that there is *no reasonable explanation except* that Mr. Trussardi committed this crime. There is no onus on Mr. Trussardi to show that he didn't commit the crime, nor that someone else committed it. It is for the prosecution to eliminate all other reasonable possibilities. The evidence called by the defense will show beyond a shadow of a doubt that the prosecution has failed to meet this obligation."

The jurors' faces, closed at the outset, are starting to open. I drive my argument home.

"In fact, the evidence will cement what is already apparent from the Crown's case—that other explanations for the murder are out there, explanations which the police chose not to investigate in their mistaken and premature theory that this crime was committed by Vincent Trussardi. The evidence will also show that Mr. Trussardi, a law-abiding citizen, had no reason to kill his wife. He loved her, and she was carrying his child. He had every reason to want her very much alive. And finally, the defense will produce evidence that Vincent Trussardi was, in fact, somewhere else when the crime was committed."

Kasmirsky nods as I make my final pitch.

"The Crown's case is a thin tissue woven from fragile threads, each of which fails upon testing. In the end, when you have heard and considered all the evidence, ladies and gentlemen of the jury, you will have no choice but to conclude that the Crown has failed to prove its case and thus failed to prove beyond a reasonable doubt that Vincent Trussardi committed the crime with which he is charged."

I return to my chair, and Jeff gives my arm a squeeze.

Justice Moulton clears his throat. "We'll take the morning recess and return to hear the first defense witness."

We have our roster. It's short. Our alibi witnesses—the yacht club waitress Sandra Day and Vincent's friend Ollie Semple—today and tomorrow. Vincent Trussardi on Friday, Monday in cross-examination. Who knows how long Cy will take with him, but with luck we'll have a verdict—for good or bad—before next week's out.

CHAPTER 48

MR. TRUSSARDI, JUST A FEW more questions."

It's Friday afternoon, and we're finishing up our examination in chief. We've been through all the big stuff, how he loved his wife, how they were looking forward to a child, how he was sailing at the time of her death.

The defense case is almost in. So far, so good. The waitress, Sandra Day, said what she had to say Wednesday afternoon. Cy toyed with her for an hour or so, filling out the day. He gave Ollie Semple a rougher ride on Thursday, but Ollie held his own.

"Sure, I was a little tipsy, but I know what I saw," he responded to Cy's probing. "I remember Vincent's jacket. He left it on my boat once last spring when I took him out . . . Sure, he was my friend—*is* my friend—but I would never lie, not even for a friend. I know what I saw."

Vincent Trussardi has thus far proved a good witness—calm, straightforward, addressing the jury eloquently. All to script.

"Let me take you back to the night of the murder, Mr. Trussardi," I say. "You came home and found your wife, called the police. How long did it take for the police to get there?"

"About ten minutes."

"And during those ten minutes, what were you doing?"

"I was in shock. I sat on the sofa, sobbing."

"Did you get up at any point?

"Yes, I went out to the terrace."

"Tell the jury, did you see anyone on the terrace, talk to anyone?"

Vincent Trussardi's eyes briefly close. "It was a terrible night. A storm had blown up out of nowhere."

"Please answer the question, Mr. Trussardi."

"The boy was there," he says, opening his eyes.

"What boy, Mr. Trussardi?"

"The boy she brought to the house once. He used to come around after the night she invited him in. The gardener would see him, lurking in the woods, staring at the house. He seemed to have a fixation on Laura."

"Did you talk to the boy on the terrace that night, Mr. Trussardi?"

"Yes."

"Tell us about it."

The jury leans forward, all attention.

"I told him to go away. That he didn't belong there, not now."

"And what did the boy say?"

"He said, 'All the police around—she's dead, isn't she?' I told him yes, and then he began ranting, and I heard him scream, 'I killed her!' "

I hear a low gasp from the jury box. My eye catches Damon at the back, ashen faced.

"Order," Moulton chides.

"Who was that boy, Mr. Trussardi?"

"It was Damon Cheskey, the boy who testified here. He looked different then—skinny, long hair matted—but it was him."

"Thank you. Your witness, Mr. Kenge."

Cy sits very still. Justice Moulton reads his shock and decides to rescue him. "Three forty," he announces. "Court will reconvene at ten o'clock Monday for cross-examination."

For once, the timing is in our favor. All weekend for the jurors to ponder the possibility that Damon killed Laura. We gather up our papers and head out.

CHAPTER 49

"I LOVED MY WIFE," VINCENT Trussardi tells Cy Kenge on Monday. "I could never have harmed her."

"Never?"

"Never."

Cy stands at the prosecution table, one hand on its leather surface to support the weight of his torso but otherwise relaxed, rested, and ready to go. He smiles at Vincent's assertion that he could not have harmed his wife.

"You maintain your wife had no reason to fear you, Mr. Trussardi. What if someone were to say that, a few days before the murder, your late wife was in the street outside your house, crying and afraid to return?"

"I would say it's nonsense. I never laid a hand on her."

"What's this about?" Jeff whispers.

"Maybe Cy's just trying to get him mad," I whisper back, but I feel nervous all the same.

Cy has been going at Vincent Trussardi for over an hour now, by turns cajoling and attacking. He's made limited headway. Trussardi remains cool and collected.

Cy shakes his head, all sympathy. "Enough to drive any man to distraction, the way your late wife was carrying on. Do you agree?"

"No, I loved her."

"I didn't ask if you loved her, Mr. Trussardi. I asked whether you liked the way she was carrying on."

"I didn't like the adultery. I hated it. But it was over."

"So you say," says Cy, with a cynical nod of his head. "We'll let the jury decide about that." He moves close to the witness box, fixes Vincent Trussardi with his stare. "Admit it, Mr. Trussardi. Your wife was doing drugs, committing adultery, and cavorting with street boys. It made you angry; it pushed you over the brink; you couldn't take it anymore." Cy's voice drops. "So you killed her."

"No," says Vincent Trussardi. "No, no, no."

He's holding his own. Still, the constant barrage is starting to wear on the witness. His face, pale a moment ago, is flushed with anger at the suggestion that his wife could have feared him.

Cy moves on.

"Let's go back to the gun—the gun that killed your wife. Did you always lock your safe?"

"Yes, of course."

"As far as you know, no one else ever opened the safe?"

"Not that I know. But someone must have."

"When was the last time you opened the safe?"

"I'm not sure. I used to check the contents every few months."

"Was the gun in the safe when you last looked?"

"Yes."

"But when the police had the safe unlocked by a locksmith after your wife's death, the gun was gone?"

"Yes. That's what I was told."

"How do you explain that, Mr. Trussardi?"

"I can't. Trevor Shore knew where I kept the code—he designed the false compartment. Damon Cheskey watched me take out the code, open the safe. And Laura knew."

"You're surely not suggesting your late wife tied herself up and shot herself," Cy scoffs. "And as for Damon Cheskey, it's lunacy to suppose a drugged-up street boy would have the wit to know the code and get the gun, don't you agree?"

"I don't know—"

"Much less that he would have reason to kill the woman he adored?"

"Objection." I rise. "Mr. Kenge is asking the witness to speculate on matters he cannot know."

Moulton nods. "Sustained."

Cy moves on to our alibi. "Let me take you back to that fateful day, Mr. Trussardi. You say you drove to the yacht club about eight thirty that morning."

"I do. I did."

"And you had breakfast there, then took your boat out."

"Yes."

"And you didn't come back until four o'clock or so." Cy proffers a sheaf of small papers. "This is a copy of the club's charge slips for that day. Have a look."

Trussardi inspects the slips.

"And as you've pointed out in your evidence-in-chief, one of them is your breakfast chit. Twelfth from the top, I believe."

He finds the chit. "Correct."

"Would you count the breakfast chits for me?"

The courtroom sits in silence while Trussardi counts the slips of paper. "Twenty-seven," he says at last, raising his head.

Cy takes the sheaf back, hands the witness a second spike of slips, much thicker. "I'm told that these are the slips from the afternoon and evening, with lunch and dinner charges. Would you be so good as to count them?"

Again Trussardi counts; this time it takes longer. "One hundred seven," he says faintly. I see where Cy is going.

"A lot of people were at the club during the late afternoon of May fifth, Mr. Trussardi."

"The inference is yours, not mine, Mr. Kenge."

"We will leave the inferences to the jury, Mr. Trussardi," Cy snaps. "Let me put it this way—the charge slips I have just given you show that there were many people in and about the Vancouver Yacht Club about the time you say you docked your boat, walked directly in front of the lounge and up to your car. Yet you have been able to produce only one witness—a man who says he is your friend and admits to being drunk at the time."

I frown, a warning. Vincent picks up on it. "All I can say is that I was there."

Cy offers the jury a sad, cynical smile. "Now let me take you back to that evening, Mr. Trussardi. You told the jury you waited for the police out on the terrace."

"Yes."

"And you saw a young man—a boy—there. A boy who said something like, 'I killed her.' Did you tell the police about this when they interviewed you, Mr. Trussardi?"

"No," Trussardi answers.

"This is vital information to your case, wouldn't you agree? Someone else saying they killed her?"

"Yes."

"Then why wouldn't you have told the police about it at the first opportunity?"

"My lawyer said to answer only the questions they asked. They didn't ask."

Excellent response.

"So you want the jury to believe that you didn't give the police the one piece of information that might have cleared you?"

"The boy was crazy, out of his head. When he said he killed her, I didn't make much of it, not at the time."

I bite my lip. *Don't undermine what Damon said.*

"So you didn't believe the boy killed your wife, Mr. Trussardi?"

"No. I thought he was just raving."

"So why are you asking the jury to believe that the boy might have killed her when you didn't believe that yourself?"

"I didn't know what to believe then. But now he admits he knew where the gun was, knew how to get in the safe. If I'd known that, I would have made more of his threat." His voice drops. "The truth is, I still don't *know* who did this terrible thing. All I know is that it wasn't me."

Good, I think, *stop there*. But he doesn't. He is looking down, lost in his memory.

"The rain was freezing. I was looking out over the ocean, the water beating against my face, the wind cutting it. The boy started screaming. I grabbed him, pushed him away. 'No,' I said, 'you didn't kill her. *I* killed her.' "

Shock descends over the court. The jury reels back in their soft red seats. I feel the blood drain from my head, the bile rise in my gut. What is he saying?

"No further questions." Cy swings triumphantly back to the counsel table.

Out of the stunned silence comes Justice Moulton's voice. "Re-examination, Ms. Truitt?"

I struggle blindly to my feet. *How can I fix this?* Then words come.

"What did you mean when you said, 'I killed her,' Mr. Trussardi?"

He is sobbing, wiping away his tears. "I meant that I let her die. I married her. I was supposed to look after her. I left her alone, went out sailing, left her there to be killed."

"Mr. Trussardi," I say, voice low. "Did you physically kill your wife?"

His body is shaking. He's falling apart; it's all over. Then he draws himself up and looks the jurors in the eye. For the first time in the trial, he is a lion, magnificent.

"I did *not* physically kill my wife," he says, emphasizing each word. "I loved her. I did not kill her."

"Thank you, Mr. Trussardi." I sink to my seat.

Cy starts to stand, but thinks better and falls back into his chair. His triumphant moment is clouded, the fatal admission qualified. Still, I fear it's the end for us. *I killed her.* The words have been uttered, seared into the jurors' brains. The explanation that came after is just so much noise.

Moulton's eye moves to the clock. "We'll take the noon break."

CHAPTER 50

MY LORD," I TELL JUSTICE Moulton when we return, "that completes the evidence for the defense."

I'm about to try for a reprieve on our address to the jury—no way to hold their attention when they're exhausted from a morning of forced concentration—when Cy heaves himself to his feet.

"My Lord, the prosecution wishes to tender evidence in rebuttal." Cy gestures to the jury. "You might wish to excuse the jury while I advise the Court of the nature of the evidence."

"Very well, the jury is excused."

"What the *hell*?" I hear Jeff breathe as the jury files out.

"What can there be to rebut?" Moulton asks. "I heard nothing over the past week that resembles a new issue."

"The new issue is this: The accused, Mr. Trussardi, in his evidence, has—for the first time—raised the issue of the absence of previous violent conduct by the accused toward the deceased."

"And you propose to rebut that, Mr. Kenge?" Justice Moulton queries.

It hits me like a blow to the belly. *Lois in the kitchen. Lois warning me of the occurrence report.*

"I do," replies Cy. "Important evidence emerged late in the case that indicates the accused was indeed violent—very violent—toward his wife and that she feared him." Cy picks up a sheet of paper that Emily has placed before him. "The evidence consists of an occurrence report filed by a member of the West Vancouver Police just two days before the murder. The officer reports that, while on a routine patrol near Marine Drive in West Vancouver that evening, he observed a woman running down the street. She was wearing high heels, and as the headlights of the police car revealed her, she fell. The officer stopped to make sure she was okay. He asked her where she lived. She pointed to a nearby house, which he later determined to be the Trussardi residence. He reports that the woman kept saying she couldn't go back, that she had to get away, but when he offered to take her to a shelter, she refused. She ran away from him, back down the drive to the house. He waited awhile and then returned to the police station and wrote up his report."

"He didn't follow her to the house to investigate?"

"Sadly, no." Cy lets his words, potent with the possibility of a murder averted, hang in the silence.

"Jilly?" Jeff whispers. It's not like me to say nothing.

I rise and smooth my gown. "Three points, my Lord. First, Mr. Kenge should have put this report to the accused in cross-examination. Second, this is not proper rebuttal evidence. The relationship between my client and his wife has been at the center of this case since the charge was laid." I take a deep breath, plow on to my final point. "Third, my Lord, the defense has had no notice of this report. The law—*Stinchcombe* to be precise—is clear. All evidence the Crown seeks to use must be disclosed to the defense well in advance of trial to allow the defense to meet it—in a word, to allow a fair trial, a right guaranteed by the Constitution. The rule is as simple as it is absolute: if evidence has not been disclosed to the defense, it cannot be admitted."

I take my seat as Moulton turns to Cy. "What do you say to that, Mr. Kenge?"

"My Lord, the evidence came to light only late in the day."

"It's up to the prosecution to ferret out the evidence and disclose it. Your failure to find the evidence is no excuse for lack of disclosure."

Cy bows his head. "The matter is somewhat delicate, but I do not think that Ms. Truitt will deny that she was made aware of the existence of this report long before she put her client on the stand."

Every eye swivels to me. Jeff stares at me in shocked disbelief.

A red tide creeps up Moulton's face. He spits his words at me like pellets of poison. "Is this *true*, Ms. Truitt?"

"The possibility that such a report existed was mentioned to me." I stand shakily. "But it was in a casual conversation with someone who is not part of this case. With Mr. Kenge's wife, to be precise. The meanderings of a person at a party do not count as formal disclosure. Not having had formal disclosure, I disregarded them."

Justice Moulton turns away, studies his bench book, looks up.

"You *knew* that this report might exist before you put your client on the stand, and now you complain that using it to bring forth the truth is unfair." He fixes me with an icy stare. "This is not a *game*, Ms. Truitt; this is a *trial.* A woman has been brutally murdered; a just verdict is at stake. Mr. Kenge, you may call your witness." He nods to the sheriff. "Bring the jury back."

It doesn't take long. Constable Cooke, a rookie cop, tells the jury what he saw and what he put in his report. Challenging his claim is futile. I cross-examine, do what I can. The officer never got the woman's name, doesn't know who she was—just that she was slender, blond, and ran back toward the Trussardi residence. Nor did she say what had happened or who she was afraid of.

But I know this is damning. After all, who *but* Laura St. John Trussardi could the woman have been? Who *but* her husband could she have been running from? Sure, she had a secret life. But crying in the street, outside the matrimonial residence?

I watch the jurors' faces harden. It's over.

CHAPTER 51

WHAT THE FUCK DID YOU think you were doing?" Jeff looms over me in our little room.

I've filled him in on my conversation with Lois at Cy's party. Finally.

"We're a team, Jilly—or so I naïvely thought. You held out on me. You fucked me over, and you fucked the case."

"I'm so sorry, Jeff," I say, and I am. "I didn't even know if the report was real. And if it was, I never dreamed Cy would try to use it, never imagined Moulton would let it in."

Jeff seizes my shoulders. "You never told me what you knew," he says. "You left me out—you let me down." He lets his hands fall to his side, turns away.

There's nothing I can say to make it right.

"I believed what I wanted to believe, that Lois would never

trick me, that Cy would never stoop so low as to use his wife just to win a case. You're right, Jeff. I've become too close to this case, addicted to proving Trussardi didn't kill Laura. I was blind." My words trail off in a whisper. "And I thought Cy was my friend, once."

Jeff studies me. But he says nothing, and it hits me that we're done, Jeff and me. He'll cross the street to Peck or somebody. He's good—he can go anywhere he wants and make more money, too.

I steel myself. I wait for Jeff to speak.

"Let's get the hell back to the office," he says, granting me a temporary reprieve.

I nod. We pick up our bags and leave.

I'M GETTING INTO A CAB outside the courthouse when Damon finds me. I motion and he slides into the seat beside me. Numbly, I give the driver the address of his condo. I should be angry with him. He let us know too little, too late; revealed his part in the saga in dribs and drabs; and then ended up testifying for the Crown. He didn't have much choice—Cy subpoenaed him—but what niggles at me is how it happened.

"I underestimated you, Damon," I say, as the pieces fall into place in my mind. "You played your cards superbly. Not guilty of killing Laura because you've sunk Trussardi. Immune from prosecution on anything else because you've made a deal with Cy. Congratulations, Damon."

"No," Damon whispers, a sob in his throat. "I don't know how Cy found out about the drugs. I think he's after me."

"Nice try, Damon."

"No, Ms. Truitt, it's not like that. I was delivering a document from Jeff, and Cy invited me in and showed me around the Crown offices. I thought he was being nice, but then he started talking about Trussardi. He said he knew that I'd delivered drugs to the Trussardis' house. I started getting uncomfortable. I told him I had to go. But he just refilled my coffee cup and smiled. 'Sit down, Damon,' he said, that soft edge in his voice. 'We know everything.' I had no choice. He didn't say much, but he made it clear—cooperate or he'd bring me in. I told myself what he was asking wasn't so bad, just the truth, after all." He shrugs.

I want to believe him. Maybe he didn't set out to betray me. Maybe Cy got what he wanted by empty threats about past deeds. I feel a chill. Or maybe not so empty. *It's over,* Damon told me that night in the hospital. Was he talking about Kellen?

The cab pulls up to Damon's building.

"Damon, we shouldn't be discussing this. Whatever Cy thinks he has on you, let it go. Lie low for a while and keep out of trouble."

He gives me a desultory wave as the cab speeds away.

CHAPTER 52

TUESDAY, DAY TWELVE OF THE trial. My closing address. But I know it's too little, too late; the image of Laura Trussardi fleeing her home in terror has snapped the jury members' minds permanently shut. I hit the weak points in the Crown's case, and there are many—the shoddy police work, the unexplored alternatives: Trevor Shore, the footprints, Damon. I talk about my client's spotless past and stellar reputation. I remind the jury of Carmelina's testament to matrimonial harmony, ask them to remember that the accused believed—rightly, as it turned out—that his wife was carrying his child. I deal, as I must, with the rebuttal evidence. It is weak and should not be relied on. All we know is that some woman who may or may not have been Laura was on the street, professed not to want to go back to the house, and then did precisely that. We do not even know for sure who she was. Such evidence cannot rebut the mountain of contrary evidence as to the happy state of affairs between the accused and his wife. And then, knowing Cy is waiting in the wings, I bear down on the theory of the Crown.

"The Crown's case rests on the supposition that Vincent Trussardi killed his wife in the deliberate and cruel fashion you have heard about for no other reason than that she accepted the delivery of drugs and that she was having an affair with Trevor Shore. That theory is absurd. You have heard the evidence. Vincent had known of the affair for some time, believed it to be over, and had reconciled with his wife.

"The Crown has the burden of disproving any other reasonable alternatives as to who killed Laura Trussardi, and it has utterly failed to do so. Other plausible theories—Trevor Shore, Damon Cheskey—are sufficient to raise not only a *reasonable* doubt, but a *substantial* doubt as to Vincent Trussardi's guilt. In a nutshell, the prosecution case against Vincent Trussardi is nothing more than speculation. Ladies and gentlemen of the jury, on a full and fair consideration of the evidence, you will conclude, as you must, that the Crown has failed to discharge the burden upon it. You must acquit the accused."

It's not a bad address, as addresses go, nor a bad defense. But in my heart, I know the jurors have decided. Now it's Cy's turn. He goes through the evidence, then sums up the Crown's theory by recounting the tale of Othello and Desdemona: the story of love—maybe too much love—betrayal, and jealousy turned to madness.

"Mr. Trussardi's wife was no longer the sweet girl he thought he had married. He says he loved her, but he had also lost her—to another man and to drugs. And we all know what happens when great love becomes great loss. It fuses into an insane burning fury that demands destruction of its cause. A fury capable of turning a gentle, civilized man into a murderer."

"Objection!" I shout, but Cy pulls back before Moulton can hammer him.

"It is for you, ladies and gentlemen of the jury," he goes on, "to decide if Vincent Trussardi was crazed with jealousy. For you to decide if he murdered his wife. All I ask is that you consider the evidence impartially. You will find the answer."

AT FOUR THIRTY, JUSTICE MOULTON, having spent the afternoon instructing the jurors on the law and the evidence, gives them his final invocation. Their verdict must be unanimous. "Ladies and gentlemen of the jury, we await your decision."

They file out, Justice Moulton descends and exits, and Jeff and I busy ourselves straightening our papers. Cy tries to catch my eye as he makes his way down the aisle to where Lois waits, but I ignore him. At 6:00 p.m., Marion finds us where we lurk in the corridor and tells us the judge is coming back. "Have they reached a verdict?" I ask.

She shakes her head. "He's decided to tell them to go to dinner and resume their deliberations tomorrow."

Jeff and I head for the parking elevators. I glimpse Raquella behind a pillar. Hildegard bends to whisper something in her ear. Raquella laughs, a short bark.

"Sis can't wait for the verdict," says Jeff.

"Got that right."

An angry pain gnaws in my stomach. Despite all my efforts, I have failed. *I will know everything,* I told Raquella. *Stupid, idle boast.* All I know is that I will never know.

CHAPTER 53

I GET HOME LATE. I turn on the TV, turn it off. A novel—a slight thing on the bestseller lists called *The Rosie Project*—lies on the coffee table in front of me, its spine cracked at page three. I flick on CBC Radio 2 hoping for something soothing—a pianist plays "The Girl with the Flaxen Hair," and I think of Mike. Numbly, I stare at my Jack Bush. I'm in full letdown mode. I hate it when I lose, hate it more when I lose and the client's innocent.

The phone rings—Vincent Trussardi, out on his last night of freedom.

"What can I do for you?" I ask coldly. I have no time for this man, even if he didn't kill his wife.

"I need to talk to you, Miss Truitt."

"It is my professional opinion that you do not need to talk to me and that I do not need to talk to you."

"Miss Truitt, we must speak."

"Mr. Trussardi, the die is cast. We have done our best. The evidence is in. You should know that things don't look good for you."

"I am aware of that. But there are things that you should know."

"Mr. Trussardi, it's late and—"

"Go to your window," he says, "look out."

Something is different about his voice. It makes me cross to the window.

"Do you see a limo?"

"Yes."

"I would not detain you if it were not important." A long silence. "Please."

I tap the screen to end the call, consider my Jack Bush—the broad vertical strokes, so clear; the swirls of pink and gray, planted erratically, shades of doubt. Five minutes later I'm outside.

A liveried chauffeur steps smartly round and pulls the back door open for me. I slide in. Trussardi does not acknowledge my presence. The dim light of the street shadows his profile, the high forehead, the aquiline nose, the grim set of mouth. I have seen him sad; I have seen him angry; I have witnessed his ineffable charm. Tonight he is all business.

"Where are we going, Mr. Trussardi?"

"For a cruise."

"I don't think so." I reach for the door, but before I can get out, the car is moving.

I sit back in my seat, face to the window. We cross the lagoon into the park, neither of us talking, and glide down the slope to the yacht club. Ahead, vessels rock against the night. The chauffeur opens the limo door and extends a hand. We walk along a pier, Trussardi and me, passing boat after boat after boat before he halts.

Above us, the hull of a yacht looms, broad and capacious. I catch her name, black letters on her starboard, *La Trilla*. Two white-jacketed men on the upper deck peer down. Trussardi waves me up the gangway and into the boat. A girl in jeans arrives with a tray laden with smoked salmon and long-stemmed glasses filled with pale nectar. I decline both, but Trussardi takes a glass, raises his drink to me. “At last, Jilly,” he says. “I have waited too long for this moment.”

My stomach clenches. *What’s going on?*

“Mr. Trussardi.” I’m angry; I’m wary. “What’s this about?”

“Your mother.”

CHAPTER 54

I ROCK BACK IN MY chair.

My mother, that dark hole at the beginning of my being. All my longing, all my searching, and here she is, evoked by Vincent Trussardi. I have a picture in my mind—a good woman, a kind woman, a woman forced by overwhelming circumstance to part with me. "I know all I need to know about her," I say.

"You know nothing," he replies flatly. "I remember the first time I saw her. She was standing in the door of a longhouse. She wore a long white dress and sandals. Her thick black hair fell over her burnished shoulders. She looked at me and smiled a slow, mysterious smile. I stood as though in the spell of a goddess. Then she held out her hand to me, and I took it."

His face is lost in another time.

"What are you trying to tell me?" I whisper. Pain moves like a wave from my stomach.

"It was 1981, and I was spending a summer cruising the West Coast with a friend who had developed a sudden passion for the art of the coastal tribes. In the south, the villages had McDonalds and Safeways, but in the north, one could still find places where people lived the old way, in communal longhouses nested among totem poles in silent forests of giant Douglas fir, in Haida Gwaii. And that's where I met her. Your mother."

This is not my story. I don't want it.

"I was sure you had figured it out, Jilly. Your visits with Edith, your trip to Hildegard, your fascination with the dark-haired woman in the photo. I'm sorry, Jilly, so sorry. Do with the truth what you will, but you must know it."

It comes together, fragment by fragment, in a mangled mental swirl. "That's why you hired me to take your case." My mother, his anguished regret. Me, his way back to her? "What happened?" I hear myself asking.

"I took her out on our boat, and when I brought her back to shore, her father was waiting. He said words to her in their language, and then he turned and left her standing on the shore, all alone. She waited a long time, but no one came from the village. I told my friend we could not leave her shunned by her people. He told me I was crazy, that they were just trying to teach her a lesson and would welcome her back before dusk. 'You cannot take a girl who has never seen a proper house, never seen a streetcar or bus, back to Vancouver,' he said. He was right, but I did not see it then. I brought her back."

Dread encompasses me. *I don't like this story, don't like where it's headed.*

"I took her to my apartment. It was a small place—I was still a student. We did all the things lovers do, went to movies, shared books, dined at little dives. She loved the city, its action, its brilliance. She plunged into my world—even though English was her second language—with gusto. But gradually things changed. We still loved each other madly, but her days alone while I studied or ran errands—my father was insisting I get into the business—were long and lonely for her. And then she told me she was pregnant."

"Me," I whisper.

"Yes, you," he says softly.

I stand in a rush of rage. "Stop, I won't listen. You seduced my mother, abandoned me," I yell. "All the foster homes, all the abusive dads. And all you wanted was your yachts and your starlets." My hand goes back to strike him.

He catches my arm and holds it. "Let me finish. I told my family of your mother. I will not repeat what they said. It was ugly, racist. I must give the girl up, they said, adopt the child out when it came. I lost my temper—I didn't need them; I would make my own way. I would quit university and get a job. I went back to the apartment and told your mother. She kissed me and cried."

I wrench my arm away. "Good intentions, but you let them win in the end. You didn't care."

"I did care! The next day, I went all over the city searching for a job, but when I returned, the apartment was empty. She was gone. I wandered around in a daze for days, searching for her everywhere—in the streets, in malls—but I did not find her."

"You made her leave!"

"Hildegard made her leave. She was young then but already the family consigliere. As much as I pressed her, she would not tell me where your mother was."

"And then you made your deal with the devil," I say.

"Yes. I agreed that I would forget about you and your mother and go back to the family firm, but I extracted two concessions. The first was that I be based in Europe—I didn't want to be anywhere near my family. The second was that I see you when you were born. Six months later, I flew back from Milan, took a cab to Vancouver General Hospital. That's when I met you. You were four days old—black hair, pink skin, eyes like a doe. I held you in my hands, marveled at you. I asked for your mother, but they told me she didn't want to see me—keeping her end of the bargain, I suppose, or perhaps just bitter about how it had all come to this. I kissed the top of your head, said goodbye, and a nurse took you away from me."

His face softens as he slips into reverie. I feel a tear slip down my cheek, wipe it away with my fingers.

"Hildegard was waiting for me with a social worker—Edith Hole. She had found a good home for you. Not an adoption—it wasn't easy to find adoptive parents for Indigenous children then—but at least a foster home. 'What about a name?' Edith asked me. 'The child needs a name.'

"Hildegard vetoed Trussardi, so I said, 'Let's make it Truitt, an Anglo Trussardi.' And that was it. I flew back to Italy."

I sit, head in hands, unable to speak.

This man—my father—looks at me with fondness in his eyes. "I know this is hard for you, Jilly."

"What do you know?" I say. "You can't know me, how it was for me."

He sighs. "Actually, I knew most of what was happening to you. Relations with my family resumed a semblance of civility, except for my sister, who remained bitter. Every six months, I came back to Vancouver. Every six months, I met with Edith. I became fond of her, and we had a relationship of sorts. Through her, I kept track of you. Once, she arranged for me to watch you at a sports event. You were ten or so. I watched you run a race, just a stranger in the crowd of parents. You came in second—I was so proud. When you were thirteen, I got a frantic call. The minister and his wife had passed away within months of each other. Edith had placed you in another home, but things hadn't worked out. The people called you—what was the terrible phrase?—a 'disruptive deviant.' Edith had found another home, and another. But you kept running, and I had to help you. 'Let me deal with it,' I told Edith. I met with my old friend from the boat trip so many years before."

"Brock Mayne," I say.

"Yes, he had married a lovely woman and had children already. 'I'll meet all the expenses,' I said, 'pay for the best schools, university when the time comes.'

" 'If we do this, she will be our child,' he told me. The rest you know."

"And Edith?" I ask. "You broke her heart."

"I suppose I did."

I slump back, unable to move. In less than an hour, this man has put the jigsaw puzzle of my life together—my mother, my father, the Maynes. I study him—his dark swept-back hair, his profile defiant against the black of the windows—this man who never took the trouble to be part of my life but now claims me.

"You've been playing with me just like you played with my mother." I see it all clearly now. "You hired me to defend you for your amusement. You didn't tell me the truth about the case either. It was you who had me followed; you who wrote that threat on my windshield. You didn't want me to find out that you were my father—not yet. I would have quit the case and spoiled your final dramatic reveal."

His face has gone white. "No, Jilly, you're wrong. I've never had you followed, never threatened you. I could never—"

"Then who the hell did?" I yell.

"I don't know," he says, quietly.

I feel my chest thickening, my throat clogging. I will not cry any more. I will not give him that satisfaction.

Then it hits me. I remember the trial. I remember Laura Trussardi. "Where is my mother?"

"She is no longer with us."

"You mean she's dead?"

"Yes," he whispers.

"How?"

"There is no good way to say this. She had started taking drugs. There's a police record, drug possession—I found it a few months ago. You should know, Jilly, that she loved you very much. It's all there in the presentence reports I read. She was wracked by guilt over abandoning you. And she was desolate, obsessed by the gnawing absence of you in her life. So she eased the pain with heroin. She was on the street, in the end—her money gone. It was a bad trick that took her. She was good with words, your mother, like you, Jilly. You can find her presentence report—Trilla James was her name—although it will break your heart to read it." He halts, unable to go on. "It did mine."

"That's what you were doing all those months in the penthouse?" I ask. "Sitting with her photo, brooding? Regretting what you did, or didn't do?"

"Yes."

He's holding out on me, still holding out. Then I remember the name, the name on Keltey's report, the name on this boat.

A moan rises up from my gut. "No, no!"

His eyes shine with tears. "Pickton, the pig farm."

I hear myself sobbing, and I cannot stop.

"My dear, my daughter."

He moves toward me, tries to cradle me in his arms, but I pull away. I saw the police reports—women shackled, mutilated, killed. I feel sick and run to the head. I kneel over the toilet bowl, weeping.

I WAKE UP IN AN unfamiliar bed. He bends over me, bathing my face with a soft cloth. My father.

"You must get up now," he says. "We're almost back to shore."

He helps me up to the railing, where he stands beside me looking across the water at West Vancouver. His face once more is calm, serene. He has the air of a man at last at peace.

My professional persona surfaces. "I should tell you, as your lawyer—if that's what I still am—that you have a good chance at a new trial. The judge erred in letting the rebuttal evidence in. Find a new lawyer. He'll appeal, get you a new trial."

"You still don't understand, Jilly. I'm guilty. Not of Laura's murder but of letting her die. I failed her." He turns to look at me. "And I'm tired. There's nothing more for me here." A rough laugh. "Who knows, I may have the pleasure of meeting Robert Pickton in prison and performing my duty of revenge."

"You won't get the chance," I say. "Too many other inmates have the same idea. They keep him in protective custody."

"Ah, a disappointment, that."

In the dark ahead, I see the ghostly arch of the Lions Gate Bridge. We glide beneath it, nose into the harbor and toward the yacht club.

"If there's one thing I can ask of you, Jilly, it's to stay away from my sister."

My mind races. "She knows I'm your daughter, doesn't she?"

"Yes, and I would never want her to hurt you."

"Did she kill Laura?"

"No, she loved Laura," he says wearily. "Laura was kind to her, liked her, but never requited her love. Raquella was upset that Laura and I were back together, livid that Laura was expecting my child. But she wouldn't have killed Laura. She *couldn't* have killed her. My sister is an addict, and the cocaine that Laura received was for her. I should have told you—Raquella was away in rehab after Laura's death, dealing with her drug addiction." He pauses. "Laura's death haunts me, will haunt me forever until I know who killed her."

The boat slows and lurches. I clutch the railing, head bent, as my mind sorts the pieces and slots them into place. Trussardi, my father. Raquella, my embittered aunt. My mother, forever gone.

"You are the only good thing ever to come of my life," my father says as *La Trilla* softly bumps against the pier.

I nod dumbly, stumble to the gangway that the men in white are putting in place.

"Joseph Quentin will be contacting you," he calls. "There are some pictures I want you to have. And a trust fund."

"Too late to buy me, Father."

I hear his laugh, short and harsh, as I jump to the pier. "Then give the money away." He throws his head back and hurls his words into the night.

I stagger into the waiting limo, hold myself together as it glides over the bridge, through Stanley Park, and down Georgia Street to Yaletown. Only when the door of my condo shuts behind me do I release the animal howl in my belly.

CHAPTER 55

MY PHONES ARE GOING CRAZY. I wrench the landline from the wall, thumb my cell phone to off, and throw it to the floor. I lie on my bed in a fetal curl. Time passes.

"Jilly, for fuck's sake." Jeff is standing over me, yelling.

"How did you get in? Go away," I say.

"I phoned Richard. He knows where you keep your secret fob. Now get your ass out of bed and come with me to court."

"I'm not going to court. Not today."

He studies me with something between compassion and contempt. "This is not the time to fall apart. Your career is on the line. You know what people will say." He bends low, spits the words into my face. "Just another woman who can't take the heat."

"You don't know, Jeff—"

"No, I don't know, and I don't care." He rips the sheets back.

"Now get up, wash your face, put on a suit, and come to court. You've got ten minutes."

I force myself up, move to the bathroom where I stand under the hot shower and think about my mother. I put on my suit, brush my black hair, and practice my smile before the mirror. How many hours did I study that photo of the girl in a white dress without seeing who she really was? I am her—all that is left of her. I put on my high heels and move to the living room.

Jeff waits, cappuccino in hand. He thrusts it at me. "'Once more unto the breach.'"

Twenty minutes later, I enter courtroom twenty. Inside, I'm a mess, but outside, I'm fine, shoulders back, head high. I look over to the prisoner's box, where my father sits. He offers me a weary smile.

Fuck you, I think. But for now, I'm his lawyer. I give a curt nod.

The jury files in, Justice Moulton enters. Marion intones the familiar words: "Ladies and gentlemen of the jury, have you reached a verdict?"

Their faces tell me nothing.

Our foreman Kasmirsky rises. "We have."

"And what is your verdict?"

"We find the accused guilty as charged."

CHAPTER 56

THE REST IS PRO FORMA. Moulton pronounces the sentence—twenty-five years without parole—thanks the jurors for their service to the state, and dismisses them. Marion cries for order, and Justice Moulton exits through his door. At the prisoner's box, the sheriff clinks the cuffs around my father's outstretched hands. He gives me the smallest of smiles before they shove his shoulder and push him toward the prisoner's door. I do the calculation—he'll get out when he's eighty, if he lasts that long.

Jeff and I pack up, stuffing papers that seemed so precious a day ago into our big leather bags like trash. Jeff hefts two brief-cases off the table; I take the third. There is nothing to say—we've lost.

Cy Kenge, magnanimous in victory, waits for us at the back of the empty courtroom. "Well fought, Jilly," he says, as if his win has miraculously restored our old camaraderie. I ignore his extended hand, stare him in the eye until his gaze falters.

"You crossed me, Cy. You short-circuited the rules." And you sent an innocent man to prison—a man who, whether I like it or not, happens to be my father.

"You were warned, Jilly."

"Sure."

"Just like you were warned about Damon."

"Damon?"

"Who else?" Cy smirks. "Cops are onto him, Jilly."

"About what, Cy?"

"Who else would want Kellen in a Dumpster?"

"Plenty of people. Why would you try to ruin an innocent kid?"

Cy looks at me like I'm a fool. "It's called justice, Jilly."

I cross the glass-sheathed atrium toward the elevator that will take me to the barristers' lounge where I can shuck my gown and tabs. The earlier rain has ceased, and now the low sun breaks through the clouds, lighting the slate and glinting off the plants that hang tier upon tier from the upper corridors.

"Jilly."

I stop.

Lois steps out from behind a pillar.

My briefcase clunks to the floor. "You fucked me, Lois. What an actress, what a performance. You were in it together, you and Cy, weren't you? I was just a game to you two, just a joke."

Her face crumbles. "Jilly, it wasn't like that; you don't understand."

"I have nothing more to say to you."

For a moment, I think she won't move. Then she turns and walks away.

I make my way up to the lounge, ditch my court regalia, and stow it in my locker. I find the parking elevators and descend into the bowels of the building where Jeff waits beside his battered van.

"What took you so long?" he asks.

"Business," I say, as I toss my briefcase on the backseat. "Taking care of business."

Jeff noses the van out of the garage, waits for a bus to pass, and eases onto the busy street. People are going about their affairs, talking and laughing as if it's just another day. I see Cy and Lois on the sidewalk ahead. She is crying, shouting, pummeling her tiny fists against his chest. He reaches to grab her wrists, but she pulls away. His body lurches, and Lois falls into the street. The squeal of brakes; the bus halts, too late.

Jeff stops the van. "Jesus!"

People run to the crumpled form. From somewhere a police car appears, then an ambulance. Lois's crushed body is strapped to a stretcher, loaded into the maw of the ambulance. Cy stands on the sidewalk, gazing blankly after the vehicle as it wails its way down the street in a cacophony of accompanying sirens.

Alone, utterly alone.

CHAPTER 57

RAQUELLA TRUSSARDI GLARES UP AT me from her chair. Her face is deeply lined; her black hair, newly streaked with white, sits askew. She's had a bad night.

"You promised I wouldn't have to throw you out a third time," she rasps.

It has cost me some effort to find her. It was Richard who said she'd be at Vincent's condo, Richard who got me in the door on the pretense of a delivery. I look through the wall of glass. Below me the city sprawls toward the sea. But I'm not here for the view.

"I told you that before this was over I would know everything. I know most of it. There are just a few details I need your help with."

She wheels away from me to the window. "So he told you that

you're his daughter." She gives a harsh laugh. "All the time you spent with him, you never picked up on it."

"On what?"

"My dear, beloved brother creates his own fantasy worlds. The truth for him is what he wants it to be. It's not impossible that he had a daughter as a result of one of his brief affairs. Apparently he's decided you're the result. Why do you think I tried to warn you off the case?"

She's smiling, shaking her head sadly. For a moment I believe her, before my gut kicks in. "I've seen delusional people—the courts are full of them. Vincent Trussardi doesn't fit the mold."

"Believe what you want, Miss Truitt. It's of no consequence to me. Just don't think you'll see a penny from his estate." Her hand presses a button on her chair, and Hildegard, stark in a dark pantsuit, emerges from a doorway, a look of intense dislike twisting her features.

"Hildegard, see Miss Truitt out."

"You've done enough damage, Miss Truitt," Hildegard says. "You've lost Vincent's case. The damage to the family and its business is incalculable." She catches Raquella's sharp look. "Raquella, you will be the new CEO. But the fact remains, to lose Vincent—to lose his experience, his judgment—will be a great blow."

I smile. Oldest mistake in the book: two allies telling different stories. "Raquella says Vincent is delusional; Hildegard vaunts his judgment. Someone's lying here."

"Just leave," says Hildegard, drawing a deep breath.

"Why do you hate me?" My gaze travels between the two women. "If the idea that I'm Vincent's daughter is a delusional fixation, why would you fear me?" I go out on a limb. "Why would you threaten Edith Hole? Why would you have my birth records removed? If I wanted to be part of this family, if I wanted your money—which I don't—I'd have to prove it. A simple DNA test would show I'm not his daughter, or that I am. "

"Then why are you here?" Hildegard asks resignedly.

"I came here to talk about Laura Trussardi and her murderer." I turn to Raquella. "You loved Laura, didn't you?"

I catch the alarm in Hildegard's face, but Raquella ignores her.

"Of course I loved her," she says. "I loved her like a sister."

"No, not like a sister," I press. "More. Like a lover."

Hildegard seizes the back of Raquella's chair. "Enough of this nonsense."

I'm not leaving without the answers I need. "It started slowly, didn't it, Raquella? Laura would come to have tea with you. She loved Vincent, but she was lonely. He was away on business so much, and afternoon visits with you turned into long evenings together. You became friends, and then more. It was only natural that when she built her new house, she would include an apartment for you, separate but connected."

"You know nothing of how it was," Raquella hisses.

"Raquella, we need to go," Hildegard says, her voice rising.

Raquella laughs, eyes flashing. "I have never run from anything in my life, and I will not run from this little bitch."

"But Laura started to withdraw," I say. "Maybe she didn't like it that you wanted more than friendship, maybe she didn't like all the drugs you were doing, maybe she didn't like procuring them for you. She had an affair with the architect, but she ended it, maybe for you? Then she got involved with the boy who brought the drugs, nothing serious, but still, he wasn't you. Finally, she returned to Vincent, and they decided to have a child." I drill down. "That final betrayal—returning to your despised brother and carrying his child—you couldn't handle it. You had a fight two days before the murder. You attacked her. People assume that because you're in a wheelchair you're weak. But you're strong. You can run a person down in your chair, and you can strike fast. Laura fled to the street, where the police officer saw her. She never told him she was running from you, though, and so his report damned your brother."

"You're mad, Miss Truitt. Utterly mad."

"We're going," says Hildegard. She tries to yank the wheelchair around, but my hands are on the arms. I lean over Raquella, watch her eyes widen.

"For two days you festered in your fury, waiting for your moment of revenge. And then it came. It was Sunday—Angela was off, Carmelina was out, and Vincent was sailing. Laura was alone at last. You took the elevator up, removed the gun from the safe, and you murdered her."

"No," she whispers. "No."

"Yes, you had it all planned. First, a lovely meal. Laura's Last Supper."

She looks up sharply.

"One of the police reports noted two glasses, two plates, two sets of cutlery in the sink."

"Nonsense!" Hildegard barks.

"Is it?" I ask.

She elbows me aside to regain control of the chair. "You've troubled Raquella long enough."

I step forward, blocking their path to the door.

"Something's been puzzling me, Raquella. How did you do it? How did you overcome her? You're strong, but so was she. But I think I understand. It was the lunch. You prepared the plates downstairs, brought them up on the little cart you keep in the kitchen. You ground up some of your pills and put them in her food—the coroner found traces of a sleeping drug in her blood. She became groggy and went to bed. After that it was easy." I think of the photos. "Easy to tie her up, easy to shoot her. I hope she did not feel too much."

Raquella is immobile, knuckles clenched on the arms of her chair.

Hildegard steps back, surveying Raquella. She finally sees it. "No," she says, with shock.

We stare at each other, three women in a frozen tableau.

Raquella's cry breaks the silence. "Laura," she moans. "I didn't want to do it. But I couldn't bear to see her back with him. Not after everything we had."

Hildegard bends to Raquella, silences her with a "Shh," then sends me a withering stare. "You've done enough damage, Miss Truitt, now go."

"Just a couple more details," I say. "You decided to make sure Vincent took the rap for the murder by having other suspects killed. Like Trevor Shore."

Raquella rouses herself. "That's—" She shakes off Hildegard's attempt to quiet her. "It doesn't matter anymore—Vincent's in prison. Trevor Shore was aware of how it was between Laura and me. He was distraught."

I take a leap. "He knew where the gun was. Is."

"You're brighter than I thought, Miss Truitt. When Shore designed the house, I asked him to put a concealed safe under the Botero. It was something my family had always had in their houses, an old-fashioned whimsy. He knew how the mechanism worked, how to make the sculpture swing to reveal the cavity below."

"So he checked the Botero? He found the gun and confronted you."

Raquella stares at me in silence. "Let's go, Hildegard."

"He came to see me," I say. "He told me to look at the family, look at the house. If I had figured out then what he meant, he'd still be alive. You wouldn't have had him killed."

Her chair whirls toward me. I step back, but it hits me in the shins. She reaches out and grabs my hand. "It's all your fault. You and your detective kept poking around." She twists my wrists in a crippling vise grip, and I buckle. "His death was your fault, Miss Truitt, all your fault."

I wrench my hand from hers, pick myself up, and straighten my skirt. "You were following me."

"Raquella?" Hildegard looks at her with surprise.

"It gave me great pleasure to frighten you, Miss Truitt, to cause you a little of the pain you caused me. I *enjoyed* it."

"Quiet!" Hildegard's pale hands grasp Raquella's wheelchair. "You've destroyed yourself," she whispers to Raquella, wheeling her away. "You've destroyed the family."

"It's all your fault, Miss Truitt, all your fault," Raquella cries as Hildegard pushes her around the door. "He should never have had you. You should never have been born!"

"Well, I was. I *exist,* whether you like it or not." I pause. "You will be hearing from the police, Raquella."

I've done it, I think. *I've found the truth.*

I click the recorder in my pocket to off and leave.

CHAPTER 58

HOURS LATER, I SIT ALONE in a narrow room lined with black-paned windows at L'Abbatoir, an industrial-chic restaurant around the corner from my office. The waiter, young and trendy with a silver ring in his ear, pours me a glass of Chablis.

"Tough day, Ms. Truitt?" he asks. I'm a regular here. Tonight, though, I'm not hungry.

"You could say that." If he only knew.

"Jilly, I thought I might find you here."

I look up. "Hey, Jeff."

He sits down and the waiter brings him a glass. "I got your message, downloaded the audio file with Raquella's confession. Unbelievable. What happens now?"

"First I tell Edith she can stop worrying. I just sent her a text letting her know she's safe, that she can come back."

"I mean about the case."

"Ah, the case. Tomorrow I take the confession to the police. Cy will have no choice but to ask Justice Moulton to set the verdict aside and release Trussardi. Raquella will plead guilty to first degree and go to prison for the rest of her life. End of story."

"You're not going straight to Cy with the confession?"

"No way. He broke all the rules. And then he pushed Lois under the bus. It's over between us."

"He didn't push Lois under the bus—she fell. And word is that she's expected to pull through."

"If you say so." I sit, considering. "I'm glad that Lois is okay."

Jeff leans forward. "There was something else on that recording, Jilly. Something about you."

I tell him, not everything but enough. A mother found and lost. A father found and discarded. My only aunt, and I'm sending her to prison.

As Jeff listens, his eyes widen. "I concede," he says when I finally wind down. "This time it wasn't just another case." He brightens. "But life goes on. Debbie's been trying to reach you. Some politician charged with strangling his daughter, big case, big money. Desperate to see you, only you."

"I'll deal with it tomorrow."

Jeff starts to protest, then stops himself. "Okay, I'm off. Jessica awaits." He bends for a quick hug.

"Goodbye, Jeff. It's been great working with you."

"What are you talking about? See you Monday, boss."

Relief mingles with deep joy. So he's staying.

He shoots me a smile. "Look after yourself, Jilly Truitt Trussardi."

I'm alone again. The wine in my glass has grown tepid. Rain

streaks the windows outside. I need to move on, but there's nowhere to go.

I nose my Mercedes aimlessly westward toward Georgia and Stanley Park, then double back onto West Hastings, past the stately Vancouver Club, where women couldn't enter the front door a few years ago, past the shops and swank hotels of Coal Harbour. I bear ever eastward and downward into narrowing strips of street, where windows are broken, lights are garish, and people in alleys hook and snort and do whatever they have to do to get through the next hour or two.

My eye catches the tall figure of a man on the sidewalk—jeans, suede jacket, long black hair swinging loose like a girl's. He's got his eye on me or maybe he likes the car. I should pass by, but I slow, pull to the curb. My finger touches a button, and the window rolls down. He leans in, and my breath catches at his beauty—skin of creamy copper, eyes of liquid black. He moves closer. He says nothing for a long moment.

"Need some help, sister?" he asks.

My throat thickens. He has taken it all in—my diamond studs, my Armani jacket, the Prada bag on the seat—and has seen me for what I am: a sister and in need. I shake my head. In the rearview mirror I see the red and blue lights of a police cruiser; a siren shrieks. I reach into my pocket and pull out my walk-around money—two hundreds—move my arm toward the man. His hand closes over mine.

"Be kind to yourself," I say.

He looks at the money in his hand, looks up, eyes wide. "You too, sister."

The police car is on my tail now. I pull forward slowly, ready to stop. I know what they're thinking: a drug deal. But the cruiser moves on to a more compelling incident up the street. I round the corner, head south into Chinatown and onto Union Street, gentrified condos springing up where Sammy Davis Jr. used to sing, only the shabby green tribute to Jimi Hendrix left to bear witness to the people who lived, loved, and made music here. I swing up the viaduct and exit into the shining-glass jungles of Yaletown, my town.

But I'm not ready to go home. I pull into a taxi zone in front of Le Provence. On my left, the glistening pleasure boats rock gently in the marinas of False Creek; on my right, happy couples exit restaurants, chatting and laughing. *Jilly Truitt, you have to be at the jail at nine to see a desperate man charged with killing his child. Go home and get an hour's sleep before you start again.*

My hand reaches for my bag; my fingers rifle the contents—I find my iPhone. I scroll through my contacts, find Michael St. John. My finger sits poised above the screen for a long moment. Then I throw the phone back in my bag. Someday, maybe. Mike's moved on from his dark place, but I still have a ways to go.

CHAPTER 59

I'M ABOUT TO MOVE FORWARD when I hear a thud on the roof. The passenger door opens and a figure slides into the seat.

"What the hell, Damon? Are you following me?" I eye his trench coat, the set of his jaw in profile. He looks older.

"We need to talk."

"What's this about?"

"About you, Jilly. About me."

A taxi honks behind me, and I pull out of the space.

"We need someplace private." He motions. "Try Pacific Boulevard."

I do a U-turn, swing up and east. The glowing globe of Science World looms to our right. *This will do*. I pull into the deserted parking lot.

Damon gets out and opens my door. "Let's go."

He steers me toward the seawall. A storm is rising. The wind tears at us; black waves crash on the concrete wall. Damon's face is strangely white in the neon of the great dome. I feel a twinge of fear.

"Why are we here, Damon?"

"I'm in trouble."

"Damon, whatever it is, I can help. You're a good kid."

His laugh cuts the air like a scythe. "I *was* good, Jilly. After my trial, you told me I could start over, and I thought I could. But I was scared. I knew there was no escaping. I would answer. Law of the street."

"Kellen."

Damon nods. "One day it hit me—a life of fear is no life at all. Kellen had won. Without even laying a hand on me."

"You let the undertow suck you back in."

"No, Jilly, I made my choice. On my own. No drugs, no clouded judgment. No bleak look down the barrel of a gun this time."

"Stop. Damon, I can't know this."

"I stalked Kellen, memorized his moves. Found his condo, learned when his boys dropped him off after the night's business. Checked the security cameras, found the blind spot." He sucks in his breath. "And then I did it. I killed him." He glances down. "You told me I was an innocent kid led astray by the temptations of the street, and for a while I almost believed you. But now I know better. I'm a criminal. I know it. And it's only a matter of time before the world will know it."

"Lots of people hated Kellen. Cy can't prove it was you."

"Unless I tell him, Jilly."

I seize his arm. "No—"

"Only way to make things right. Tomorrow I'm going down to

Cy's office to turn myself in. Don't worry. I won't need a lawyer. I intend to plead guilty."

Good, I should say. I'm an officer of the court, after all, sworn to uphold the law. *Confess, Damon, end the cycle. Let justice be done.* But my words, when they finally emerge, startle me.

"What a waste, Damon. You rot in jail for the rest of your life at the public's expense. You've made choices in the past, some of them bad. Now you face another decision." I pause. "You still have a life. You can do good things with it, help people, make the world a better place."

"There you go again, Jilly—"

"No, listen to me. These labels we put on ourselves, like criminal or orphan or deviant, they mean nothing. The only way we know who we are is by confronting the waves that crash over us and beating our way on, until we can go no further. You did something criminal, Damon. Maybe that's who you were. But it's not who you are."

"Easy for you to say, Jilly—successful lawyer, everybody's golden girl."

"No," I cry. "I have my own dark places. I'm still a work in progress." I grab Damon's shoulders, feel them shudder beneath my hands. "But I'm not giving up, I'm not going down."

"It's the law," he shouts over the wind. "You kill; you pay."

Words from a distant shore come back to me. "Sometimes, Damon, the law doesn't matter a damn."

I hook my arm through his and steer him toward the car. Faces set against the rain, we press on.

ACKNOWLEDGMENTS

Thank you to my editors, Brendan May and Sarah St. Pierre, who helped me discover the novel within my sprawling manuscript.

Thank you to fellow author Simon Gervais, who read an early draft and helped me believe in this book, and to my staunch agent and ally, Eric Myers.

Enormous and abiding gratitude to my husband, Frank McArdle, whose love and unfailing support made this book possible; and to my son, Angus McLachlin, and sister, Judi Dalling, for making me believe I could write it.